The
DOWRY
OF LADY
ELIZA

To Colleen—
God Bless!
Anita Stansfield
2021

OTHER BOOKS AND AUDIOBOOKS
BY ANITA STANSFIELD

First Love and Forever
First Love, Second Chances
When Forever Comes
For Love Alone
The Three Gifts of Christmas
Towers of Brierley
Where the Heart Leads
When Hearts Meet
Someone to Hold
Reflections: A Collection of Personal Essays Gables of Legacy, Six Volumes
A Timeless Waltz
A Time to Dance
Dancing in the Light
A Dance to Remember
The Barrington Family Saga, Four Volumes
Emma: Woman of Faith
The Jayson Wolfe Story, Five Volumes
The Dickens Inn Series, Five Volumes
Shadows of Brierley Series, Four
Volumes Passage on the Titanic
The Wishing Garden
The Garden Path
Legally and Lawfully Yours
Now and Always Yours
Heir of Brownlee Manor
The Color of Love
Lily of the Manor
Love and Loss at Whitmore Manor
The Stars above Northumberland
The Heart of Thornewell
The Lady of Astoria Abbey
The Empty Manger
The House of Stone and Ivy
The Emerald Heart of Courtenay
The Angel of Grey Garden
All Hearts Come Home for Christmas
Home to Sommersby
The Heart of Hampton House

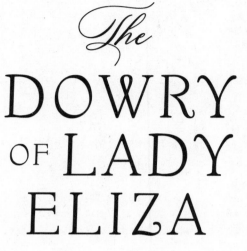

The DOWRY OF LADY ELIZA

ANITA STANSFIELD

A REGENCY ROMANCE

Covenant Communications, Inc.

Cover Images: *Historical Woman Holding Flowers in Grand House* © Ilina Simeonova / Trevillion Images; *Victorian Wallpaper* © Ridderhof / Pixabay. Interior Image: *Invitation Greeting Card with Floral Background. Wedding Invitation, Thank You Card, Save the Date Cards.* © All-about-Flowers / Shutterstock

Cover and interior design by Kimberly Kay © 2021 by Covenant Communications, Inc.

Published by Covenant Communications, Inc.
American Fork, Utah

Printed in the United States of America
First Printing: January 2021

28 27 26 25 24 23 22 21   10 9 8 7 6 5 4 3 2 1

ISBN: 978-1-52441-342-2

Chapter One

THE ABANDONED BRIDE

London, England—1808

ELIZA MELODIOUS GRENVILLE WAS CHERISHING every facet of her wedding day, constantly aware of the ethereal perfection of each moment. She had dreamt of this day since she'd barely been old enough to understand the purpose of weddings. How clearly she recalled attending the wedding of a distant cousin, and even then she had imagined herself as a bride one day; and from that time forward she had been planning the perfect wedding in anticipation of finding the man with whom she would spend the rest of her life. A blissful life with her dearly beloved was all a part of her flawless plan, and the very day she'd met Joshua Downing, she'd known the missing piece of her life had fallen into place. Along with his brother, Matthias, and her sister, Mia, the four of them had been friends for a handful of years. Joshua had courted Eliza for an appropriate number of months, he had proposed marriage with all the devotion of his soul, and together they had embarked upon putting all of Eliza's plans for the perfect wedding into place—although Joshua readily admitted that he preferred to let Eliza, her sister, Mia, and Mrs. Simpkin—Eliza's trusted housekeeper—do most of the planning. He only wanted to marry Eliza, and his attitude about this and so many other things made her feel adored and loved in ways she could never adequately describe.

Now that the great day had finally arrived, Eliza was more than pleased to see all her plans falling neatly into place. Even the weather was cooperating; the May sky was blue with intermittent picturesque clouds adding beauty to the ambience of the day. Every detail of the morning remained exactly on schedule as Eliza enjoyed a delicious breakfast, relished a long, luxurious bath, and got ready for her wedding with the help of Prudence, who surely had to be the most efficient and skilled lady's maid in the great city of London—if not the entire country. The two of them rarely had much to say to each other, despite the hours they spent together throughout the course of any given day with Prudence making certain that Eliza had everything she needed and every possible comfort. Still, Eliza felt completely at ease with the maid, and she was glad now for her special expertise in styling a lady's hair as she twisted and pinned and wove white ribbons into Eliza's nearly black tresses, creating a coiffure so thoroughly unique and stylish that Eliza wondered if she'd ever felt more beautiful.

Once they had both agreed that Eliza's hair was perfect, Prudence helped Eliza into her gown—a work of art constructed from satin and lace that was also everything Eliza had imagined her wedding gown might be. Prudence then carefully pinned the wedding veil into Eliza's hair; it fit perfectly into place right at the crown of her head where Prudence had purposely styled her hair to accommodate the veil. With satin slippers on her feet, and an exquisite lace handkerchief tucked into her sleeve where it was completely undetected, Eliza studied her reflection in the long mirror and had to force back the threat of tears. She felt beautiful and blissfully happy. Everything was perfect.

At that very moment, Eliza's sister rushed into the room, the petticoats and skirts of her lavender gown rustling as she hurried to Eliza's side to examine her appearance.

"Oh, dear sister!" she declared and let out a girlish giggle. "You look divine! The perfect bride!"

"Do you really think so?" Eliza asked; even though she agreed, she'd always sought her sister's approval.

"I do indeed!" Mia assured her and giggled again.

Mia was less than two years younger than Eliza's age of twenty-one; nevertheless, she'd always maintained a girlish nature that was completely endearing. They looked nothing like sisters, since Mia entirely favored their mother with her blonde hair and thin figure, and she was a few inches taller than Eliza, who was shorter than the average woman. Eliza's figure was much curvier than her sister's, although they had both always agreed that they were each fair enough in appearance and one was not more beautiful than the other. Their parents had always said so with great sincerity, and they both believed it. Even though their mother had passed on nearly ten years earlier, and their father had followed a few years ago, Eliza and Mia both had precious and tender memories of their parents, and despite missing them terribly to this day, they cherished having each other. Together they shared the same perfect empathy over the loss of their parents—each to different illnesses—and they had always helped take care of each other during the years they'd been alone. Being in a manor house where dozens of people were employed to help care for them, they were never physically alone, but Eliza and Mia had no other siblings; therefore, they were the only ones who truly understood each other. The closeness they shared was incomparable.

Eliza and Mia had both talked a great deal about how Eliza's marriage would change their relationship, but since Joshua would be living in the home of his new wife, the sisters would still live under the same roof and would therefore be able to remain close even though Joshua would now become the most important person in Eliza's life—just as it should be in marriage. But Joshua Downing had been spending most of his time at Eliza's home for many months now, and they'd all become accustomed to sharing meals and tea with him and his brother, as well as going riding together or for walks in the garden when the weather was favorable. Joshua and Mia had become very much like a brother and sister, and they were both completely comfortable with the prospect of officially becoming family. Eliza doubted she could have married a man who didn't feel comfortable with having her remain close to her sister, which was one of the countless reasons she loved and appreciated Joshua so much. And even though Mia and Eliza were not quite as comfortable with Joshua's brother, Matthias, they had still grown to care for him—and he for them—and they were all prepared to become a family. The reality that her wedding day had finally come filled Eliza with jittery excitement and she could barely keep herself from giggling, much as Mia kept doing. But as they hurried downstairs to get into the carriage that was waiting to take them to the church, Eliza left the giggling to her sister and instead held her joy close to her heart, wanting to memorize every moment of this day, knowing it was the most important day of her life. Of course, she and Joshua were just embarking on a lifetime of happiness, but it was this day that determined the path they were taking together, and quite simply she felt elated from the tips of her fingers and toes, to the very center of her heart and mind.

The ride in the carriage with Mia and Prudence was brief, since the church they attended was only a short distance through the busy London streets from the grand home in which they lived. Once the carriage had halted, one of the footmen helped Prudence and Mia step out of the carriage, with Eliza descending last and the other women making certain that her veil and the train of her gown both emerged from the carriage unscathed. As Eliza ascended the front steps of the church while the bells in the tower above were ringing, she felt as if she were at the center of a dream—a perfect, beautiful dream, which would surely be among her most precious memories for the rest of her life.

Once inside the church, the three women went into a room furnished with a mirror and several comfortable chairs, a room that had been constructed especially so that a bride and those attending her could make certain all was perfection while they waited for the groom, the vicar, and the guests to all be ready for the ceremony to begin. A clock on the wall let Eliza know that they'd arrived right on time, since she wanted a few minutes to catch her breath and feel prepared, but she didn't want to have to wait too long. Once the big hand on the clock was pointing straight up, Eliza expected to hear the music of the organ shift from the gentle strains she could hear in the distance to the bolder notes of the wedding march. The vicar was also a dear friend to all of them, and he was known for wanting everything to be punctual. Eliza and Joshua had spoken to Simon just two days ago, a conversation in which they'd rehearsed all their plans and he'd assured them that everything would go perfectly. But a minute passed, and then another, and another, and nothing happened.

"What's wrong?" Eliza demanded, her voice even more panicked than she'd intended as she looked at her sister, then Prudence, then at her sister again. "Something's wrong."

"A few minutes' delay doesn't mean something's wrong," Mia insisted.

"I agree with your sister, m'lady," Prudence said softly but with more conviction than she was generally known to assert.

Eliza was soothed by their reassurances until more minutes had passed and nothing had changed. She should have been at the head of the chapel by now, exchanging her vows with Joshua! Where was he? Where was the vicar? What had gone wrong? The very moment she was ready to blurt these questions aloud—as opposed to just restraining them to swim around in her mind—the vicar entered the room, and all three women turned toward him expectantly. Simon Law was an unmarried man in his early thirties and average looking in nearly every way: average build, average height, average brown hair. Except that his eyes—which were framed by spectacles—held a kindness and wisdom that had never been average. While Eliza was fully prepared for Simon to offer some kind of reassurance that there was a simple and perfectly logical explanation for the delay, her heart began thumping painfully hard as she took in his countenance. *Something was wrong. Something had gone* terribly *wrong!*

"What?" she demanded.

"Eliza, my dear," he said and gently took hold of her arm to guide her into a nearby chair. He sat next to her, looked into her eyes in a very vicar-like way, and added, "He's not here, and no one seems to know *where* he is, or *why* he's not arrived by now."

The passing of seconds felt like minutes as Eliza's mind recounted every tiny detail of all that had led to this moment, all the careful planning of her wedding, and most importantly, the tender care she had put into choosing the man with whom she wanted to spend her life. While her dreams of an idyllic wedding shattered around her like a crystal goblet crashing onto a marble floor, all of that felt trivial and insignificant in contrast to the fact that the man she loved was missing. Joshua was nothing if not punctual and dependable. That fact alone made it clear that something *was* terribly wrong.

If only to try and convince herself that she was mistaken, Eliza said, "Surely there's just been some kind of delay in his being able to get here. I'm certain if we just wait a little longer, he will—"

"Eliza, my dear," the vicar said again, "his brother arrived just before I came in here. Matthias has been searching for Joshua since breakfast; apparently Joshua went out late last night and never came home."

"What?" Eliza muttered, her voice somewhere between a gasp and a squeak. She then laughed—a sound that felt completely out of place, but it was the only way she could express her reaction to the absolute absurdity of her precious fiancé going out late on the night before his wedding for *any* reason, and then disappearing. "That just can't be right," Eliza said. "He told me he would be spending the evening with his brother and going to bed early. Why on earth would he have gone *out*?" She realized her breathing had become labored and fought to get it under control. "This is just not like him!" Eliza protested, as if doing so might immediately eliminate this problem, and her beloved Joshua would appear instantaneously, ready to proceed with the ceremony. "He's . . . dependable, and . . . he loves me, and . . ." Her voice quavered and she feared continuing would tempt her to erupt into uncontrollable sobbing. She was not only devastated, she felt terrified. "Something's wrong," she declared aloud with some measure of composure. "He would not have *chosen* to abandon me this way . . . to abandon our wedding. He *wouldn't!*" she insisted. "Something's terribly wrong."

"I agree," the vicar said with compassion. "And we will do everything we can to get to the bottom of it. Matthias has gone for the police and—"

"That's good," Eliza agreed vehemently. Joshua's brother was lacking in some of the admirable character traits Joshua possessed, but he dearly loved his brother and he would surely do whatever might be required to resolve this problem. Although, the very possibility that the assistance of the police might be necessary pressed Eliza toward panic. She fought to breathe evenly with little success despite Simon sitting on one side of her with his comforting hand over her arm, and her sister sitting on the other side with her arm around Eliza's shoulders.

"In the meantime," the vicar said with a deepening compassion in his voice, "even though I know it's terribly difficult for you, perhaps it would be best for you to wait for any news at home. You will be more comfortable there, and I promise you I will send word of anything I learn, and—"

"No!" Eliza insisted. "Surely he will be here soon." Even as she spoke, she recognized a certain lack of logic in her reasoning, but at the moment she couldn't accept any other possibility. "Surely there's a simple explanation; they will find him soon and we can go on with the wedding."

Eliza chose to ignore the concerned glances exchanged by the vicar, her sister, and Prudence. Right now, she focused only on the image of walking down the aisle of the chapel toward her precious Joshua so they could exchange their marriage vows, just as she'd been dreaming about for many months now. No one spoke, as if not one of those she trusted who were surrounding her wanted to be the one to dash her hopes. The quiet became strained until the vicar finally said, "Very well, Eliza. We'll wait a while longer." Simon rose to his feet and visibly mustered the strength to be assertive before adding, "But if he doesn't arrive within a reasonable amount of time, I must insist that you return home to wait for news. As I said, I know it's difficult for you, nevertheless it's simply not practical for you to wait here much longer; we just don't have the amenities available here to keep you comfortable."

Eliza couldn't find the strength to respond to such an edict, even though she knew Simon was right. If Joshua was truly missing, she couldn't wait here at the church indefinitely, especially dressed as she was in a gown and veil that felt fragile and constricting.

"Thank you," Mia said to Simon.

He nodded and moved toward the door as he added, "I will inform the guests that we will wait a short while and then determine what to do next. I'll check back soon."

Soon after the vicar left, Eliza found it impossible to sit still. She stood and began pacing frantically while her mind conjured up all kinds of terrible things that could have happened to Joshua. The only truly logical explanation she could settle on was that he had likely felt restless the night before his wedding and had gone for a late-evening walk and there had been some kind of accident. Perhaps he was injured somewhere and couldn't move enough to get help, although the streets of London would be busy enough by now that this possibility didn't seem likely, unless he was in some alleyway or on a back street where there was little traffic. Perhaps he'd been accosted and robbed, and that was the reason he needed assistance. She refused to think that the situation might be any worse than that. She longed for the police to hurry and become involved so he could be found and given the assistance he needed. She imagined him being discovered and properly aided, and even if he'd been injured, he would recover quickly enough, and their wedding would only be postponed a number of days. It was a scenario she could make peace with, and she simply couldn't think about any other possibility. Truthfully, she couldn't even *imagine* any other possibility. This was just not like Joshua at all, and there surely had to be some kind of logical explanation.

The minutes continued to tick by while Eliza paced herself into exhaustion, then stumbled into a chair, fearing she might faint otherwise. The tighter-than-usual corset she was wearing with her wedding gown didn't help matters any. Mia and Prudence each offered an occasional reassurance that surely all would be well, but each time they spoke, the strength of conviction in their voices waned a little until no one spoke at all. More than an hour after the ceremony should have begun, the vicar returned to report that he'd sent the guests home, and the police were engaged in a vigorous search for the missing groom. Only then did Eliza start to cry. Inside her own mind she could hear herself screaming and sobbing, but on the outside, she simply allowed silent tears to trickle down her face, while she made use of the handkerchief that had been tucked into her sleeve.

"I must insist that you ladies return home," Simon said firmly but with compassion. "There is nothing that can be done here, and the three of you should wait for news where you can be comfortable. I assure you that I will remain closely in contact with the police; the constable has agreed to keep me updated personally, and I told him I would either be here or at your home. I will meet you there once I've made certain I've done everything that I can."

Eliza heard everything Simon had said, and she nodded toward him, attempting to convey her appreciation, but she felt so thoroughly numb with terror and disappointment that she could hardly breathe, let alone speak. She was grateful for the way Prudence and Mia assertively guided Eliza to the waiting carriage. Once inside, Eliza abandoned any effort to keep herself from sobbing. She should have been married by now; instead, the man she loved was missing with the assumption that he'd encountered some kind of danger. Both Prudence and Mia did their best to comfort Eliza and offer reassurances that there was surely some kind of simple explanation, that Joshua would be found well and safe. Eliza wanted to believe them, and a part of her couldn't imagine any other possibility, but there was something deep inside herself—something she never could have explained—that lured her to suspect something was terribly, terribly wrong, and this problem would not be as easily solved as everyone seemed to believe.

Back in her own rooms, Eliza would have never been able to get out of her wedding apparel if not for the assistance of Prudence and her sister. She stood like a statue, unable to feel, or move, or think while they removed the veil, unbuttoned the dress, and slid it off her arms so that it fell in a heap around her. The huge petticoats soon followed, then her corset was removed from over her chemise, which helped her breathe more deeply but she still felt incapable of moving. Prudence made the suggestion that Eliza should perhaps remain in her underclothing and get into bed, but Eliza summoned enough strength to respond, insisting that she needed to be presentable when the vicar came, and she also hoped someone from the police might come with a report. Even though she wasn't able to speak her deepest hope, she imagined Joshua arriving with some kind of reasonable explanation for this horrible misadventure, which would bring a conclusion to all this drama and fear.

Wearing a suitable day dress with a lavender skirt and white bodice, Eliza paced her sitting room only long enough for Mia to change her clothes before she went with her sister to the drawing room, while Prudence went with instructions to speak to the housekeeper about what had happened, so that the entire staff would be on alert for the inevitable visits of the vicar and the police. It had occurred to her that the police might want to question members of the staff, although she felt certain there would be no information to be gained by doing so. Surely not one of them knew any more than she did. Joshua and Matthias had shared dinner the previous evening with her and Mia; they had visited over coffee in the parlor—as they always did when the brothers came for dinner. Then they had left at the usual time to return to their home, which was no more than a ten-minute ride by horse through the streets of London. The vicar had said at the church that Matthias had seen Joshua later the previous evening, so they'd made it home safely. But Joshua had gone out after that for reasons no one knew. Eliza held to her theory that he'd gone out to take a walk, given that he'd likely been afflicted with some nerves prior to the wedding, as any groom might be. Eliza herself had certainly felt a little jittery since her fiancé had kissed her good night before he'd left to return to his home after dinner. She'd even had trouble sleeping due to the giddiness she'd been feeling. She could understand how Joshua might have been feeling, but whatever had happened to him since she'd last seen him, she couldn't begin to imagine.

Eliza paced the drawing room while Mia sat in silence. She'd made some attempts to reassure Eliza that all would be well until Eliza had become so impatient with what only felt like platitudes that she'd asked her sister to be quiet. Thankfully Mia was not offended; she knew Eliza was upset. But now the silence beyond the noise of Eliza's feet moving back and forth on the carpet had an irritating quality in and of itself.

Lunchtime came and went with no news and no visitors. Eliza attempted to eat but could hardly choke down more than a couple of bites. She noted that Mia also barely touched her meal and knew that her sister was upset and deeply concerned, perhaps almost as much as Eliza herself. They returned to the drawing room and continued to wait, although now Eliza was slumped on a sofa, unable to move, drained of the strength to do any more pacing.

More than an hour after they'd come back to this room following lunch, Mia broke the silence by saying, "We can't wait here forever, Liza. You know someone will come for us if we're needed. Perhaps we would be more comfortable upstairs. If nothing else, it would be a change of scenery."

It took Eliza another twenty minutes or so to be convinced, as if her physical closeness to the main entrance of the house might somehow help solve the problem of finding Joshua and solving the mystery of his disappearance. She finally gave in to Mia's urging and was grateful for her sister's strength as she wrapped an arm around Eliza while they walked slowly together up the stairs to Eliza's sitting room. Eliza felt tempted once again to begin pacing, but the strain of the day was beginning to take its toll and she dropped gratefully into her favorite comfortable chair, which faced a trio of high windows that looked out over the leafy treetops in the midst of the grand garden that was hidden from the view of passersby in this prestigious area of London in which they lived.

Once she was back in the safety of her own rooms, Eliza leaned her head into the high, cushioned back of the chair and wept, wondering what horrible thing might have happened to the man she loved. They should have been celebrating their marriage, surrounded by friends and loved ones, dancing and drinking champagne. Instead she felt as if she were in the center of a nightmare, and nothing but the reappearance of her precious Joshua could solve this problem.

When Prudence brought tea to the sitting room, Eliza was startled to realize how many hours had passed since Joshua's absence had become painfully obvious. She felt shocked and frightened and confused, but she gave in to Mia's gentle prodding to eat something when her rumbling hunger due to hardly touching her lunch suddenly made her feel ill. She feared if she *didn't* eat, she would never have the strength to face whatever the remainder of the day might bring. She couldn't even consider the possibility that this mystery might not be solved before the day ended.

Eliza felt physically better after her stomach was full and she'd enjoyed an extra cup of tea. The warm, savory liquid helped soothe her nerves, perhaps due simply to the familiar taste and fragrance. Only a few minutes after Prudence had taken the tea tray back to the kitchen, another maid appeared to inform Eliza and Mia that the vicar had arrived and wished to speak with them.

"Oh, my goodness!" Eliza exclaimed. "I do pray they've found him . . . that he's all right."

"As do I," Mia said, and Eliza hurried toward the stairs with her sister right behind her.

Eliza doubted she had ever descended the stairs so quickly in all her life and considered it a miracle that she'd not fallen and injured herself. She entered the drawing room out of breath and found not only the vicar, but two uniformed police officers.

"Simon?" Eliza squeaked, looking at the vicar's trusted countenance. She and her sister had known Simon for years since he had grown up attending church with them, and they'd come to know him even better since he'd taken over the care of this particular parish a few years earlier. He had been invited frequently to share teas and meals in their home, and they had surely become close friends. Despite her absolute reverence for the religious position he held, Eliza was not at all unfamiliar with calling him by his given name. The officers in the room were strangers to her, but Simon was a friend, and it was from him that she sought answers. But his visage was grave, and Eliza's heart pounded painfully as she waited for him to answer.

"We've been unable to find him," Simon said quickly, as if to get the most important news out first before he relayed any details. "The finest of London's police force have been searching all day with the help of Matthias who likely knew his habits best. It's as if he's just . . . disappeared, but . . ."

"But?" Eliza echoed impatiently, reaching for her sister's hand, which she squeezed tightly, fearing that worse news was about to come forth. Seeing the vicar exchange concerned glances with the two officers heightened her fear and contributed to the pounding of her heart.

"But . . . we have no reason to believe that he *chose* to not be there for the wedding," Simon stated. Eliza took some comfort from this until she perceived the deeper implication of his words even before Simon went on to explain. "Every possible means of transportation out of the city has been carefully reviewed by the police. No carriages were hired by anyone matching his description. His own carriage and horses are accounted for."

"Which means he's still in the city?" Eliza asked, not certain if the hope in her voice was warranted. Just because he hadn't left London didn't mean he hadn't *chosen* to not be at the wedding; he could be hiding somewhere if he'd changed his mind. Was that what all of this was about? Had he simply decided to not marry her, and not had the courage to tell her so he'd skulked into hiding instead? Or had something horrible happened to him? If that were the case—and she chose to believe it was—rather than believing he had any aversion toward the marriage—then his absence combined with his not having left the city didn't sound like good news at all. It was a very big city, with many unsavory places and despicable people. Something terrible could have happened to Joshua. He could be suffering greatly right now. Or perhaps worse, he could be . . . No! Eliza couldn't even consider the possibility that he might be dead. The very idea was ludicrous. A late-night walk ending in his death on the night before his wedding? It was absurd!

"So, what do we do now?" Eliza asked, suddenly aware that they were all still standing. The weakening of her own knees lured her toward a sofa, and she motioned with her hand for the others to be seated. Mia sat beside Eliza, but the men all remained on their feet.

"We will keep searching, m'lady," one of the officers said. Eliza didn't know their names since no one had told her, but she believed that was just as well since she doubted she would be able to remember them. "There is surely a logical explanation. Your fiancé is a respected gentleman in this city, and we'll not stop looking until we find him."

"Thank you," Eliza muttered, wondering why his promise sounded futile. Deep inside, she felt her hope dwindling that Joshua would be found safe and well. She hoped such a feeling was due simply to her fears and exhaustion as opposed to any kind of actual premonition.

"I just wanted you to hear it from the officers personally," Simon stated. "I'll see them out and be right back."

"Thank you," Mia muttered this time and Eliza leaned toward her sister, depleted of strength. Mia put an arm around Eliza and whispered the reassurance that all *would* be well, but Eliza couldn't bring herself to believe it. A few hours ago, she had been clinging desperately to the belief that all would be well, but in this moment, she found no inner strength that enabled her to hold on to that belief.

Eliza didn't realize Simon had come back into the room and had sat down across from them until he said, "Is there anything I can do?"

Eliza couldn't speak. Her thoughts were drawn to how Simon was the vicar who would have performed her marriage ceremony earlier today—if the groom had been present. Because he was also a friend, he had been greatly involved in plans for the wedding celebrations that had now all dwindled away. She found herself distracted by wondering what had been done with all the food that had been prepared for wedding guests. Where was the cake? The flowers? Likely all hidden from Eliza's view so as not to remind her of what should have been. And knowing the efficiency and attitude of the cook and housekeeper, Eliza suspected that the food had been sent out with every available servant to be distributed among the hungry and homeless in the parts of London most people might never dare enter. But it was common practice for such things to happen when there was a surplus of food in the kitchens of this house. The tradition had begun with Eliza's grandmother, and Eliza and Mia were nothing but pleased and eager to continue such a fine tradition. But in that moment, Eliza felt unsettled to think of her wedding feast being distributed among the poor. Not that she resented the poor having something fine to eat; but she certainly resented the fact that her wedding had not taken place, and the groom could be seriously injured—or dead, for all she knew. *No!* She reminded herself again. *Not dead!* The very idea was too preposterous to even consider.

Eliza was glad for the way Mia thanked Simon for sitting with them, and she was also grateful for the way that Mia and the vicar managed to find trivial things to talk about that avoided any mention of the mystery they were all thinking about but didn't want to discuss. There was nothing to say that hadn't already been spoken many times, and Eliza far preferred the distraction of hearing about ordinary news regarding what was going on in the lives of other parishioners, as well as some of the political happenings in London—something over which Simon always maintained an interest. Eliza didn't share his interest personally, but she generally enjoyed his stories since they had a way of making the simplest matters entertaining, and sometimes even humorous. And right now, his casual conversation was a welcome means of distraction.

When the shadows in the room and the clock on the mantel both agreed that evening was approaching, Eliza could hardly grasp that Joshua had not yet been found. Hearing Mia invite the vicar to stay and eat with them was further evidence of how the day was coming to an end, but Eliza was glad that Simon accepted the invitation, since he was skilled at keeping her distracted, whereas Mia and Eliza would have likely been driving each other mad with nothing at all to say to each other except expressions of worry and concern.

In spite of having very little appetite, Eliza managed to eat a fair amount of her meal, reminding herself with each bite that she needed to keep up her strength. She had no idea what had happened to Joshua—or what the coming hours would bring—but logically she knew she didn't want to be vulnerable to feeling ill or faint when she was required to face whatever news might come to them.

Simon stayed long after Eliza and Mia would have normally gone to bed. Eliza felt certain she could never be able to sleep without having some answers, but at the same time she wanted to just curl up in bed and allow oblivion to free her from this terrible, terrible day.

Eliza was grateful when Mia said to Simon, "We truly appreciate your staying with us, and all your efforts on our behalf, but I don't believe sitting here trying to make polite conversation will solve this mystery any more quickly. I think Eliza needs to rest . . . or at least try and rest." Mia stood up, which prompted Simon to do the same. "Please come or send word if you hear anything. In the meantime, we will do our best to get some sleep, and you should do the same."

"Of course," Simon replied and exchanged proper farewells and a heartfelt declaration that he would be praying for everyone involved.

The moment the vicar left the room, Mia was hurrying Eliza up the stairs, as if they might both collapse if they didn't get there quickly enough. In truth, Eliza was so suddenly overcome with exhaustion that she feared such a thing might actually happen. In her room they found Prudence waiting to help Eliza prepare for bed. Mia remained and helped make certain Eliza was as well as she could be under the circumstances before she went down the hall to her own room.

Once alone in the dark, Eliza curled up in her bed, attempting to comprehend the present reality. This should have been her wedding night; today should have been the happiest of her life. Instead, it had all turned into a nightmare. She prayed both silently and aloud that her dear Joshua was safe and well and would soon be found. As exhaustion settled in more deeply, she told herself that she would surely be awakened in the night with news that this mystery had been solved and all was well—even though Eliza could no longer come up with any logical explanation for what might have happened.

Eliza took advantage of being alone in her bed to cry long and hard, wanting to vent her tears and release them into the open, which she figured would make it less likely for them to burst forth unexpectedly at a time when others were around. Crying in such a way could be seen as unseemly for a lady, if not wholly embarrassing. Her tears finally settled into a numbing shock. As she saw it, there were only two likely possibilities: Joshua had either made the decision to leave London and not marry her, although the police had told her there was no evidence of this. *Or* he'd met with some kind of unspeakable harm while walking the streets the night before their marriage. She tried to consider which would be worse for her to accept—that he was dead, or that he had betrayed her. Either possibility was too devastating to consider. She only knew that she had no idea how she was going to get through the following day; she only hoped that it would bring answers. For all that the outcome would be horrifying no matter what it might be, the uncertainty felt unbearable, simply a stressful delay for being able to face the truth and come to terms with it.

Eliza's sleep was sporadically mixed with frightening dreams that would awaken her with a pounding heart and difficulty breathing. It took great effort to calm herself down and relax, and she did little but doze off here and there between her nightmarish episodes. When daylight finally came, she couldn't keep herself from getting out of bed so that she could pace the room with the hope of releasing some of her nervous energy, even though she felt so exhausted that she feared she might collapse if she didn't force herself to relax. More than once she attempted to get comfortable sitting down, but her efforts didn't last when she simply couldn't sit still.

Prudence arrived earlier than usual to help her get dressed and to style her hair, but the maid wore a countenance that alarmed Eliza. "What?" she asked before anything else had been said between them.

"The vicar is here . . . with the constable," Prudence announced solemnly. "They apologize for arriving so early, but they wish to speak with you as soon as you're presentable."

"Oh my," Eliza gasped and put a hand unwillingly over her heart. Somehow, she knew in that moment these men had come with the worst possible news. But thankfully she felt blanketed with a deep layer of shock that she hoped would remain in place so she could maintain her composure no matter what they'd come to tell her. Perhaps Joshua had been found injured and he was recuperating. Perhaps they'd come with *good* news. She held onto the tiniest bit of hope for the possibility of hearing *good news*, but she couldn't ignore the nagging of her deepest instincts telling her that once she heard what these men had come to tell her, nothing in her life would ever be the same.

"Let me help you," Prudence said, startling Eliza from her grim thoughts.

"Of course," Eliza said, and the maid efficiently helped Eliza into a dark-gray dress; she had the thought that the color was appropriate for mourning, then she immediately scolded herself for thinking that Joshua could actually be dead. Surely that was just her imagination coming up with the worst scenario.

In an effort to hurry, Prudence quickly brushed through Eliza's hair and wound it into a long braid, tying it at the bottom with a black ribbon and promising to style it more appropriately later on when she had more time. Eliza thanked Prudence for her efficiency and kindness before she hurried to the drawing room where the vicar and the constable were waiting. She considered that perhaps they'd simply come to tell her that there was *no* news, that nothing had changed. But the earliness of their visit contradicted that theory and she had trouble keeping her heartbeat calm and her breathing normal as she moved at a steady pace toward her destination. She wished that her sister was here and wondered if Mia too had been summoned, but she didn't want to wait long enough to find out.

The moment Eliza entered the room, the two men came to their feet and looked directly at her. Their expressions alone told her that the news was not good; still, she clung to the hope that somehow all would be well.

"Forgive the intrusion at such an early hour," Simon said. "Please sit down." He motioned toward a sofa and Eliza hurried to follow his suggestion, alarmed over the very fact that he had invited her to be seated when this was *her* home, and it should be her offering such invitations.

Once she was seated on the sofa, Simon took his seat next to Eliza. And the man who was obviously the constable sat in a chair across from them. Simon offered an introduction, but Eliza barely heard him above the pulsebeats in her ears.

"Eliza, my dear," Simon said and took her hand in a way he'd never done before, but Eliza felt certain it was a vicar's way of offering spiritual support in the most dire of situations; this only made her heart thump all the more loudly. "Joshua has been found, but—"

"You found him?" Eliza interrupted, hearing a gleeful tone in her voice that contradicted the deepest instincts she was trying to ignore. The grave looks of Simon and the constable made it clear that she needed to allow the vicar to finish what he'd been trying to say, and her brief moment of hope shattered as she forced herself to be silent and listen.

"But . . ." Simon repeated and tightened his hold on Eliza's fingers, "I'm so sorry to have to tell you this, my dear . . . but Joshua is dead."

Chapter Two

THE DUPLICITOUS JOSHUA DOWNING

ELIZA COULD NO LONGER FORCE herself to maintain any kind of dignity. She heard herself gasping for breath and lowered her head to her knees when she began to see flashes of light swirling around her and she feared losing consciousness. She could hear Simon offering reassurances, but his words were muddled, and she couldn't decipher exactly what he was saying. She suspected the constable had come to give her details of the situation, but she couldn't very well take in *any* kind of information when she had no ability to even remain upright.

Eliza began to fear that her dizziness would not relent, and she would never be able to breathe normally. She was just wishing that she'd had the good sense to wait for Mia to accompany her to this early-morning, ominous visit when her sister rushed into the room, immediately taking a seat next to Eliza, at the same time demanding, "What's happened?"

"Joshua is dead," Simon informed her, and Eliza heard a quaver in his voice. Simon had become good friends with Joshua and his brother, just as he had with her and Mia. This was unspeakably horrible for all of them. Eliza had a hundred questions she wanted to ask, but she could barely breathe.

"What happened?" Mia asked breathlessly on the wave of a harsh gasp. Before anyone had a chance to answer, Mia urged Eliza into her arms and Eliza let go of Simon's hand in order to take hold of her sister, as if Mia could prevent her from drowning in this horrifying whirlpool of her desperate attempt to accept that Joshua was truly dead.

Through the haze of attempting to draw in breath and maintain her equilibrium, Eliza could hear Mia asking questions with a trembling voice. The constable's answers were toneless and succinct, and Eliza barely heard that Joshua's body had been found in an alley; he'd been shot and by all appearances had died instantly, since the bullet had entered his heart. His body had then apparently been dragged into a corner where two buildings met and had been covered with piles of trash that had been left in the alley, which explained why it had taken so long for the police to discover him. Eliza had to fight back waves of nausea to think of her precious Joshua shot dead and abandoned in a trash heap, no less. More and more questions filed through her mind, but she couldn't find the voice to speak them. She was grateful when Mia asked, "Who would have done such a thing? And why?"

"We're putting all our resources into answering those very questions, Miss," the constable said, a sliver of compassion creeping into his voice. "And we will keep you apprised of any developments. I promise you that as soon as we have any information at all, I will either send one of my senior officers to speak with you, or I will come personally if it's at all possible."

"Thank you," Mia said, again saying what Eliza couldn't.

"You ladies have my deepest sympathies," the constable said and stood up.

"Thank you," Mia said once more, and Simon stood as well, offering to show him out. In the absence of having a brother, Eliza was grateful for Simon's trusted friendship, and that he was here now to help them through this.

Once the constable had left, Simon returned to the drawing room where Eliza continued to cling to her sister while they both wept without restraint. "Oh, my dears!" Simon murmured sitting across from them. "I wish I had any idea what to say. There are no words to assuage such grief."

"We are so very grateful for your assistance," Mia said to him.

"Yes," Eliza managed to mutter.

"Forgive me if this sounds insensitive," Simon added, "but I hope there will at least be some relief in not having to *wonder*."

"I confess I had the same thought," Mia admitted. She tightened her arms around Eliza and added, "It's all unspeakably horrible, dearest, but at least you know he didn't leave you by choice. He surely loved you."

Eliza had thought the same thing, but hearing it spoken deepened the evidence that Joshua was dead, and Eliza lost what little measure of composure she'd been managing to gain. Sobbing in her sister's arms, she was relieved to hear Mia tell Simon, "I think we need some time alone . . . and I should see that Eliza gets some rest."

"Of course." Simon rose to his feet and said his goodbyes, promising to check on them the following day to see what he could do to help.

Once Eliza was alone with her sister, it seemed to take forever to get upstairs to her bedroom. Prudence was waiting there as always to see if Eliza needed help with anything, and she was understandably shocked when Mia gave her the constable's report. Eliza was grateful when Mia sent Prudence to get some hot tea and scones from the kitchen, insisting that Eliza needed to eat some kind of breakfast, even though she accurately guessed that Eliza had no appetite.

"Have a good cry," Mia said as if it were an order. "You're certainly entitled. And you can cry all you need to. But you also need to eat. So once Prudence comes back you *will* eat something; you've got to keep up your strength, and I will force a decent amount of breakfast down your throat if I have to. So do your best to calm down for now and you can cry some more after you've eaten."

Eliza felt strangely grateful in being told exactly what she needed to do, since she doubted she could think for herself *at all*. By the time Prudence returned with a large tray which she set on a table in the sitting room, Eliza had settled into a state of shock that held back her tears, and she was able to sit with her sister and slowly eat some buttered scones with marmalade, and drink three cups of warm tea that helped soothe her. Once she'd had her fill, Mia insisted that Eliza take off her shoes and get back into bed.

"You might not be able to sleep," Mia said, "but at least you can rest while you try to come to terms with all of this." Eliza nodded and felt tears creeping up again as she followed her sister's instructions and slipped beneath the bedcovers.

"Stay with me," Eliza pleaded, allowing her head to sink down into the pillow.

"Of course, my dear sister," Mia said and slipped beneath the covers on the opposite side of the bed.

"I can't believe it's true," Eliza admitted. "How can I believe what I'm being told if I don't see the evidence for myself?"

"I'm not certain you'd really want that," Mia said, "would you?"

"I don't know," Eliza said. "But . . . it doesn't feel real. How will I know it's real?"

"Just rest," Mia urged. "We'll talk about this later."

Eliza nodded and more tears came, making it difficult to speak, but her sister was there beside her, and for now, there was nothing more important to do than try to accept that the man she loved had been killed, shot through the heart and left in a heap of trash in an alley. These images, connected to what she'd been told, haunted her mind, and she wondered if she would ever be able to sleep again. But all her crying had taken a toll, and she gradually drifted into oblivion.

Eliza spent the remainder of the day dozing here and there and eating very little of the food that was brought to her sitting room. Either Mia or Prudence were with her continually, and she was barely aware of the fact that they were concerned about leaving her alone. Beyond her vacillation between a numbing shock and the need to cry so hard she could barely breathe, Eliza found herself preoccupied with the notion that this just didn't seem real. A part of her simply couldn't believe Joshua was truly dead. She shared her concerns with her sister over and over, until Mia gently said, "Do you actually believe the police and the vicar are conspiring to play some kind of cruel trick on you, Liza? The very idea is absurd!"

Eliza thought about it and admitted, "I know, but . . ."

"But?" Mia echoed.

"It just doesn't feel real. It feels as if . . ." Eliza couldn't finish as tears overtook her again. "I should be on my honeymoon by now," she muttered through her weeping. "What could have gone so terribly wrong, Mia? How could this have happened?"

"I don't know, darling," Mia said gently, "but I'm certain the police will get to the bottom of it."

The day dragged by with no further news until Mia and Eliza had just finished their supper in the sitting room. Then a maid came to tell them the vicar was here and waiting in the drawing room.

"Oh, my," Eliza said, coming to her feet so abruptly she almost felt dizzy. She quickly checked her appearance in a mirror, then decided that she didn't care if she looked as if she'd been crying all day. She had no reason for pretenses with Simon.

Eliza and Mia hurried to the drawing room and entered to see two men come to their feet. For only a second Eliza thought it might be a police officer, then she recognized Joshua's brother, and it was evident that he too had been crying. She'd never seen him so distressed, and the red splotches around his eyes were unmistakable. His wavy brown hair was more rumpled than usual, and his green eyes looked as if they'd aged a decade since she'd last seen him only a couple of days ago. His attire was fine and stylish as always, but he looked as if he'd not changed his clothes for more than a day, which she assumed to mean he'd likely not slept—or if he had, he'd done so sporadically in his clothes. The vicar too looked utterly exhausted and somewhat unkempt, and she doubted that he too had gotten much sleep since Joshua had disappeared and then been found dead.

Impulsively Eliza rushed toward Matthias and hugged him tightly, even though she never had before. Doing so was certainly not considered appropriate social decorum, but right now they shared the grief of losing Joshua and she didn't care at all about anything else. Strangely enough, she noticed that he didn't smell like the cigar smoke that generally clung to his clothes, and she wondered if the drama had made him suddenly stop smoking. She'd always disliked the disagreeable smell that had hovered around him, even though he'd never actually smoked in her presence. But the aroma had also always clung to Joshua's clothes since he and his brother spent so much time together. Knowing it was a petty observation in light of all that was happening, Eliza didn't comment. Instead she murmured while still holding to Matthias, "Are you all right?"

"Not at all," he said and relinquished their embrace to step back and look at her with narrowed eyes. "And neither are you; that's evident enough." He motioned toward a sofa. "We should sit."

"Do you have news?" she asked and thankfully sat down, which eased the perpetual weakness in her knees.

Matthias sat beside Eliza while Simon and Mia took chairs nearby. The way Matthias took Eliza's hand made her nervous, but he spoke with compassion. "I have nothing new to tell you," he said, "but I understand that you're having difficulty believing that he's really gone . . . that it's really true . . ."

Eliza glanced toward Mia who said, "Yes, I sent word to Simon that I was concerned about you for this very reason."

Eliza turned back to look at Matthias. "Simon and I discussed the matter with the constable, and we all agreed that we did *not* want you to see Joshua like that. So . . ." He took a deep breath and Eliza could hear it quavering as he let it out. "So . . . the constable took Simon and me to see the body."

Eliza put a hand over her mouth to hold back a gasp. She couldn't imagine how difficult that must have been for Matthias; if she'd had any doubt, it was erased by the hollow grief in his eyes. "Please allow us to assure you, Eliza, that Joshua is indeed dead. There is absolutely no question about that. However, it's believed he didn't suffer. From the way he was . . . shot . . . he would have died instantly. We can find some peace in that."

"Indeed we can," Simon murmured, but Eliza could only hang her head and cry. She was surprised to find Matthias's comforting arm around her as he guided her head to his shoulder, and even more surprised by how accepting and grateful she was for his comfort. She'd never liked Joshua's brother very much, but now that Joshua was gone, they shared the same sorrow, and at least for now, any differences between them were irrelevant.

After Eliza had summoned her composure, she sat up straight and patted her cheeks with her handkerchief to dry them before she pressed the handkerchief beneath her nose. She was glad when Simon broke the silence by saying, "Matthias and I have already spoken with the undertaker, and we will take care of the funeral arrangements—unless there is something specific you would like to contribute."

Eliza thought about it for a moment and said decisively, "No, but thank you. I'm just glad to know you'll be taking care of it."

"You know, of course," Simon added gently, "that it is not required for a lady to attend a funeral, and to some it's not even considered appropriate. Nevertheless, you also know that I personally advise my parishioners to make their own choice on such matters, and I am aware—because you told me—that you both attended your father's funeral. I simply want you to know that I will support your decision to be there, if that's what you decide to do."

"Yes, of course I will be there," Eliza said firmly. "I *need* to be there!"

"I understand," Simon said.

"And I will be by her side," Mia insisted, and Eliza was once again overcome with the sensation that this didn't feel real. While she was frequently preoccupied with the reality that she should have been on her honeymoon with Joshua, she could hardly cope with the prospect of being able to attend his funeral, even though she instinctively knew that *not* attending would only contribute to her inability to be able to accept that he was actually dead. She felt deeply grateful that she had no need to be involved with any of the arrangements. She had a black dress hanging in her closet that she'd worn to her father's funeral a few years earlier. It only had to be aired out and pressed. Beyond that, she was only too glad to leave the rest up to the vicar and Joshua's brother. Since Eliza and Joshua hadn't actually been married, she wasn't related to the deceased; therefore, it was more proper for his brother to take care of such details. And of course, the vicar of their particular parish would be involved in these things whether or not he happened to be a friend of those who were grieving.

Eliza felt the verification of Joshua's death sinking into her with the growing reality that she could no longer wonder if it was true, and therefore perhaps hold onto the tiniest bit of hope that there had been a mistake. A combination of despair and exhaustion made her feel as if she might slip off the sofa onto the floor, and all she could do was say, "Mia . . . help me. I need . . . to lie down and . . ."

"Oh, dearest!" Mia stood and rushed toward Eliza and helped her to her feet with a little assistance from Matthias. "Thank you, gentlemen," Mia said to their guests while she guided Eliza out of the room. "Please keep us apprised of any information regarding the funeral or . . ." Eliza knew she meant to add something about their desire to learn about the reasons Joshua had been murdered, but she simply said, ". . . anything else."

Eliza heard both men make statements of agreement before they murmured appropriate farewells, and then Eliza felt a brief burst of strength surge through her which surely originated with her desire to be within the safety of her own rooms where she could once again cry freely. She marveled that a human being could hold so many tears, but she knew from the experience of her parents' deaths that such grief was normal, and she certainly loved Joshua no less than her mother or father.

Over the next few days Eliza allowed herself to grieve deeply, not only over Joshua's death, but for the loss of all her hopes and dreams for a future in which he had been the center. She'd anticipated spending her life with Joshua, having children, growing old together. And all of that was lost to her now. She doubted she would ever find another man as fine as Joshua, and wondered if she would end up a spinster, spending her life alone now that her one true love had been brutally murdered.

The funeral was more difficult to get through than she had expected—and she had considered herself well prepared for the experience to be gruesome. Eliza was deeply grateful for the black lace veil that hung over her face, which concealed her steady flow of tears, even if the way she kept easing her handkerchief beneath the veil surely gave away the fact that she couldn't stop crying. Thankfully, Mia was constantly by her side, and Matthias was more often than not beside her as well. The three of them sat together through the service, having nothing to say except that Simon was an excellent vicar and he did well at paying a fine tribute to Joshua. Since Matthias and Joshua had no other siblings, and their parents were also deceased, Matthias had no other family with whom to share his grief. She suspected that was the biggest reason he remained near Mia and Eliza, and she found the three of them to be a strange little group—especially since she had generally disliked having Matthias around when his brother had been alive. But Matthias and Joshua had been as inseparable as Mia and Eliza. When Eliza considered how it might be for her to lose her sister to death—especially such a horrible and tragic death—her heart ached so deeply for Matthias that it was difficult not to break out into fresh sobbing on his behalf. Whether she liked him or not, she knew that he loved his brother and they'd shared a deep loyalty to each other. How could she not feel compassion for his loss, especially when they were grieving for a man they had both loved, a man who had been the center of their lives in different ways?

Eliza had difficulty forcing herself to leave the cemetery once every aspect of the service was over. Mia and Matthias remained there with her in patient silence, until a ridiculous amount of time had passed, and Mia whispered to

Eliza that they needed to leave so the sexton could finish his work. This brought to mind the fact that Joshua's body would be buried beneath a great deal of earth, and Eliza suddenly couldn't leave quickly enough. Matthias helped the ladies into the waiting carriage, insisting that he would escort them home and make certain all was well.

Even though the drive from the churchyard wasn't terribly long, Eliza took advantage of it to ask Matthias a question that had been circling in her head all day, but with the funeral taking place, she hadn't wanted to speak of it. Now the formalities were all behind them, and she looked at Matthias and asked, "Has there been any news from the police? I know you said you would keep us apprised, but I also know you might not want to burden us with anything unsavory. If you know something . . . please . . ."

Eliza was stunned to see in his eyes that he *did* know something, and he very much didn't want to say it. She realized then that she'd been hoping for some kind of reassurance that his death had been completely random, or perhaps that she would prefer it to remain a mystery. She wasn't at all prepared to hear Matthias say, compassion evident in his voice, "Eliza my dear, my brother . . . was not entirely the man you believed him to be."

"What?" Mia squawked in a very unladylike manner, perfectly expressing Eliza's own reaction. More quietly she asked, "What on earth is that supposed to mean, and what does it have to do with his death?"

Matthias swallowed hard and looked as if he were weighing his words very carefully. He finally said, "Perhaps you would prefer to remember him as the man you knew, and I should keep the information I have to myself. Does it really matter *why* he died, or—"

"Yes!" Eliza blurted. "It matters! What are you saying, Matthias?" she demanded, already wondering if she could trust whatever he might tell her. Joshua had told her many times that Matthias was not necessarily a man of high character. But that didn't necessarily mean he wouldn't tell her the truth about *this*. In fact, she believed he would have nothing to gain by maligning his brother's memory.

"I'm saying," Matthias murmured with obvious trepidation, but looking directly at Eliza, "that Joshua had a problem with . . . a very *severe* problem with . . . gambling and—"

"That is *ludicrous!*" Eliza blurted with a sardonic laugh; it wasn't at all funny, but the very notion was completely absurd.

"*And,*" Matthias continued as if he were determined to finish his point in spite of Eliza's protest—which he seemed to have expected, "I have reason to believe—and so do the police—that his death was connected to an enormous amount of money he owed to some very bad people. I'm certain it would be easier for us to believe that he was randomly murdered simply because he happened to be in the wrong place at the wrong time, but the truth is that his death was the result of his own choices, and our desire to believe otherwise will not change that fact."

Eliza gasped and shook her head and once again let out a burst of astonished laughter. "I don't know what you're trying to accomplish by saying such things," she said to Matthias while she felt Mia take hold of her arm, as if that might keep her calm, "but I don't believe you. It's as simple as that; I don't believe you. He was a good man, the *best* of men. And I'll not tolerate having you tarnish his memory for the sake of . . . of . . . I have no idea why you would do such a thing."

"I have no ulterior motives, Eliza," Matthias insisted, sounding mildly angry, "except that I believe you deserve to know the truth. Whether or not you believe me is entirely up to you. Perhaps you'll believe Constable Harrison when he tells you; I was hoping to give you some warning before that happens . . . to prepare you for the truth."

Eliza was relieved beyond measure when the carriage came to a halt, since she had no idea how to counter such bizarre accusations against the man she loved and cherished so dearly. She exited as quickly as she could manage, with Mia coming right after her, then the carriage moved on to take Matthias home. She hurried upstairs to her bedroom and Mia remained with her; it was evident her sister knew they needed to talk about what Matthias had just said. Eliza found Prudence waiting to help her, but Eliza sent the maid away, declaring she needed to be alone. Prudence left the room, and Mia closed the doors. Eliza began to pace the floor in a frenzy, frantically pulling off her black lace gloves and the veiled hat she was wearing, tossing them to the floor.

"I cannot *believe* Matthias would dare say such a thing!" Eliza spouted angrily. "I know he's a cad, but . . . why would he make up such a despicable story when his own brother is barely in the ground. I wish I'd had the nerve to slap him good and hard for saying such a thing and—"

"But what if it's true?" Mia interrupted, and Eliza stopped pacing so abruptly she nearly tripped. She turned to face her sister who was sitting with her hands holding so tightly to the arms of her chair that her fingers were white. When Eliza couldn't think of any words adequate enough to scold her sister for believing such things could even be possible, Mia added, "I'm not certain Matthias is nearly the cad that Joshua would have liked us to believe, and I see no reason why Matthias would have said *anything* to hurt you for no good reason. You want answers as to why Joshua died this way. Matthias said he wanted to warn you before you speak to the constable. Therefore, I think we need to hear what the police have discovered before we simply conclude that Matthias is lying."

Eliza couldn't believe what she was hearing, but when she was unable to contradict it, she was overcome with a sudden weakness and sank into a chair. Her mind began to spin with the horrifying possibility that what Matthias had said might be true. She was startled to hear Mia say with trepidation, "Liza, darling, there's something I need to say, and I ask you to hear me out." Eliza couldn't speak but she nodded toward her sister who took a deep breath and added, "I know how much you loved Joshua—*love* him still, of course—but I must say that there were times I wasn't entirely comfortable with him; times when I wasn't certain he could be trusted, and I . . . felt concerned."

"What?" Eliza practically choked on the word, or perhaps she was choking more on what her sister had just said. "If that's true, then why didn't you say something? Why would you want me to marry a man you believed to be less than trustworthy?"

"I *tried* to tell you, Liza," Mia said, sounding upset while she still gripped the arms of the chair as if they might save her from some kind of monster threatening to devour them both. "I tried multiple times to tell you I wasn't comfortable with things he said . . . or the way he behaved, but you wouldn't hear it; you only got angry with me for daring to malign your precious Joshua. I finally accepted that you had no interest in what I had to say unless it was what you wanted to hear, so I kept my opinions to myself and did my best to be supportive of your decisions. But now that he's gone, I have to speak up and tell you that I agree with Matthias, and I'm not at all surprised to hear what he had to say. We *do* need to hear what the police have to say, and you need to be prepared for the possibility that you will not at all *like* what you hear, but you're going to have to accept it."

Eliza suddenly found it difficult to breathe. Could it be possible? Had she truly been so arrogant and stubborn that she'd so unkindly disregarded her sister's observations? For that matter, had she been so blind as to be oblivious to any signs that Joshua was not the perfectly wonderful man she'd believed him to be? Nausea began to churn in her stomach as she wondered if she had nearly married a man who had not possessed the high moral character she'd considered most important in choosing a husband.

A knock at the door startled both her and Mia and they gasped in unison. "Come in," Eliza called, and Prudence entered to tell them that Constable Harrison and two officers were there and wished to speak with them. She was glad to hear Prudence mention his name, since she had been too upset to recall what it was from their first meeting and any other reference to him.

"Thank you," Eliza said calmly to Prudence. "Tell them we'll be down shortly."

Prudence curtsied slightly and left the room, closing the door behind her. Eliza looked at her sister, unable to hold her facade of forbearance in place now that they were alone. "Oh, Mia!" Eliza murmured. "What if it's true? What if Joshua *wasn't* the man I believed him to be? What if he *did* make choices that contributed to his dying? Being murdered in an alley?" She struggled to take in enough breath to fill her lungs. "Am I really such a fool? Have I been so blind?"

"Oh, darling," Mia said, crossing the room to take hold of Eliza's hands and help her to her feet, "you mustn't blame yourself. I believe he was a very good actor."

"But . . . you just said that I . . . ignored what *you* tried to tell me. How could I have been so unkind to my own sister, and—"

"Eliza!" Mia interrupted. "There is nothing wrong between me and you that cannot be fixed. But right now, the police are here and we need to speak with them. We simply need to be composed and hear what they have to say, and we will contend with our feelings over the matter later on."

"Of course," Eliza said and nodded stoutly, grateful for her sister's sound counsel and strength. Given the likelihood that the police were going to tell them something unseemly about Joshua, she was suddenly grateful for Matthias's warning and wished she hadn't been so unkind. But she would make certain she found an opportunity to apologize to him. Right now, she had to follow Mia's advice and pull herself together enough to get through the impending doom of whatever the constable had come to tell them.

Eliza held tightly to her sister's arm as they made the trek to the drawing room. Never had the size of their home felt so ominous to Eliza than now when it seemed to take forever to arrive at their destination, and the pounding of her heart increased with each step she took. Outside the closed doors of the drawing room, they paused to draw in deep breaths, and Mia offered Eliza some reassuring words that helped Eliza believe she might actually survive this. For now, she only had to think of surviving her conversation with the police. She couldn't even fathom anything at all beyond that—especially if what they had to tell her was in the same realms as what Matthias and Mia had both suggested.

"I think I can remain upright," Eliza said to Mia. "Let's get this over with, and then I'm going to bed until . . . I don't know when; maybe next year."

"And I will take very good care of you," Mia promised.

Eliza gave her sister a wan smile and squeezed her hand. "You always do."

Mia returned a weak smile and opened the door. The three men waiting for them all came to their feet as the ladies entered the room and Mia closed the door behind them. Following appropriate greetings, they were all seated and the constable looked directly at Eliza, saying gravely, "I know this has been very trying for you, m'lady, and I apologize for coming on the day of the funeral. You must surely be exhausted, and I will keep this as brief as possible, but I believed it was imperative for you to know what we've discovered, and for you to hear it from me, because the story will be in tomorrow's newspaper, and I certainly did not want you to receive the news in such a way."

Eliza focused on trying to keep her breathing even as she listened to the constable. She wanted to thank him for his thoughtfulness, given what she'd just heard. In her mind she could see herself and her sister sharing breakfast in one of their sitting rooms, passing the newspaper back and forth as they often did, and reading about the scandal surrounding her fiancé's death. The fact that Joshua's life—and his brutal end—were surrounded in scandal was something she had barely begun to accept, but she had a feeling that fact was about to become very real. She simply nodded toward the constable, hoping he understood her gratitude as well as her permission for him to go on, because she simply couldn't speak without revealing how she was barely managing to keep herself from becoming faint.

"We have apprehended the killer, m'lady," the constable said. "He's been arrested, and he will finally meet justice."

"Finally?" Mia asked what Eliza wanted to but couldn't.

"He is a mercenary; a man who gets paid to kill people who find themselves in trouble by consorting with men who control a powerful gambling operation here in the city. We've been tracking this man for several months; it was evidence we found in the death of your fiancé that helped us finally capture him."

"Oh, my!" Mia said on the wave of a gasp. Eliza just inhaled sharply and put a hand over her heart as if that might help slow down its pounding. "What does this mean exactly . . . regarding Joshua?"

The constable drew in a loud breath and let out it even more loudly. His eyes showed regret as he glanced from Eliza to Mia, and then back to Eliza. "I'm afraid it means that Mr. Downing was heavily involved in this gambling operation, m'lady. He was deeply in debt due to years of gambling, and these people . . . well . . . when they don't get paid, they . . . hire someone to . . ."

"Oh my!" Mia said again with even greater alarm.

"I had no idea," Eliza said in little more than a whisper, even though it was with all the strength she could muster. But she felt the need to make certain the police knew she had nothing to do with this, that she had been completely ignorant—even if that made her look like a fool.

"We're certain you didn't," the constable said. "I'm afraid it's common for those with terrible gambling habits to indulge in them without their loved ones knowing."

Constable Harrison stood as if to declare that he'd said all he needed to say. The other two men followed his lead, while Eliza and Mia remained sitting. Eliza felt completely drained of strength, and with the way Mia was clutching Eliza's hand, she knew that Mia was struggling as well. Now that the police officers had delivered the unhappy news, it seemed they wanted to leave as quickly as possible, and Eliza felt sure they wanted to be away from the awkwardness of having to deliver such terrible information. Eliza didn't mind, since she was so overcome with what she'd just learned that she wanted nothing but to be left alone with her sister.

"I believe that concludes our business with you," the constable stated with forced formality. "But of course, if you have any questions for me—or any kind of difficulty—I assume you still have the information I gave you . . . so that you know how to contact me."

"We do, yes," Mia said when Eliza didn't answer. "Thank you for everything."

Mia's words seemed to give the men permission to leave and they hurried out of the drawing room, closing the door behind them. Eliza had the urge—and even the need—to burst into heaving sobs with the futile hope of expelling her grief and horror over what she'd just learned; in her mind she could see herself crying helplessly, unable to function. But shock encompassed her entirely, and she couldn't even make a sound. Mia urged Eliza to her feet and she was surprised that she could even move, but she leaned against her sister as they slowly made their way back to Eliza's bedroom where Mia sat Eliza on the edge of the bed and knelt down to ease Eliza's feet out of her slippers.

"Get into bed," Mia said. "You're in shock; I know you are. But it's going to wear off, and you need to stay here and rest until you're able to come to terms with all of this. No one will question your need to stay in your rooms for days—or weeks if you need to. And I'll take care of everything." Eliza put her head on one pillow and held another close, curling around it while Mia tucked the covers up to her chin. "I'll be close by whenever you need to talk—or cry, or scream." Mia pressed a kiss to Eliza's brow. "I'm here, dear sister; I'm here."

Eliza could only nod as the first hint of tears crept from her eyes and trickled toward the pillow. But the sorrow she felt over Joshua's death was quickly swallowed by the horror of how he'd died, which was all gulped down mercilessly by the reality that he had not been the man she'd believed him to be. The weeping of grief merged into the need to scream into her pillow so that no one except Mia could possibly hear her audible response to this news that felt much worse than being abandoned on her wedding day, and even worse than Joshua's untimely and gruesome death. She felt indescribably angry with Joshua for his deceptions, and even more angry with herself for being such a fool. She might have found some consolation over her ignorance if Mia too had been fooled, but Eliza had *chosen* to not pay any heed to her sister's observations, and she'd allowed herself to remain blind to any possible hints that Joshua had been a duplicitous man, and she had naively made the choice to entangle her life with his.

Over the next two days, Eliza hardly left her bed. She vacillated between a sinking shock that engulfed her in numbness, and a debilitating grief that had the capacity to produce endless tears. She lost track of night and day except for the meals being brought to her room—which Mia forced her to eat—since Eliza refused to have the draperies opened, and she didn't want any of the maids coming into the room, not even Prudence. Eliza was endlessly grateful for her sister, who slept on the other side of the huge bed and was there to listen whenever Eliza needed to talk about her feelings, even if her words often came out mixed into sobbing or screaming and were likely indiscernible.

On the third day after the funeral, Eliza felt the sudden need to speak with Matthias. She had dismissed him unkindly when he'd warned her about what the police would tell her, and she felt the need to apologize to him as much as she wanted to find out what else he might know. She and Mia both agreed that attaining more information about Joshua's life would help them come to terms with his death and the reasons for it. Mia suggested that they could send a message to Joshua's brother and ask him to come and visit, but Eliza felt the need to make an effort to go and see *him*, as if that might make up for her bad behavior toward him. "And getting out of the house will do us both good," Eliza concluded.

"I cannot dispute that," Mia replied with enthusiasm.

Prudence beamed with pleasure when she was called into the room and asked to prepare a bath for Eliza, and to inform the necessary members of the staff that the sisters would be going out and would need the carriage. While Eliza bathed, Mia went to her own rooms and did the same. By the time they were both dressed and had their hair styled, it was nearing lunch, so they ate before going out. The distance by carriage from their home to that of Matthias was not very many minutes, but Eliza and Mia knew from experience that it could be an exhausting walk, especially contending with the number of people that crowded the streets at this time of day. And there were always people in such a hurry that Eliza felt safer inside the carriage, not to mention that the presence of a driver and a footman also aided her sense of feeling safe and protected. This was not a new concept, but since Joshua's death she'd felt instinctively more afraid of going beyond the safe parameters of her home.

As the carriage stopped in front of the grand Downing home, Eliza had to consciously remind herself that Joshua was dead and would not be here. She'd come with her sister to visit Joshua here more times than she could count, and now it felt as if he should be here. But he wasn't. He was dead. He was a *scoundrel* and a *blackguard!* But she couldn't think about any of that or she would not be able to remain composed enough to have a polite conversation with Matthias.

The ladies were helped down from the carriage and went through the front gate and up the steps before Mia put a hand on Eliza's arm to stop her. Eliza looked at the front door and gasped at the same moment that she felt her sister's hand tighten on her arm. There was a notice tacked on the door that was clearly some kind of legal declaration, but the only word that Eliza took in was: FORECLOSED.

"What does that mean?" Eliza asked Mia.

"It means the house was taken to pay off debtors," Mia said, her voice trembling.

"Oh, no!" Eliza muttered, finding it more difficult to fight back the urge to cry. "What will Matthias do? Where might he have gone? They have no relatives to speak of!"

Eliza heard the panic in her own voice and was glad for the way Mia urged Eliza back to the carriage, but before Mia stepped inside to join her sister, Eliza heard her speaking quietly to Clint the footman, a man whom they knew well and trusted and who assisted with many things in their household. They waited inside the carriage for a few minutes while Eliza couldn't think of anything to say that wasn't simply repeating the questions she'd already posed to Mia, which Mia clearly couldn't answer. Clint returned to report that he'd checked all the entrances to the house, and it was locked up tight, and he had peered into windows only to find that all of the furnishings were covered. The house had obviously been vacated.

"Oh no!" Eliza murmured again as the carriage moved forward to take them home. She felt sick at heart to think of how she'd spoken to Matthias, and she wondered if he was now without a home due to his brother's indiscretions. The very idea sickened her. And then it occurred to her that if she'd married Joshua, his enormous gambling debts would have affected her. She couldn't even think about that. For now, she just knew they had to find Matthias—if only she knew how to go about it.

Chapter Three

IN THE WAKE OF INDISCRETION

THE MOMENT ELIZA AND MIA had returned home they went directly up to Eliza's sitting room where they always spent the majority of their time, especially when they needed to talk or contend with a problem. And this was certainly a problem. In fact, since Eliza's supposed wedding day, they'd done nothing but contend with one problem after another and all their related emotions— and every challenge came down to the unseemly and despicable indiscretions of Joshua Downing. Eliza had expected to be married and enjoying a blissful honeymoon right now, but instead she was steeped in shock and grief, and was unbelievably grateful that she'd been miraculously prevented from marrying such a duplicitous man. Because she'd not married Joshua, the fortune she'd inherited from her father was safe from his enormous debts, and she had no legal accountability for his crimes. But Matthias had clearly not been so blessed. And Eliza felt anxiously compelled to find him and be certain he was all right.

"Where do we begin?" Eliza asked her sister as she removed her hatpin and set the pin and hat on the table beside the sofa where she sat down, as worn out as if she'd been running a long distance. "Does this truly mean he's without a home? Or would he simply have been forced to move to a place more conservative? But how do we find him? I must know he's all right!"

"I believe we have two possible sources for assistance that are quite obvious," Mia said sitting across from Eliza while she too removed her hat. "If our good friend the vicar doesn't know where one of his parishioners might have gone, then perhaps Constable Harrison would be able to use his resources to locate Matthias for us."

"Oh, of course," Eliza said with enthusiasm. "How right you are! What would I ever do without you to help think matters through? I feel as if my brain has turned to porridge."

"Understandably so," Mia said with compassion and stood again. "I'm going to send a message to both of them and we'll see what turns up."

"Thank you," Eliza said with sincere gratitude.

"And perhaps you should rest," Mia suggested. "You look so tired."

"I *am* tired," Eliza said with a sigh, "but I'm also tired of resting. I think I'll go out to the garden and take in some sun."

"I'll see you later, then," Mia said and left the room.

It took Eliza a few minutes to work up the motivation to stand and do as she'd said she would and go out to the garden. The moment she stepped out onto the patio behind the house, where lovely clusters of trees and flowering shrubberies spread out before her, she took in a deep breath of fresh air and walked slowly toward a bench conveniently located beneath the largest tree. But given the time of day, the bench was not shaded and she sat on the warm stone, turning her face towards the sun, her eyes closed against the light while she contemplated the enormous changes that had taken place in her life. When such contemplation tempted her to start crying, Eliza forced away any thoughts of Joshua and his impact on her world. Instead she just listened to the sounds of the birds singing in the nearby trees, and the not-so-distant sounds from the street in front of the house where carriages and people were continually passing.

Eliza thought back to the death of her mother. Eliza had been nearly eleven years old, and her father had made the decision to sell their country estate and live permanently in their London home. Eliza and Mia's father had always preferred the city, and once his beloved wife had passed, everything about their country estate had only reminded him of her. He had considered it a prudent decision to not waste money on the upkeep of two enormous homes when one was more than sufficient for himself and his two daughters and the servants required to care for them. Eliza's father had inherited an enormous fortune, and there had certainly been no need to be concerned about being financially frugal, but he had been a practical man who held firmly to the attitude that they were blessed to be able to live in such comfort and luxury, but there was no need to be gluttonous or wasteful. By selling the country estate, the three of them would have more than enough money to live a comfortable life, provide a good living for the people they hired to care for them and their home, and still leave a great fortune for generations to come. Other than their father, the sisters were in the unique situation of having no living male relatives to which the estate would be passed following his eventual death, an event for which he'd planned very carefully so that his daughters would be cared for in every respect. Although he couldn't have known that he would pass away at such a young age. Eliza's father had two sisters who had never married, and her mother had a sister who had also given birth only to daughters. Now, every member of the generation before Eliza had passed on. She and Mia had a few female cousins they had met only once who lived in the most northern part of England. Eliza and Mia only had each other. But oh! How grateful Eliza was to have her sister! She thought for a moment that Joshua should have been a part of their family by now, but she pushed the thought away as quickly as it appeared in her mind. Right now she focused only on the warmth of the sun bathing her face and the peacefulness of the garden in which she sat, which was surrounded by a high fence that met with the corners of the house so that it was completely private and separated from the large and beautiful yards of their opulent neighbors.

Eliza was just starting to feel a little too warm when she heard the rustling of skirts and opened her eyes to see Mia approaching. Before her sister sat down Eliza said, "Let's find a shadier spot."

"The shade would suit me better," Mia said, and they moved a short distance to where a different bench sat facing in the opposite direction beneath a different tree so that it was completely shielded from the sun.

"I wrote messages to the constable and Simon and they've been dispatched," Mia said the moment they were seated. "Now all we can do is wait."

"And pray," Eliza said with a weighted sigh. "I'm truly worried about him."

"As am I," Mia muttered with an even heavier sigh.

"I shouldn't have been so unkind to him in the carriage following the funeral," Eliza added, voicing the regret that kept circling around in her head.

"What he said was shocking," Mia said. "It was difficult for you to hear. I'm certain he understands why you would have been upset."

"But it wasn't shocking for *you* to hear," Eliza said, looking directly at her sister. "You weren't as surprised to hear of Joshua's indiscretions because you were wise enough to not be blind to his weaknesses as I was."

"They say love *is* blind," Mia said, taking hold of Eliza's hand with some attempt to offer comfort.

"Well, it shouldn't be!" Eliza insisted. "*Real* love should be anything *but* blind; it should be the opposite of blind. If two people truly love each other, they should be able to see each other clearly; they should be willing to be completely vulnerable with each other, and entirely honest."

"Yes, they should," Mia said, sounding mildly angry, "and Joshua purposely deceived you, Liza. You can't blame yourself for believing his lies when he was so thoroughly convincing."

"*You* didn't believe them," Eliza said with self-recrimination. "*You* were able to see past his deception."

Mia looked away and sighed. "I wasn't in love with him. I can understand why you would only want to see the best in him."

"To the point that I would be unkind to my sister when she was only trying to help me?" Eliza said with *deeper* self-recrimination. "What if I had married him? What if he'd lived and his deceptions had only grown more and more elaborate? Can you imagine the disaster it would have created for us? Matthias lost his home, and for all we know, his belongings as well. When I marry, all that we have will legally become my husband's. What if the entire fortune our parents worked so hard to manage well and preserve had gone to pay for the gambling debts incurred by my poor choice in a husband?"

"We can be grateful that didn't happen," Mia said.

"Yes, I consider it nothing short of a miracle that we were saved from my own foolishness," Eliza declared, hearing her own anger growing. "And yet the only reason we were saved was due to the man I loved being *murdered*. How will I ever make peace with the fact that I was such a fool? How can I ever trust myself again to know what's real and what isn't? How do I know if he even loved me? Was that too a lie?"

"I believe he *did* love you," Mia insisted.

"Did he?" Eliza asked, amazed at the depth of her own cynicism when she had never been prone to being cynical before. "Or did he love the money that would have become his once he'd married me? How will I ever be able to trust anyone, ever again?"

Mia didn't answer, which Eliza took to mean that she couldn't answer such questions any more than Eliza could. But the possible depth and breadth of Joshua's deception haunted Eliza, and she truly doubted that she would ever recover.

Following several minutes of silence Mia said, "You are wiser now, Liza. You mustn't go forward with your life assuming that everyone you encounter has the intention to deceive you the way that Joshua did."

Eliza knew her sister was right, but in that moment, she felt thoroughly damaged—and anything but wise. She felt deceived and lost and broken, and she doubted that she would ever be the same.

Due to the perpetual exhaustion that she just couldn't shake off, Eliza decided to take a nap and was glad when she awoke to realize that she'd actually been able to sleep. Being asleep meant that her mind had been given a rest from the constant swirling of difficult thoughts and memories and speculations. And she'd slept without any troubling dreams, which was even more of a blessing.

Eliza had just freshened up when Prudence came with the message that Mia would be having tea in the winter parlor and asked that Eliza join her if she was awake. Eliza found her sister sitting in one of their favorite rooms, reaching for the teapot that a maid had just delivered along with everything else needed for an enjoyable tea.

"I confess that I've grown somewhat weary of hiding away upstairs for our meals and teas," Mia said as Eliza sat across the table from her. "Perhaps it's time we attempt to return to our normal routine, even if we don't feel normal."

"I'm certain you're right," Eliza said, and Mia passed a cup of steaming tea across the table. Eliza added sugar to her liking and put some little cakes and sandwiches on her plate while she waited for the tea to cool enough for her to drink it. Overcome with a recently familiar lack of appetite, she had to talk herself into eating what was in front of her and was glad that the first bite tasted so good that it was easier to keep eating.

The sisters said practically nothing to each other while they enjoyed their afternoon respite, as if their thoughts were thoroughly consumed with things that neither of them wanted to talk about. There was nothing to be said about the present circumstances that hadn't already been said many times. Eliza knew she had far to go in being able to come to terms with all that had happened, but a part of her doubted that she would *ever* be able to heal, that she could ever be the same. And she didn't want to talk about it.

Long after Eliza had eaten her fill and the tea had gone cold, she sat at the table with her sister, still locked in silence. She sensed that Mia longed to be able to say something—anything—that might help Eliza feel better. But they both knew there was nothing to say; surely it would just take time for all of this to even feel real, and it would likely take much longer for Eliza to find healing—if such a thing were even possible; right now she doubted such a possibility.

A maid entering the room startled Eliza out of a dazed stupor. Both Eliza and Mia turned toward her as she announced that the vicar was here to see them.

"Thank you," Mia said and stood. "We'll be right there."

The maid curtsied and nodded before she left the room.

"Do you suppose he knows anything about Matthias?" Eliza asked, standing as well. "Or perhaps he's just come for a visit."

"There's only one way to find out," Mia said and hurried out of the parlor and toward the drawing room with Eliza right beside her. Eliza was surprised by the pounding of her heart as her concern for Matthias rushed to the surface of her thoughts. Oh, how she hoped the vicar had some news of him! The very idea of not knowing where he'd gone or what was happening made her feel almost as sick as she'd felt when Joshua hadn't shown up for the wedding. The comparison took her off guard, since it didn't seem logical. But nothing at all had felt logical since her wedding had fallen apart, and everything that had happened since seemed mostly like a bad dream.

"Oh, thank you for coming!" Mia said as they entered the drawing room and Simon came to his feet to greet them, bowing slightly. While Eliza closed the door, Mia asked, "Did you get my message? Do you know if—"

"I *did* get your message," Simon said as they all sat down, "and I came as soon as I could. I'm afraid I have nothing to tell you." Eliza felt so disheartened she feared she might dissolve from the combination of disappointment and fatigue that had been accumulating for days now. "I had no idea he'd been expelled from his home until I received your message," Simon went on. "I immediately set out to speak with those in the parish who knew him best, but it seems he slipped away without notifying anyone. Putting the pieces together, I can only assume that he's surely upset by his brother's death, and undoubtedly all of Joshua's problems that have come to light must make everything even more upsetting; perhaps he's even embarrassed over the matter, which would explain why he didn't tell anyone what was happening. No one I have any connection to has any idea where he's gone, and I fear I didn't know him well enough personally to be able to even guess how he might have responded to such a situation."

"Oh, it's just dreadful!" Eliza exclaimed, comfortable enough with Simon that she made no effort to conceal how upset she felt. "We must find him; we must make certain he's all right . . . that he has what he needs."

"Perhaps we should ask the constable for help," Simon suggested. "He was very kind and offered to—"

"I've already sent him a message," Mia interrupted, "although I'm certain he's a very busy man. Who can say when he might have time to look into it . . . or to let us know. I fear the police have far more pressing matters than the whereabouts of a man who has done nothing criminal."

"We can only *hope* he's done nothing criminal," Simon muttered.

Eliza felt indignant over the comment and wondered why; she'd believed for as long as she'd known Joshua and Matthias that the younger brother was a scoundrel and she'd not necessarily liked him. Why would she have changed her mind now? Finding out Joshua was not what he'd pretended to be didn't mean that Matthias was suddenly any different than what she'd believed. Still she had to say, "Why would you assume he's done something wrong, simply because his brother did? Perhaps he's merely a victim of Joshua's vile indiscretions."

"Perhaps he is," Simon stated apologetically. "You're right, Eliza; we shouldn't judge or jump to conclusions. I suppose learning all of this about Joshua has made me . . ."

"Skeptical?" Mia guessed, and Simon nodded. "Well, we both certainly understand that feeling, but we mustn't allow Joshua's misdeeds to cause us to judge others accordingly."

"How right you are," Simon said somewhat sheepishly. "Here I'm the vicar, and you are reminding me not to pass judgment. I should be more mindful of my own beliefs and live up to them with more conviction."

"Your feelings are understandable," Eliza said. "I don't know whether Matthias had anything to do with this, but I do know that I have to do everything possible to just make certain he's all right. I fear I may have misjudged him all along; maybe, maybe not. But I was unkind to him after the funeral, and . . ." Eliza was taken off guard by a surge of tears and pressed a handkerchief briefly over her mouth before she dabbed at her eyes. "Whatever he may or may not have done wrong, he's lost his brother to a murderer. And he's lost his home." Eliza took hold of her sister's hand. "I daresay that no matter what our loved ones might do or not do, it would not change our love for them—or it shouldn't. Matthias is surely heartbroken, and I need to know that he's not out on the streets."

"Then we will do everything we can to find him," Simon assured her firmly.

"Thank you," Eliza said. "I'm certain it's far more appropriate for a man to be making such inquiries. Any help you can give us would be much appreciated."

"Of course," Simon said as if helping them would be the greatest privilege of his life. "And a vicar is naturally allowed to have valid concern over a missing parishioner. It will not be a problem for me to keep probing for answers."

"You're so very good to us," Mia declared. "I wonder what we would do without you."

"The feeling is mutual," Simon murmured with a little smile toward Mia, and Eliza was completely taken aback by the realization that overcame her. Had she been so caught up in her own relationship with Joshua—and the planning of her wedding—that she had completely missed what was taking place with her own sister, right in front of her eyes? Once again, she had mounting evidence that she'd been blind. Mia and Simon shared a mutual attraction! She knew they did. She could see it as plain as day now that she'd actually bothered to pay attention. How long had it been going on? And how did Mia actually feel? Eliza now felt she had a fairly good idea about that. It was no wonder the vicar visited so frequently and made such a point of being helpful to them in every possible way! Eliza knew Simon was a good man and he would have been willing to help them regardless. But still! He was obviously attracted to Mia, and the attraction was clearly shared.

Eliza cleared her throat quietly with the hope of startling Mia and Simon out of gazing at each other in a way that was beginning to create a palpable tension in the room. They each looked toward Eliza in the same moment, both showing a mild embarrassment that quickly disappeared as soon as Simon said firmly, "I will check in with Constable Harrison myself, and if he's too busy to work on trying to find Matthias, perhaps he can at least give me some suggestions on how I might go about finding him myself. I'll take Peter with me; I believe it might be prudent to not be alone in such an endeavor, given the kind of people we know to have been involved with Joshua."

"Oh, you mustn't put yourself in any danger!" Mia insisted vehemently.

"I'll be very careful, of course," Simon reassured her. "And Peter has some experience interacting with people on the streets. I'm certain he'll be happy to help."

Eliza and Mia both knew that Peter was a member of their congregation who had been orphaned at the age of twelve and had been forced to live on the streets until he'd wandered into Simon's church at the age of seventeen—which had been just the previous year. Peter was tall and strong and had taken on many responsibilities of caring for the church building and assisting Simon in a variety of ways in exchange for having a safe place to sleep and food to eat. Peter was a kind and naturally helpful young man, and he'd become a loved member of the congregation. Eliza was glad to know that Simon had someone like Peter to help him on this quest to find Matthias, and she hoped that the constable might be able to offer some real help. A part of her feared that Matthias would never be found, and they would forever be left wondering what had happened to him, but she tried to think more positively and hold onto the hope that this mystery would be solved and she could have the peace of knowing that Matthias was safe and well in spite of what his brother's indiscretions might have done to send his life into such upheaval.

Eliza and Mia did their best over the next few days to resume a normal routine, even if it felt as if they were simply going through the motions of daily life while the absence of any company made it clear that their lives had changed in ways that were anything but normal. For months prior to Eliza's planned marriage to Joshua, her fiancé and his brother visited nearly every day, and often shared meals or tea or with both Eliza and her sister. Sometimes Eliza and Mia went to the Downing home to visit or enjoy tea or dinner. And Simon often joined them at either of their homes, since he was a good friend to all of them. Occasionally Peter came along with Simon, and when the entire group was together, they had the most fun of all. They'd enjoyed delightful conversation and sometimes played silly games that made them all laugh a great deal, or sometimes they relished musical entertainment since Simon, Eliza, and Mia all had some degree of training at the piano, and there were lovely pianos in both homes where they met to socialize.

Now, the silence of long days became deafening. The absence of Joshua and Matthias spoke of the horrors that had taken place. And Simon's absence was keen evidence of the mysteries still hanging over them. He'd sent more than one message to let Eliza and Mia know that he was doing all he could to find Matthias, but he'd been confronted with some significant challenges among his other parishioners, which were taking up a great deal of his time. He wrote to say that Peter was doing some investigating on Simon's behalf, but as of yet they'd not been able to uncover his whereabouts. He also wrote that the constable was very busy as well and had promised to look into the matter at the first opportunity, but he had other more pressing investigations that needed his attention. Constable Harrison had sent a message to Eliza stating that very thing and expressing his apology at not being able to help them straightaway, but he did promise to do all he could just as soon as time allowed. Eliza and Mia both understood that these men were extremely busy and they were doing the best they could, but it still felt frustrating to not be getting any assistance while days were passing and Matthias's welfare was foremost on Eliza's mind—especially while she was doing everything in her power to not think about Joshua at all. Thinking of the man she'd nearly married, how he'd deceived her, and how he'd died did nothing but cause Eliza anxiety; therefore, she pushed all thoughts of him away and chose to focus on other things. And she felt certain that once she knew Matthias was all right she would be able to put a more concentrated effort into getting her life back to normal—even if she wasn't certain what that might be like, given all that had changed.

Eliza was glad for the distraction of a ladies' luncheon that she and Mia were invited to attend. It had been a tradition among their local peers ever since they'd been old enough to come out into society. But sharing an opulent lunch and card games with frivolous and light-minded young ladies didn't prove to be as satisfying as Eliza had hoped. It was as if all that had happened recently in her life had left her with a perspective these other ladies could never understand when their greatest concerns were the latest fashions, the grandest social events, and the pursuit of husbands with fine fortunes and great reputations. More than once Eliza had to stop herself from blurting out that men could not be trusted, that the very institution of marriage was a gamble, and a woman could be gambling away everything of value by legally uniting herself with a man who would then immediately take possession of her every belonging and her financial security. Eliza's ability to keep quiet was aided by frequent meaningful glances from her sister, which let her know that Mia's thoughts were much the same. And Eliza marveled over the very idea that not so long ago she had shared the ideas and priorities of these young women with whom she regularly associated. But now that her fiancé had been murdered and left in an alley due to his own dishonesty and despicable habits, Eliza felt as if she'd become a completely different species.

In the carriage on the way home from the luncheon, Eliza shared her feelings with Mia and wasn't surprised to hear that Mia had observed much of the same. "Also," Mia added, "did you notice how not one of them said a word to either of us about Joshua's death? Not a single syllable of sympathy for your loss!" Mia sounded angry. Eliza hadn't even thought about *that*, but now that Mia had mentioned it, she was appalled to realize that her sister was right. "No doubt they've all heard about the scandal surrounding the situation, but do they believe that your grief over losing the man you love is any less because he died so ignobly? If anything, there is *more* grief involved in contending with the discoveries that have come to light. And yet these paltry women can't offer a single word of compassion. I don't believe I'll be wanting to attend any more of these luncheons. Whether or not you choose to do so is up to you."

"Oh, I agree with you completely!" Eliza declared, hearing an anger in her voice that she felt sure was rooted in a much deeper sorrow. "I would rather read a good book than waste time associating with such women." She reached for her sister's hand and squeezed it. "I'm so very glad we have each other."

"As am I," Mia agreed and squeezed back.

After returning home, Eliza was assaulted by a fresh wave of grief—which was not a surprise considering that it hadn't been so many days since Joshua's death. And despite everything she'd discovered, she'd loved him deeply and his absence in her life felt devastating. But Eliza was shocked by the amount of anger that came with this particular onslaught of tears. She sent Prudence away somewhat sharply and wasn't surprised to have Mia enter her sitting room a minute later, since Prudence had likely run to tell Mia that Eliza was upset. Eliza initially wanted to snap at Mia and send her away as well, but she quickly realized that her sister's presence offered a listening ear to all the things Eliza needed to say. Words that had been senselessly circling in her mind for days suddenly burst forth with a rage unlike anything Eliza had ever experienced. She ranted about Joshua's deception, his despicable gambling habit, and his apparent intention to gamble away *her* fortune, as well.

"Now, you don't know for certain that's true!" Mia protested. "Joshua loved you! I'm certain of it!"

"I believe he loved me," Eliza growled, pacing sporadically about the room, "but that doesn't change the fact that he would have legally gained possession of my every asset, and we could have been financially destitute in no time."

"Surely he would not have done that to you!" Mia insisted. "To us!"

"Just as surely as he would not have done that to his *brother*?" Eliza snapped, and Mia gasped as if she had not fully made the connection in her mind until that moment.

"Oh, good heavens!" Mia muttered and fell into a chair, putting a hand over her heart. "Do you really believe that Joshua would have . . ." She couldn't finish.

"I do *not* believe he would have had a dramatic change of character simply because we exchanged marriage vows." As Eliza stated a truth that had been difficult to even think about, she felt a momentum building inside her that made it easier to continue talking about the terrible truths she'd been forced to accept about the man she'd nearly married. "Every conversation we shared about our relationship . . . our future . . . was filled with the implication that there were no secrets between us, that we knew everything about each other." Eliza sat down as if being able to finally say these things aloud made it feel less necessary to pace as a means of trying to expel her anxiety. "I've gone over and over those conversations in my head. He had every possible opportunity to admit to me that he had a problem that was negatively impacting his life . . . and that it would very well end up impacting mine. He didn't offer the slightest intimation that such was the case. He purposely deceived me, Mia." She paused to wipe away the ongoing flow of tears with her handkerchief. "He deceived all of us."

"Do you think Matthias knew?" Mia asked fearfully. "If he knew and said nothing to warn you, is he not also guilty of deceiving you?"

"I don't know," Eliza snapped, deeply uncomfortable with a question that had haunted her. "He admitted in the carriage that he knew *something* of Joshua's problems, but we have no idea how much. Whether or not he knew . . . I need to know he's all right. If he was involved in any way, then perhaps his losing everything is simply a matter of justice. Perhaps he's on the run—afraid that what happened to Joshua could happen to him—and we'll *never* find him, and never know all of the truth. Or perhaps he's as much a victim as the rest of us. Unless we find him and have the opportunity to speak with him, we will never know for certain."

Mia erupted to her feet and took over Eliza's usual role of pacing the room. It was clear that what Eliza had said about Matthias had upset her. "I don't know how we could *ever* trust him again! How could he not have known of Joshua's unscrupulous involvements?"

"Not so long ago you were defending him!" Eliza countered.

"And now I've had more time to think about it," Mia rumbled. "He admitted that he knew something about what Joshua was doing. They're brothers, for goodness sake! If either you or I were sneaking around, or lying, or spending ridiculous amounts of money, the other would absolutely know!"

"Yes," Eliza agreed, "but for all that Matthias frequently socialized alongside his brother, they were not necessarily as close in their personal lives as you and I."

"Why are you defending Matthias?" Mia demanded and stopped pacing to glare at her sister, planting her fists firmly onto her hips. "You don't even *like* him."

Eliza was startled by her sudden urge to hotly and boldly defend Matthias, but she smoothed her response down to a more suitable level. "It's not that I dislike him," Eliza corrected. "I've never really known whether or not I could trust him."

"Exactly!" Mia said, pointing a finger at Eliza.

"And yet," Eliza drawled in a loud voice that she hoped would really get her sister's attention, "I realize now that everything negative I'd heard or perceived about Matthias came from Joshua. He was regularly telling me about his brother's misadventures, about his concerns that Matthias would end up in ruin. Is it not possible that Joshua told me such things to somehow attempt to . . . I don't know . . . perhaps to deflect any attention from his *own* misdeeds? Could he have spoken ill of his brother as some kind of insurance that on the chance that his deceits were discovered, he could somehow lay the blame at Matthias's feet? How can I assume that Matthias is a bad person when I've believed for so long that Joshua was practically perfect in every way?"

"You make a fair point," Mia said, "but I still don't feel at all convinced that Matthias couldn't have known a great deal about what was going on, or more likely that they were involved in these terrible things together. It's my opinion that he's left London for the sake of his own safety and we will never see him again. And now that I've had some time to think about it, I believe it would be best for all of us if that were the case. I don't *want* to see him again! I don't want to have to figure out whether he was involved . . . or whether we can trust him. I want to put all of this behind us and just . . . try to put our lives back together . . . and somehow return to some kind of normalcy."

Eliza sighed and sank back farther into her chair. "That might be possible for you," she said and sighed again. "You aren't tainted with having been betrothed to a man who was murdered because he was a blackguard associating with other blackguards. I'm not certain it's possible to recover socially from such an event."

"What on earth are you saying?" Mia asked, astonished. "You've done nothing wrong, Eliza! You don't deserve to be tainted by this! You deserve the deepest compassion!"

"Oh?" Eliza chuckled sardonically with no hint of humor. "Do you mean like the compassion I received at the luncheon we attended? At best the situation will be ignored by those with whom we associate, but I believe it's more likely that no honorable man will be interested in a woman who has proven to be such a fool. The gossip about me has likely blossomed into a firm belief that I too was involved in this gambling scheme . . . that I couldn't possibly have been betrothed to a man and not had some awareness of his shady dealings; therefore, no respectable family would want anything to do with me, let alone consider me a suitable prospect for marriage."

"How can people simply assume you would be guilty only because you were betrothed to him? As I've heard, it's not uncommon at all for men to be involved in all kinds of unpropitious behaviors while their wives remain ignorant. And you were not even married yet."

"So, you believe Matthias must surely be guilty to some degree because they are brothers, but society should assume me to be innocent even though we were betrothed?"

Mia sighed and looked away, a deep sorrow consuming her countenance. Eliza appreciated her sister's compassion, but at the same time she didn't want Mia to be so burdened by all of this; Eliza felt plenty burdened enough for both of them. Still, as long as they were already steeped in this difficult conversation, she felt the need to tell her sister the remainder of the thoughts that had been troubling her. "All things considered," Eliza said, "it's likely best if I just come to accept that I will never marry, and—"

"How can you even think such a thing?" Mia demanded, backing into a chair as if her legs might cease to support her.

"For the reasons I just stated," Eliza said, "the possibility of finding a suitable husband has become highly unlikely." She was surprised by how calm she sounded, when the very notion of living out her life without the fulfillment of marriage and children threatened to crack her heart completely in two. "And even *if* a man showed an interest in me, Mia, I'm not certain I could ever bring myself to trust him. I was fooled so terribly . . . embarrassingly . . . and . . ."

"And you are wiser now; stronger," Mia protested.

"Am I?" Eliza emitted another humorless chuckle. "I don't feel strong at all; I feel as if I will crumble like shattered glass at any given moment." She took in a deep breath and drew back her shoulders. "But I must be realistic; I must accept what's happened and move forward and make the most of my life as it is. As you know, I'm in the rare position of being a woman in possession of a great fortune. It's only in the absence of any male relatives that such a thing happens."

"Yes, of course," Mia said. "We've often talked about this."

"Yes, and you know that according to our parents' wishes, you and I have equal claim to all that they left behind—even though I am the legal heiress due to being the eldest. But . . . we also know that according to the law, once I marry, everything that is mine will belong to my husband, and I will have no right or claim to it." She sighed again and felt her shoulders slump as the air slid out of her lungs. She consciously drew her shoulders back again, needing every bit of strength and courage she could muster in order to face all the damage Joshua had left in the wake of his death. "I want to believe he was marrying me because he loved me, and perhaps he did. But I cannot deny—putting together all that I now know—that for a man like him, with his particular addictions, he was very likely *more* in love with my money. I have to ask myself if he would have married me if I'd been poor, and the answer is absolutely not. So, for all that

I truly loved him, I can feel my love turning cold, and I don't know if I can ever love again when I could never be certain of being able to trust a man with all that he would stand to gain by becoming my husband. Therefore, remaining unmarried is absolutely the best solution . . . and realistic by all counts. I shall find great joy in being an aunt to *your* children, and they will inherit all that our parents left to us. That's all there is to be said."

Eliza turned to look at her sister, whose hands were folded in her lap while silent tears slid down her cheeks. Mia clearly had nothing to say that might offer a reasonable recourse to Eliza's edict. But her sorrow over the situation was evident. Eliza shared Mia's sorrow; in fact she felt it so deeply that she had the sudden need to be alone, fearing she would burst into one of her all-too-frequent bouts of sobbing, and she was sick to death of crying in front of her sister. She'd grieved for Joshua's death, and for the discovery of what kind of man he'd really been. And now she needed to grieve for the future she had always hoped for and the reality that it would never be. But she preferred to keep this particular grief to herself. Mia now knew where her thoughts had been, and having made her declaration, she excused herself and went to her bedroom, locking both doors before she kicked off her shoes and crawled into bed, wishing she might never have to get out again.

Chapter Four

THE PRODIGAL BROTHER

Despite her reluctance to get out of bed and try to go on living, Eliza did so when it was time for tea. She knew Mia would still be upset regarding their earlier conversation, and Eliza wanted to put on a brave face for her sister's sake so that they could work together to move forward. Since Mia had just spent some time with the housekeeper for the sake of going over menus and household business in Eliza's stead, she came to tea with a few tidbits of household gossip that gave them something to talk about besides the ever-persistent drama with which they'd been contending. Neither of them approved of gossip in the sense of talking maliciously about the difficulties in other people's lives; for them it was more a matter of keeping up on the news and events of people they knew. One of their kitchen maids had just become engaged to a young man who worked with his father in a family bakery that was only a short distance from the house. Following their marriage, the couple would live above the bakery and the maid would continue with her job—at least for the time being. Both Eliza and Mia were happy for the maid, even though they barely knew her. And they avoided even mentioning Eliza's disappointments regarding marriage; accepting her own inevitable spinsterhood didn't mean she couldn't be happy that someone else had found the right person with whom to spend her life. Eliza knew that she and Mia were very blessed regarding the financial abundance they'd inherited, but there were moments when she envied the simplicity of having a life where love alone could determine choices related to marriage, and matters such as needing to pass over her entire fortune to a husband were irrelevant.

The housekeeper had also told Mia about how the butcher's wife had given birth to a healthy girl; since this particular butcher made regular deliveries to their home, most of the servants knew him well and they were all pleased with the news. Each member of the staff would be contributing a small amount of money to collectively purchase a gift for the baby, and Mia had told the house-keeper that she and Eliza would also like to contribute. This pleased Eliza, since she liked to be involved in such things as much as possible. She often wished that she and Mia could be more involved in the socializing they knew took place among the members of their household staff, but there were distinct lines drawn between Eliza and Mia and the people who worked for them. However, being able to offer a contribution toward a gift for the butcher's new baby was a small thing that made them feel a little more a part of the community.

Both Eliza and Mia loitered over their tea much longer than usual. Eliza couldn't help but think how quiet it was. Joshua was dead, Matthias was missing, and both Simon and Peter were very busy helping search for Matthias, as well as caring for other matters among the members of the parish. The absence of any company created a silence that was difficult to fill with their own conversation once they had exhausted all there was to say. A maid brought a fresh, hot pot of tea for which Eliza was grateful. She poured some into her cup following the small amount of milk she'd added first, then focused fully on adding just the right amount of sugar. She then cradled the warm cup in her hands while it cooled to the perfect temperature for her to begin sipping. While Mia gave her own cup of tea the same excessive attention, their absence of conversation didn't seem quite so stark, but once they'd both finished drinking all the tea any lady could possibly handle, the silence became ridiculous.

Determined to do something about it, Eliza stood and declared, "I think we should go to the library and find a good novel. There are surely a hundred books or more in there that we've never read; we used to read together a great deal and we've not done so for a long time."

"We've had other things to fill our time," Mia said, standing as well.

"Yes," Eliza swallowed her temptation to either cry or get angry, "but we're not going to talk about that; I'd prefer not to even *think* about that. What we need is a distraction. Until we hear from Simon or the constable—or both— there is absolutely nothing we can do; and it's possible that even when we *do* hear from them, there will be nothing helpful in what they have to report. Surely sitting around and aimlessly waiting will only make us both go mad."

"I cannot dispute that," Mia said with chagrin.

"Come along," Eliza said, taking Mia's hand. "Let's get ourselves lost in a good book and we'll both feel better. Perhaps we can find one good enough that even when we're not reading, we'll be thinking about the characters and it will be all the more helpful in keeping us from thinking too much about things over which we have no control."

"I cannot dispute that either," Mia said as they made their way across the house to the library.

The room was dim when they entered since all the drapes were closed, but they each took on a couple of windows and pulled back the draperies, which unfortunately didn't help as much as Eliza had hoped; clouds had settled heavily over the city, blocking the sunlight in a way that seemed to mimic the dark mood Eliza was fighting to ignore. In spite of the clouds, the beauty of the library could not be disguised. Eliza considered it to be one of the loveliest rooms in the house. She loved the endless shelves of books that were situated between and around the windows; in fact, it was as if every space in the room had been cleverly filled with bookshelves and there was hardly an inch of actual wall. In the center of the room were three sofas and a number of comfortable chairs, all of which had been arranged in a kind of semicircle that faced the enormous fireplace. Even though it was summer, the clouds that blocked the sun had left the house mildly chilly and Eliza was glad that everything needed for a fire had already been stacked neatly on the grate and she only had to strike a match and touch it to the kindling for a fire to begin building, adding warmth and also some light to the area within its reach.

Eliza and Mia began searching the shelves for anything that might catch their interest, both of them every bit as silent as they'd been at tea. It took nearly an hour for each of them to find a couple of possible titles that might be worth their time, but at least their search had filled some time that would have otherwise been fraught with tension. They sat together near the fire to look over their choices and decide which book they would actually read, provoking enough conversation to increase Eliza's hope that this project would keep them increasingly distracted from all the things that neither of them wanted to think about; things over which there was nothing left to say that hadn't already been said repeatedly.

They finally decided on a book to start reading aloud together and Mia did the honors of engaging in a tradition that had started when they were young children and their father would read stories to them in this very room. On a small, ornately carved table between two of the sofas sat an exquisite hourglass made from finely crafted silver, embedded with tiny emeralds, diamonds, sapphires, and rubies, creating a magnificent housing for the glass that held an hour's worth of sand that would slip from one end to the other until it was turned over, after which it would go back in the other direction. Eliza and Mia's father had often told them the story of how this hourglass had been a gift from his grandfather to his grandmother when they had married, and he had been fortunate enough to

inherit the piece. Even though its monetary value was enormous, its sentimental
value was absolutely priceless. Eliza and her sister had never indulged in stories
here with their father—or each other—without turning over the hourglass so
the sand would begin to fall and mark the amount of time they were reading.
As children they had known that when the sand had all fallen to the bottom half,
it was time for them to go to bed. As they'd grown older it had simply been a way
of holding onto cherished memories. For both of them, the hourglass was likely
the most precious item in the house. And now that they'd settled on a book, Mia
turned the hourglass over, the sand began to fall, and she started reading aloud.
But it was only a few minutes later when a knock at the door startled them, and
they turned just as a maid entered and announced, "The vicar is here to see the
both of you. He's waiting in the drawing room."

"Thank you," Eliza said as both she and Mia came to their feet.

After the maid left, Eliza met her sister's eyes and found her own nervousness reflected there. She admitted readily, "I'm as nervous to think that he
has some kind of sound information as I am that he'll tell us Matthias is nowhere
to be found. I'm not certain which would be worse."

"When we have no idea what to expect—or what Matthias's involvement
may or may not have been—it's impossible to know."

"Come along," Eliza said to her sister and led the way out of the room.
"Perhaps his visit is nothing more than a desire to simply check in on us and
see how we're doing."

"If nothing else, it will be nice to have some conversation beyond our
own." Mia chuckled wryly. "It's not that I don't enjoy your company, Liza, but
you're surely as bored of me as I am of you."

"More just bored than bored of *you*," Eliza said and chuckled in return. "I'll
try not to be insulted by *your* boredom of *me*."

"You know very well what I meant," Mia said lightly; they were both
teasing and they both knew it, but they also knew they were indeed bored and
struggling with anxiety over Matthias's whereabouts as well as their ongoing grief
over all that had happened with Joshua. Although Eliza had to wonder, given
all that Mia had said about her mistrust of Matthias, whether Mia would truly
prefer that Matthias would never be found, whereas Eliza desperately wanted to
know of his whereabouts and be able to speak with him.

"Of course," Eliza said, focusing only on the present interaction with her
sister, and they entered the drawing room.

Simon stood to greet them, and his smile felt like a welcome reprieve to
Eliza. She then noticed an especially warm smile pass between Mia and Simon

and recalled what she'd forgotten in the midst of her own self-absorbed thoughts. There was undoubtedly something more than friendship evolving between the vicar and her sister, and she wondered if it might actually lead to marriage. She wondered whether she should tell Mia that she had figured out her secret, but she would give that some more thought later.

"Oh, it's so good to see you!" Eliza declared.

"It is indeed!" Mia said with unmasked enthusiasm.

"The two of you look as lovely as always," Simon said. "I confess I feel deprived when I go too long without being able to enjoy your company."

"We feel the same," Mia stated as they all sat down, although Eliza believed Mia experienced a different kind of enjoyment of Simon's company than that which Eliza felt.

"I apologize for not coming by sooner," Simon said. "It seems that as a vicar I either have far too much time on my hands, or I am needed immeasurably more than I am able to handle. Peter has been very helpful in assisting where he can, but there are some matters that only I can see to."

"Of course," Eliza said. "The needs of your parishioners must always come first."

"And the two of you are among my parishioners," he stated. "Our friendship aside, I know that you're going through a terrible time, and I sincerely wish I could have been here more to assist you in your grief, and also in your concerns regarding Matthias's absence. However, I have finally been able to connect with Constable Harrison—twice in fact; first to discuss the problem with him and our reasons for concern, and again when he sent word to me that he had some information. I met with him and he asked me to pass along the apology that he didn't have the time to respond personally to the message you had sent him, but he has asked that I share on his behalf the information he found."

"So, there is news of Matthias?" Eliza asked anxiously.

"Yes," Simon said with a smile that made her heart quicken; surely, he wouldn't smile if the news was bad. "The constable has given me the location of Matthias's new residence. He is still in the city, and an officer spoke with him just yesterday to see if he had any further information regarding all that happened with Joshua. I know nothing about the latter, but the officer reported that Matthias is well."

"Oh, I'm so relieved!" Eliza declared, putting a hand over her heart as she let out a sound that combined a heavy sigh with some kind of gasp. "I've been so worried."

"As have I!" Mia declared. Her words surprised Eliza a little, given how negatively she'd spoken of Matthias earlier. At the very least, Mia was clearly confused regarding her opinions of Matthias; but then, so was Eliza.

"As have *I!*" Simon echoed, winking at Mia as if he considered it terribly significant and humorous that they had said the same thing. Mia smiled at him in a way that was almost simpering. Eliza found their unmistakable mutual attraction mildly annoying, and she wondered whether she and Joshua had been so annoyingly obvious when they had been falling in love. For a brief moment she allowed herself to recall that happy time when all she had been able to see was every possibility of a bright and fulfilling future with a man she had believed to be good in every respect. Now her dreams for the future had been shattered and her every memory of Joshua was tainted with the likelihood that he had been deceiving her. While a part of her believed he had truly loved her in spite of everything else, given the depth of his deceptions, she couldn't be certain, and since he was now dead, she would never know.

"If we have the location of his new residence," Eliza said, "then we must call on him. At the very least we must offer our condolences for how negatively this has all impacted his life. We have been friends for a long time; surely it's only right for us to offer support regarding his changed circumstances."

"That's all very true," Simon said with a caution in his voice that let Eliza know he intended to say something contrary to her thinking, "however, I wonder if he might be feeling some embarrassment over his changed circumstances."

"Are you saying he might not want to see us?" Eliza asked.

"I sincerely don't know," Simon said. "I don't know if your visit would be considered welcome or intrusive."

Eliza thought about that for a minute, wishing Mia might express an opinion on the matter—but she didn't. Eliza finally said, "I believe we should err on the side of being charitable. It's no secret among the three of us that we've often wondered if we could even trust Matthias, and I can't deny that for all his ability to be enjoyable company, I've always wondered whether he was trustworthy. And yet I trusted Joshua completely, and look where that got me. I suppose I'm saying that until I have reason to believe otherwise, I'm going to assume that Matthias is a victim of his brother's indiscretions, just as we are. Surely visiting him and taking some kind of friendly offering would be appropriate."

"And perhaps," Mia said, "being able to speak to him will help us gain some understanding of his level of involvement—or ignorance—regarding the trouble that Joshua had gotten himself into." Although it was subtle, Eliza could tell from her sister's tone of voice that she believed Matthias was not to be trusted, but she was struggling to be impartial regarding the matter.

"Assuming he tells us the truth," Eliza stated, trying not to sound cynical, and perhaps attempting to validate her sister's concerns. For all that Eliza herself felt concerned about Matthias and wanted to believe he *was* a victim of Joshua's deceitful choices, she couldn't deny that something inside her had become less trusting. In truth, she believed that inquiring after Matthias's welfare was simply the right thing to do, but whether they continued to associate with him beyond that would depend a great deal on how she felt once they were able to speak face-to-face.

As if he had read her mind, Simon suggested, "Surely among the three of us we have enough insight and wisdom to discern Matthias's motives. I think it's an excellent idea to visit him; however, I will insist on accompanying you. The location of his residence is not in a favorable part of the city."

"What?" Eliza blurted, initially surprised by what this meant, then immediately wondering what she might have expected. If Matthias had lost his home and had been in a position where he'd simply needed to find a place to live, why should it have been surprising that he'd been forced to take up residence where two ladies should not visit without a man to accompany them? Eliza knew there were many places in London that were considered unsuitable for proper young ladies to venture into, but until now she'd never thought very deeply on what that might mean exactly. With her determination to call on Matthias, perhaps they were about to find out.

According to the plans they'd made the previous evening, Simon arrived at eleven o'clock the next morning and, following the information given to Simon by the constable, the three of them traveled by carriage to the location where Matthias was apparently now living. Eliza watched from the carriage window as they moved from streets lined with large, beautiful homes, past shops and boutiques where they had often shopped, and into an area that just looked darker, as if the sun had moved behind clouds when the carriage had left the pristine part of the city where only the wealthy and privileged lived and shopped. Eliza felt so shocked by what she was seeing that she instinctively reached for her sister's hand. Mia was looking out the opposite window and seemed to be having the same reaction. Simon seemed unaffected, and Eliza realized that as a vicar he had likely witnessed more than his share of the impact of poverty. For Eliza, she never could have imagined what she was seeing—likely because she'd simply never seen anything like this before. She felt mildly angry over the fact that young ladies of privilege would be kept from even observing how the poor lived. How could she possibly make informed decisions about life if she had no awareness of anything but her own sheltered world, which existed not so far from children begging in the streets, and every person going about their business looking older than their years, with hunger and hardship showing literally on their faces? The buildings were crammed close together, as if they'd been shoved against each other by some kind of malevolent giant who had been trying to crowd as many people together into tiny spaces as possible. The storefronts were dark and the windows dirty, implying that when people were just trying to survive, there was no time to worry about the appearances of where they lived and worked. When many faces glared at the passing of a fine carriage, Eliza and Mia both shrank back from the windows, and Eliza felt grateful not only to have Simon with them, but also for the driver and footman who were both strong men. She hated the way she felt unsafe, not necessarily because the people on the streets were bad, but rather because they looked desperate. And the visible evidence of such a fine carriage—which represented people living in ignorance of any real want—likely created resentment.

In the space of a minute or two, Eliza felt her entire perception of the world shift, and she also felt as if she had the tiniest glimpse inside the minds of people who lived this way, and how it might be to see life through such eyes. Of course, at the same time she was well aware that she truly had no idea. One carriage ride through a poverty-stricken area of the city surely did not have the power to give her empathy for living in such conditions, but it had certainly given her a hefty dose of perspective. And gratitude. She'd always felt blessed for being born into privilege, and her parents had taught her and Mia to never take such a life for granted but to use it for good. Still, she could see now that their teachings had never included any kind of real comparison on which to base such gratitude. Now, Eliza felt more grateful than ever for the luxurious life they lived, but she also felt a keen desire to do more for people who were not so blessed.

Her mind was spinning with a great many thoughts when the carriage came to a halt and people around them showed increasing curiosity and suspicion. But Eliza was distracted by the appearance of the tall, sinister building standing beside them.

"He lives *here*?" she said to Simon, who looked more keenly out the window.

"This is the location the constable gave me," Simon said. "I have a flat number. I believe it's up two flights of stairs."

"Oh, my," Mia muttered as Ferris opened the carriage door and briefly blocked the opening as he said, "I'll be going in with the three of you to help make certain all is well." Ferris not only drove the carriage whenever that task was needed, but he did other things to help wherever the necessity presented itself; he'd been around as long as Eliza could remember, and she trusted him completely. "Clint'll stay with the carriage to keep it safe," Ferris added.

"Thank you," Eliza said, and Ferris stepped back, holding out his hand to help Eliza, then Mia, descend from the carriage. Simon followed without any assistance.

Simon led the way into the open doorway of the building, with Ferris coming behind the ladies, carrying the basket they'd brought along that contained some simple offerings for Matthias. The stairs going up were barely visible from the light that shone through a dirty window. The place was noisy with the sound of babies crying, children playing a little too boisterously, and adults shouting. Eliza and Mia remained close together as they headed up the stairs, although Eliza had to go ahead since the stairs were not wide enough for more than one person. Eliza kept her eyes focused on her feet, fearing that she might miss a step seeing as they were much narrower than those to which she was accustomed. She also lifted her skirts higher than she normally would when ascending stairs, perhaps hoping to keep them from brushing against the floors of such a place. She knew the idea was irrational. She walked in dirt and sometimes mud all the time while traversing the usual places she went on foot in the city. And she never minded having the hems of her skirt getting soiled. In this case, she knew it was more an emotional response to her personal repulsion for this place. The very idea of Matthias living here was making her stomach churn. Whether she liked him or not—trusted him or not—she hated the very idea of Joshua's brother being reduced to such circumstances, especially when it was most likely that Joshua's atrocious behavior had been the reason for it.

They finally arrived at the correct floor and Eliza took her sister's hand as they followed Simon down a dingy hallway lit only by a dirty window at the end of the hall. Simon paused in front of a door and looked at the number painted on it as he said, "I believe this is it."

"Oh, I do hope he's at home," Eliza said quietly, not wanting all their efforts in getting here to be wasted.

"As do I," Simon said and knocked. Eliza was aware of a woman and her three children passing them in the hall, eying them skeptically. They were dressed so poorly that their clothing could literally be called rags. Eliza had never imagined such a thing. She wanted to chase after the woman and give her the small amount of money she always carried in her handbag when she went out in public. But she knew such behavior would be ridiculous and probably inappropriate. She turned her attention back toward the door, which she hoped desperately would come open, and she felt heartened to hear some noise on the other side that indicated someone was there. She hoped they had the right place, and that they were indeed about to be certain that Matthias was all right. Her argument with Matthias in the carriage right after the funeral rushed through her mind like a hot wind and she wanted so badly to just apologize for not believing what he'd told her.

The door came open abruptly and startled Eliza from her thoughts. For a long moment of tortuous silence, the little group in the hallway stared at Matthias with the same kind of surprise he wore on his face as he stared back. He clearly had not expected to be found by his friends, and his embarrassment was immediately evident. His feet were bare, and his dark breeches looked as if they could use a good laundering, as did the white shirt he wore which was untucked and only partially buttoned; she suspected he had hurried to put it on when he'd heard a knock at his door. His wavy hair looked more unkempt than usual, and for the first time ever he sported a beard; or perhaps it was more accurate to say that he'd simply chosen not to shave since the funeral. His green eyes looked cynical and suspicious, and Eliza hurried to try and ease his concerns.

"Forgive us for arriving unannounced this way," she said. "We've all been . . . concerned, and . . . the constable helped us find where you were living. I just . . . well . . . I owe you an apology, and—"

"What on earth for?" Matthias demanded.

"For not believing what you told me after the funeral," Eliza explained, taking a step forward to face Matthias more directly while the other three stood at her sides. "I know now that you were right, and you were only trying to help me, and . . . forgive me for the way I was so . . . unkind."

"There is no apology necessary, Eliza," he said. "I know the news was shocking and you were upset; in truth you reacted exactly as I expected you would. All of it was shocking; it's still shocking. I'm so sorry for what you've had to go through because of Joshua's poor habits."

Eliza took a quick glance around and an even quicker glance beyond him into what little she could see of his living quarters. She could see a tiny table and a chair, both made of wood with the paint mostly worn off, and she could see the corner of a bed. Given the depth of the room between the door and the window she could see, and the space between doors in the hallway, she knew it was only one room, and a small one at that. Is this what he'd been reduced to? Given what he'd just said, it was easy for her to say, "And I'm so sorry for what *you* have had to go through because of his poor habits." Matthias drew back his shoulders and lifted his chin as if he'd just been struck by an invisible blow. When he didn't speak, she hurried to add, "Is that how we politely describe what he did that brought him—and us—to this end? Poor habits? It was surely much worse than that if it resulted in his death, and your losing *everything*."

"I'm all right," he insisted, but Eliza recognized the clear indication in his voice *and* in his countenance that his declaration was more out of pride than an honest answer regarding his present situation.

Knowing this was not the place for them to have the kind of conversation she knew they needed to have, she hurried to say, "Will you come to dinner? We want to see you . . . we need to talk, and—"

"I'd invite you in," he interrupted, sounding less defensive, "but . . . it's not an appropriate place to invite company and . . ."

"It's all right," Mia said, and Eliza was glad for her support, even though her voice was toneless. Eliza guessed that Mia wanted to be appropriate, and she considered it necessary to give Matthias a fair chance to explain himself, but she sincerely did not trust him. "Please come to dinner. We've all suffered from what Joshua did . . . and his death. We need to talk."

"I concur with the ladies," Simon said, and the two men exchanged a cordial nod.

"I can't this evening," Matthias said. "I . . ." he hesitated and cleared his throat uncomfortably, "I . . . need to work." Eliza was glad that she'd kept herself from gasping. Matthias had been born into a wealthy and privileged family, and he'd lived his life as a gentleman. She admired and respected those who worked for their living, but this was such a drastic change for him; she knew the situation had to be dreadful if he'd started working to support himself, and if all he could afford for living quarters was what she saw before her.

"We understand," she hurried to say, not wanting him to be embarrassed by his admission. "When *can* you come? Tell us when it would be convenient for you and we will accommodate your schedule."

"You're very kind," he said. "The pub where I work is closed on Sundays. May I call Sunday evening?"

"That would be perfect," Eliza said with enthusiasm, glad that it was Friday so they didn't have to wait too many days. "Would you be able to come for tea and stay through the evening for dinner?" She wanted to have plenty of time for them to talk about all these changes as much as possible, and she also felt suddenly concerned about whether or not he was eating properly. Being able to feed him *twice* in one visit gave her some kind of strange comfort.

"Yes, I can do that," he said. "Thank you for the invitation. I will be there."

Eliza felt a gentle prod and turned to see that Ferris had nudged her with the basket he was holding; since he'd remained a short distance away, mostly in the shadows, Matthias hadn't likely even noticed him or the basket in his hands.

"Oh," Eliza said, taking the basket from Ferris and holding it toward Matthias, "we brought you a few things that we stole from the kitchen." She saw the slightest hint of a smile on his face; they'd often joked about stealing food from the kitchen between meals, even though it was ludicrous to use any reference to theft when Eliza and Mia owned everything in the house. Fearing he might be embarrassed over the prospect of being offered charity, she hurried to add, "Don't be proud about accepting a few baked goods and some preserves. We know you've been through a great deal, and we also know how you love Mrs. Miles's scones and biscuits."

"That I do," Matthias said and took the basket, offering a gracious nod. "Thank you; every bite will be very much enjoyed and appreciated."

Eliza smiled at him, wishing she could think of something else to say because she didn't want to say goodbye. It was as if she'd grown to feel responsible for his well-being, and as long as they were standing here facing each other she knew he was all right. Through a few seconds of silence, it occurred to her—just as it had the last time she'd seen him—that there was an absence of the smell of cigar smoke that had always been a part of who he was. Perhaps he could no longer afford them, she thought, then hurried to break the silence that was beginning to feel awkward.

"I'm glad you're all right," she said to Matthias, even while she thought that *all right* was relative. He was safe and sheltered, but he was likely *far* from all right.

"I hope you are all the same," he said as if his plight might be equal to the grief and shock that Eliza, Mia, and Simon had been contending with regarding Joshua's death and all that was related to it.

Eliza was relieved to have Simon reach out his hand toward Matthias, who set the basket down in order to receive the vicar's firm handshake. "It's good to see you, my friend. You know where to find me if you need anything, anything at all."

"Thank you," Matthias said.

"We will look forward to seeing you on Sunday," Eliza said; Mia repeated something to the same effect, and they left Matthias standing in the doorway of his room. They'd only walked a few steps when Eliza heard the door close, and she couldn't get to the carriage fast enough. Not only did she want to be out of that wretched building, but she had the sudden urge to burst into tears and wanted to be within the safety of the carriage before she even considered allowing her grief out into the open.

Eliza was relieved that by the time they were in the carriage and it was moving toward home, her temptation to cry had settled into that numbing sensation of shock that had recently become far too familiar. She had grieved over Joshua's death, *and* his betrayal. And it had been the most painful thing she'd ever endured. She knew it would be irrational to think that she didn't have a great deal more grieving to do before she had any hope of making peace with all of this. But the impact of Joshua's choices on his brother made her feel literally sick to her stomach. She wanted to know exactly how all of this had happened, and she prayed he would be forthcoming with information when they were able to share a much-needed conversation. She couldn't imagine *his* grief considering that he'd not only lost his brother, but he'd lost *everything*. He'd been forced to change his entire life, and Eliza couldn't begin to fathom how that might feel. Thinking of her interactions with Matthias since Joshua's death, she found it difficult to imagine how she had always mildly disliked him prior to that time. She wondered now just how much Joshua might have lied to her regarding his brother's character. The churning in her stomach calmed down slightly when she formed the determination to make a fresh start with Matthias and get to know him based on his own merits and her own discernment of them, rather than anything she'd been told in the past. She was already counting the hours until Sunday's tea, and imaging how glad she would be for the opportunity to have a real conversation with Matthias Downing.

While Eliza forced herself to adhere to a more normal routine with the hope that doing so would help her life return to normal, she found herself thinking a great deal about Matthias. She felt confused over her impressions of him prior to Joshua's death, and how those impressions might have impacted the way she'd treated him. An uneasiness began to rise inside her as she considered the possibility that she had been unkind to him based on the things that Joshua had told her about his brother. She didn't want to think of herself as an unkind person, but as she prayed to see herself realistically—without any rationalization or justification—she found her prayers being answered as memories came clearly to her mind of times when she had been terse or abrupt with Matthias, if only mildly so. But mild or not, she knew him to be a perceptive man and he surely would have noticed even the slightest rebuff from her. Considering his present circumstances made her regret any kind of negative behavior she might have shown toward him in the past, although it occurred to her that she shouldn't be unkind to *anyone* no matter their station or circumstances.

Strangely obsessed with counting the hours until she could speak with Matthias when he came to visit on Sunday, Eliza was drawn to reading from the Bible. Her father had often read from the Bible with Mia and Eliza, but since his death that habit had dissolved. However, Eliza could easily recognize that she was in the midst of some extremely tumultuous circumstances in her life, and both of her parents had taught her plainly that the Bible held many words of understanding and comfort if a person earnestly and humbly searched for those answers.

Eliza wasn't surprised when Mia declared the need for some time alone; they'd been spending almost every waking minute together since Joshua's death. Eliza had needed her sister's support, and Mia had been there. But Eliza knew this had been difficult for Mia as well, and it was completely understandable that her sister may have grown weary of being constantly available to help sustain Eliza in her grief. They saw each other at meals and tea, and otherwise kept to themselves, each needing time to simply think and ponder all that had happened and its effect on their lives.

Except for sharing meals with her sister, Eliza spent every waking moment on Saturday alone in her sitting room, exploring the Bible, amazed at how she seemed to be led directly to the passages she needed. The pages of the New Testament practically fell open to a concept that she found fascinating, even though she had to read the verses multiple times before their meaning in regard to her began to make sense.

And why beholdest thou the mote that is in thy brother's eye, but considerest not the beam that is in thine own eye? Or how wilt thou say to thy brother, Let me pull out the mote out of thine eye; and, behold, a beam is in thine own eye? Thou hypocrite, first cast out the beam out of thine own eye; and then shalt thou see clearly to cast out the mote out of thy brother's eye.

Eliza felt a strange inner intuition which implied that the meaning was important for her to understand regarding herself, but despite staring at the words and reading them over and over, she couldn't quite put a finger on what it meant exactly. She decided to set it aside for now and perhaps discuss it with Simon the next time she saw him. She was pleased when Prudence came to tell her that the vicar had come to call on them, but Mia had lain down after tea and appeared to be sleeping.

"Thank you," Eliza said to Prudence. "Tell him I'll be right down."

Prudence curtsied and hurried away. Eliza took a few minutes to freshen up and check her appearance in the mirror before she went to the drawing room, taking the Bible with her.

"Oh, I'm so glad you came," Eliza said as she entered and Simon stood to greet her. "Why *did* you come?" she asked, realizing that he had no idea she'd been studying the Bible and had questions.

"I just felt the need to check on you and your sister," he said as they were both seated across from each other, "and I had some free time. I knew that if it wasn't a good time you would have one of the servants tell me."

"Well, it's a perfect time," Eliza said, "for me, at least. Mia is resting."

"I know our visit to Matthias yesterday must have been very difficult for you, but on the way home none of us had much to say; perhaps we were in shock. Now that we've had some time to think about it, I wondered how you're feeling."

"It's very upsetting," Eliza said. "I've had two very prominent thoughts on my mind. First of all, I want to be able to help him, but I don't know how I could go about that appropriately. I know he would not be happy to accept anything more from me than a basket of scones and preserves. So I would be glad to hear any ideas you might have in that regard. You're in the business of helping people."

"I've been giving that matter some thought myself," Simon said. "I don't have any specific ideas, but I'll keep thinking and we'll talk about it some more."

"Good," Eliza said. "Thank you."

"And the other thought?" he asked. She felt momentarily confused and he clarified, "You said you had two prominent thoughts on your mind."

"Oh," Eliza said and looked down at the Bible she had set on her lap with her finger tucked between the pages where she'd been reading. She quickly explained how she'd spent many hours with the Bible, and her desire to find answers that would help her become a better person, and to come to terms with all that had happened.

"That's excellent," Simon said with a smile. "A vicar can't likely hear better words than that."

Eliza returned his smile before she went on. "I've read this passage over and over; I'm drawn to it and fascinated by it, but I'm not certain I understand it completely." She paused and asked, "What is a *mote* exactly?"

"Ah," Simon chuckled. "Beams and motes. It's a fascinating concept. I'm always amazed at how such powerful messages are summarized in such simple concepts. A mote is a tiny sliver, or perhaps even a speck of dust. Think of how it feels to have even the tiniest speck of something foreign in your eye."

"Oh, it's dreadful!" Eliza declared.

"Now consider the size of any piece of wood that could be called a *beam*, and how that would affect your vision if it were directly in front of your eyes."

"You couldn't see at all."

"Exactly," Simon said with enthusiasm. He clearly enjoyed engaging in conversation that centered around spiritual principles, but then he wouldn't make a very good vicar if that weren't the case. "So, say for instance that I had a mote in my eye, and it was causing me distress and making it difficult for me to see clearly, but your vision was blocked by a beam. How could you possibly be in a position to tell me how I'm feeling or what my perspective about life might be when you can't even see me?"

Eliza thought about that for a long moment and felt the concept sink in with a heart-quickening validation of its truthfulness. "Good heavens, that's remarkable," she said. "So . . . the passage is telling us that we need to work on removing the beams—and even the motes—from our own eyes in order to be certain that we're seeing clearly before we attempt to help our brother—which would mean any other human being."

"Exactly," Simon said. "And it's important to take any specific teaching in the Bible and combine it with *all* the teachings in order to discern the meaning clearly."

"How can I do that when I know so little of the Bible?"

"Well, I believe it's a good thing for any person who has access to a Bible to study regularly, and I'm certainly happy to help you answer any questions. I suppose the most important thing to understand is charity. Even after we've put the effort into being able to see clearly—and that can take a great deal of effort, in my opinion—we need to *always* view the challenges and behaviors of others through a lens of charity. And we need to be charitable toward ourselves as well as others; a proper balance is important."

Simon leaned forward and carefully placed his forearms on his thighs. "I feel like I'm trying to give you a dozen sermons in one conversation, and we can certainly talk these things through as much as you need. I will always be your friend as well as your vicar, and I know you've been through some terrible things of late, and it will take time to come to terms with those things. But our trials can indeed make us stronger and wiser if we embrace the opportunity to allow them to teach us, rather than letting trials make us cynical and angry."

Eliza nodded, understanding what he meant but also trying very hard to take in everything he was saying in a way that *would* help her become stronger and wiser rather than allowing the opposite to happen. One thought stood out and she said, "Tell me more about being charitable."

"It's rather simple but incredibly powerful," Simon went on, becoming more somber, or perhaps more reverent. "Be charitable to others, Eliza, in the way that Jesus taught. While we use the word *charity* to often describe giving to those in need . . . to those lacking the basic necessities of life who require assistance, when you study the descriptions of charity in the Bible carefully, it's clear that there is a deeper definition. I believe that being charitable means quite simply to treat others as Jesus would treat them. He did not tolerate hypocrisy or deceit, and yet he was always kind and respectful—even to those who had committed grievous sins. The Apostle Paul taught that 'charity never faileth.' I believe those three words are sufficient to describe how we should live and treat others."

Simon maintained his silence, allowing Eliza to think about everything he had said. She felt her understanding being enhanced by his insights, but she also knew she needed more time to ponder everything he'd said. When the silence grew long, Simon finally spoke in a soft voice, as if he didn't want to detract from the reverent mood of their conversation. "May I share something else with you? Something that's been on my mind regarding the present situation?"

"Yes, of course," Eliza said eagerly. She always appreciated Simon's insights.

"You know the story of the prodigal son," he stated as fact. She'd attended the same church as Simon for as long as they had lived in London, and she'd watched him evolve into the vicar of their parish. She'd heard the story growing up, and she'd heard Simon himself preach more than one sermon based on its principles of acceptance and forgiveness.

"We don't know whether Matthias was actively involved in Joshua's dishonorable activities. Perhaps he too made bad choices, and perhaps he's simply a victim. Either way, he is clearly in a difficult situation. He has no family to go to for help. We are the closest thing to family he has now that his brother is dead. I don't believe that trust is a requirement of forgiveness, Eliza. It might take time for us to know if we can trust him . . . to know if he had unsavory involvement in these things. But regardless of that, I believe we need to be very mindful of forgiving him. Whether he's done anything that requires forgiveness or not, we should receive him back into our circle of friendship with an attitude of acceptance, and *then* we will do our best to determine whether he is trustworthy—as opposed to the other way around. Do you understand what I'm trying to say or—"

"Yes," Eliza said, feeling humbled by his perception. She'd been struggling with this very thing, vacillating back and forth between believing Matthias to be innocent and deserving of their support and kindness, or perhaps guilty and not deserving of anything, least of all their trust. But Simon had just shared the most basic of Christian principles that helped her put her own difficult feelings aside and consider how all of this had affected Matthias before she jumped headlong into any judgment or assumptions about him. Forgiveness and charity needed to remain most prominent in her thinking, and she felt grateful to have found some answers that helped soothe her concerns, and she anticipated Matthias's visit even more for a number of reasons.

Chapter Five

THE TRAITOR

SUNDAY MORNING ELIZA WOKE UP very early, finding her room barely filled with the hints of predawn light. Her mind went immediately to Joshua, and she was overcome with how much she missed him. He'd been at the center of her life for several years now. At first as friends, and then through a lengthy period of courting, and also a long engagement. She'd grown to love him dearly, and even though her discovery of his deception and appalling behavior had been shocking and difficult to accept, it hadn't changed the fact that she *had* loved him, and she missed having him around. She'd lost track of how many days it had been since they should have been married and instead he'd been found dead, but it certainly hadn't been nearly long enough to adequately grieve the loss of a beloved fiancé—nor to come to terms with her sorrow over learning that he was not the man she'd believed him to be. Eliza cried into her pillow over losing the man she loved to an atrocious death, and she cried over the disillusionment she'd been assaulted with following his death. She could see now that she'd lost her naivete, her gullibility, and some of her innocence; and perhaps that was good in the respect that she had grown wiser and more discerning. But she had also lost some of her trust in people and the world around her, and she hated the way she seemed to be seeing her life through a veil that perhaps distorted her view of what was going on around her and the people she encountered.

When Eliza grew weary of just lying in bed crying, she put on a dressing gown and slippers and went to her sitting room where she sat near a window and opened the Bible, thumbing through pages with the hope of finding something that might soothe the pain hovering inside her. She read a little here and there by the light coming through the window that was growing brighter, but she found nothing that caught her attention. The clock on the mantel chimed and she glanced toward it, realizing she would soon need to get ready for the day if she hoped to enjoy her breakfast and get to church on time. With only a few minutes left to read, she thumbed through more pages and saw a passage that caught her eye. She read the simple words and felt her heart quicken at the same time a warmth surrounded her as if a blanket had been wrapped around her shoulders. Tears stung her eyes, but they were not the tears of grief and sorrow that she had been crying every day since Joshua's death; instead these were tears of a calm and soothing joy that she could never describe, but she knew her pain had been diminished, at least to a degree.

Eliza blinked several times to release the tears and allow them to slide down her face so that she could read the words again. *Peace I leave with you, my peace I give unto you: not as the world giveth, give I unto you. Let not your heart be troubled, neither let it be afraid.* Reading the words yet again, somehow Eliza knew that she would find peace regarding all that had happened, even if it came slowly and with time. She also knew there was no reason to fear that other people would betray her the way Joshua had. She knew in her heart that these experiences *had* left her wiser and more discerning, and she needed to be observant and careful, but she also needed to be kind and trusting; she needed to be charitable to others, just as Simon had taught her.

In the carriage on the way to church, Eliza shared her experience with Mia, and it was no surprise that her sister was deeply touched by all that Eliza had learned and felt—even if Eliza was only able to share a very condensed version since the distance to the church wasn't very long. But they promised to talk about these things later in more detail, and they both agreed they were very much looking forward to Matthias's visit that afternoon. However, Eliza sensed something reserved and perhaps mildly skeptical in Mia—even if it was too subtle for Eliza to address openly. She believed that Mia was doing her best to be appropriate in regard to Matthias, but that she was consciously reserving judgment, or perhaps she had already decided he simply could not be trusted. However, she didn't want to make such an audacious statement. Eliza felt certain that with time everything would work itself out. So she let the matter rest.

"I'm hoping he can help answer some questions," Mia said with the barest hint of cynicism in her voice just as the carriage came to a halt. "There's so much about what happened that I don't understand . . . so many holes in the story."

Ferris helped the ladies step out of the carriage, holding an umbrella over their heads to ward off the rain that had begun to fall since they'd left home. He shifted the umbrella into Eliza's hand once she had her feet on the ground. She thanked him, then she and Mia moved toward the open doors of the church, both huddling beneath the umbrella and holding their skirts up just enough to try and keep the hems from getting wet.

"I agree," Eliza said to her sister as they stepped carefully around some growing puddles on the uneven cobblestone. "Now that Joshua is gone, I hope that Matthias will be forthcoming about what he knows, and I do hope he's not involved in any way."

"Oh, I hope for that too!" Mia said, giving Eliza hope that her sister's cynicism toward Matthias was not too severe. "I want to trust him . . . and I believe he needs us . . . and perhaps we need him. Although, I confess . . . I'm struggling over his possible involvement. Still, I don't want anything to get in the way of our continuing to be friends, despite all that's happened."

"I agree," Eliza said again, and they stopped talking as they entered the church to the sound of gentle organ music, and Eliza left their umbrella near the door before they walked to their usual pew. They'd both offered Simon a little wave as they'd passed him on their way in, but he'd been busy greeting other parishioners and they generally left him to do so since they were blessed enough to be able to visit with him regularly at other times throughout the week.

Eliza enjoyed the service, even though her mind kept wandering to the passage she'd found this morning in the Bible and the way it had made her feel. Simon gave an excellent sermon about being charitable, which had much the same message as what he'd told her the previous afternoon. She wondered if their conversation had been inspiration for his sermon, or if he'd been sharing a portion of his ideas for what he had already planned on preaching. Either way, it was a very fine sermon and Eliza told him so as they were leaving the chapel, and she made certain he knew that he too was invited to tea and dinner since he was also a good friend to Matthias. Simon had assumed he was meant to be included, but Eliza couldn't recall whether she'd officially extended an invitation or not.

Once again Eliza and Mia huddled beneath the umbrella to make their way through the continuing rain to the waiting carriage. Ferris was loyally waiting there to help them inside while remaining as dry as possible, and they were home and sheltered from the storm within a matter of minutes. Once Eliza and Mia had both changed into more comfortable dresses, they visited and shared lunch, and Eliza was glad to be able to tell Mia more about what she'd learned from studying the Bible, and also from her lengthy conversation with Simon the previous day. She was grateful for Mia's genuine interest in what she had to say, and they agreed that they would like to discuss these principles in more detail but they were both feeling tired and decided that indulging in a nap prior to tea would likely make it possible for them to more fully enjoy Matthias's visit.

Eliza was surprised to awaken and realize not only how quickly she'd fallen asleep, but how long she'd slept. She'd barely sat up in bed, attempting to become fully awake when Prudence knocked at the door, then entered timidly, telling her that she needed to hurry and freshen up in order to be ready for tea. A few minutes later, while Prudence was attending to Eliza's hair in an attempt to smooth over the damage done by her nap, a maid came to announce that Mr. Matthias Downing had arrived and was waiting in the drawing room.

Eliza let out a deep sigh of relief, not realizing until that moment how much she'd feared he might not come. If there were things about the situation he didn't want them to know, or if he was overly embarrassed about his present circumstances, he might very well have preferred to avoid the people he'd once considered friends. But Matthias was here, once again in her home, and Eliza was taken off guard by a sudden fluttering in her stomach at the thought of seeing him. Glancing at her reflection in the dressing-table mirror while Prudence attended to her hair, Eliza noted that she looked flushed. She was glad to see that Prudence was too busy to have noticed, even though her reaction was surely nothing but relief to finally be able to talk to Matthias and reassure him that their friendship would go on despite Joshua's death. Eliza also hoped Matthias would be able to offer insights into the situation that might help them all come to terms with the confusing string of events that had deeply affected all their lives.

"Thank you," Eliza said to Prudence once she was finished, and Eliza hurried out of her room with the intention of going to find Mia before she went to meet Matthias. In most cases they preferred to be together when receiving company, and Eliza knew this was certainly one of those cases. She was surprised to find Mia in the hall waiting for her. They took each other's hands and squeezed tightly while they both took in a deep breath at the same time.

"I do hope and pray this goes well," Eliza said.

"As do I," Mia added, sounding more nervous than Eliza felt. "I want him to feel comfortable despite all that's happened . . . and I want to be able to help him if that's possible, but I confess . . . at the same time I'm genuinely struggling with the fact that . . . well . . . how do we know he isn't at least partly to blame? How do we really know if he'll tell us the truth or—"

"We talked about this earlier," Eliza said, hearing evidence once again that Mia was confused about the situation with Matthias, wavering back and forth between feeling distrustful and wanting to help him. She couldn't deny her own confusion at times, although she had settled more firmly into what she felt the need to state very clearly. "We will be *charitable* as Simon so wisely suggested, and we will also be discerning. Being kind and helping someone in need doesn't mean being taken for a fool. Between the two of us—and with Simon's wisdom on our side—we will surely be able to know what's true and right—and what's best. Now, until we have evidence to the contrary, let's just assume that Matthias needs our friendship and support, and simply enjoy our time together."

"Of course," Mia said and nodded stoutly before they went together to the drawing room.

Matthias stood as they entered, as did Simon who had obviously arrived while Matthias had been waiting. They exchanged appropriate greetings and were all seated before Eliza said to Matthias, "I'm so very glad you came; I believe we all are." Simon and Mia made noises of agreement. "So much has changed in so short a time, and I think we're all overdue for a long conversation that might help us all catch up. But that doesn't mean I want our time together to be glum and macabre; it would be nice to just talk and laugh as friends again, don't you think?"

"I would like that very much," Matthias said, seeming surprised over Eliza's last comment. She wondered if he'd believed he'd been invited here for some kind of interrogation, indicating they had no desire to continue their friendship. "And yes," he added, "I believe there is much we need to talk about and—"

A maid brought the tea cart into the room and carefully set dishes out on the little table situated within reach of where everyone was seated. After the maid left, they all took turns pouring out their milk and tea and adding sugar to their liking, and they managed to maintain some trivial small talk while they enjoyed a variety of little cakes and sandwiches.

"Your kitchen always produces the most appetizing components of a good tea," Matthias said, overtly savoring his food in a way that made Eliza wonder what he'd been living on since his life had been reduced to such a menial status.

"Indeed they do," Simon added. "Mrs. Miles is not only a precious soul; she is a most excellent cook and she manages her kitchen staff well."

"We are very blessed," Eliza said, increasingly conscious of just how blessed they were while she sat across from Matthias, recalling the living conditions they'd found him in two days ago.

When everyone had finished eating and relaxed more into their chairs, Eliza wondered how she could possibly begin to ask Matthias the innumerable questions she had simmering in her mind. She was relieved beyond words when he cleared his throat, clasped his hands onto his lap in a gesture of some kind of resignation, and said firmly, "If it's all right with you, I'm just going to tell you everything I know . . . tell you all that's happened and why . . . and then we can hopefully be free of this cloud hanging over us. And with any luck, once you've heard what I have to say, you'll still allow me to stay for dinner."

Eliza wondered if that was some kind of warning that he had an unsavory confession to make, or if he was simply nervous. She was glad that he hurried on so she didn't have time to wonder.

"I've known for a long time that we needed to have this conversation," Matthias said, looking down at his hands. "In fact, I very much wanted to have it long before the wedding plans were made official, but Joshua had sworn me to secrecy, and he was very convincing whenever he made the case to me that as his brother I had a special obligation to never reveal what I knew to anyone else. In fact, he went so far as to threaten me with the possibility that if I betrayed him . . . that if he went down, I would go down with him." Matthias sighed loudly while Eliza could hardly breathe. He lifted his eyes and looked directly at her. "It seems he was right. I didn't betray his secrets, but he certainly took me down with him."

Matthias kept his gaze locked with Eliza's and she could almost feel him daring her to ask him any question, as if he *wanted* to be able to speak freely and be free of the burdens he'd been carrying. The lengthening silence provoked her to speak. She knew before the words came through her lips that they might sound offensive, but she had to say them. "So . . . you're telling me that you knew . . . even before Joshua and I became engaged to be married . . . that he was . . . what? Deceiving me? Deceiving all of us?" She motioned toward Mia and Simon.

"Yes, m'lady, that's what I'm saying," Matthias stated, the quivering in his voice a distinct contradiction to his firmly set jaw and the courage in his eyes.

"M'lady?" Eliza echoed. "You've called me by my given name for years."

"After what I've done, I no longer feel worthy to do so," Matthias said. "I feel honored that you would even invite me into your home because you surely suspected that I knew far more than I had told you. Even from what I said to you after the funeral you must have known. I expected you to be furious with me, and yet you showed up at my door with nothing but kindness—all of you." His eyes darted to the others but came back to Eliza; because she had very nearly become his brother's wife, it seemed he felt he owed her the most direct explanations. "Once you hear everything I have to say, I will leave and never come back if that's what you feel is most appropriate, and I will understand.

However, I am indeed grateful that you are at least giving me the opportunity to speak my piece."

Again, there was taut silence until Simon said with compassion, "It's clear you felt obligated to keep your promises to your brother, even though you disagreed with what he was doing. The dilemma must have been a terrible burden for you to carry."

Matthias looked as surprised by the comment as if he'd been assaulted with a bucket of icy water. Had he truly come here expecting anything but kindness and understanding? Had he sincerely believed it was a possibility Eliza would kick him out of the house once she heard what he had to say? For all she knew, they'd not heard *everything* yet, she could understand why he'd felt compelled to keep Joshua's secrets.

Believing that Matthias—at the very least—needed the opportunity to tell them all that he knew, Eliza motioned toward him with her hand and said kindly, "Please . . . tell us all you know. He's gone now; there's no reason to keep secrets for his sake. I think we just . . . want to understand what happened . . . and why."

"Yes," Mia agreed, and they all looked expectantly toward Matthias who cleared his throat again and once more looked at his hands in his lap as he pressed his palms over his thighs as if to wipe away their sweatness. Then he clasped his hands again but didn't look up.

"I had so many arguments with him," Matthias said, the regret in his voice evident. "I can't count how many times I begged him to stop getting involved in these betting schemes . . . in these late-night secretive games of cards and dice. And I told him over and over that he needed to be honest with you." He lifted his eyes briefly to look at Eliza, then looked down again, as if he were ashamed. "I told him it was nothing short of cruel to go into marriage while keeping such terrible secrets from a potential wife. He arrogantly disagreed and embraced his bad habits above all else." Matthias sighed and shifted in his chair but still kept his eyes turned downward. "I knew there was debt, and I knew he was selling valuable items our parents had left to us. I suspected the people he dealt with were unsavory and lacking in integrity, but . . ." He looked up with naked desperation showing in his eyes, as if nothing mattered more to him in this world than having them believe he was telling the truth. "But . . . I swear to God I had no idea how bad it was. If I'd had even the tiniest inclination that his debt was so deep . . . and that the people to whom he owed money would actually resort to murder if they were not paid . . . I would have gone to the police myself a long time ago—if only to keep him alive. If I'd known these secrets I helped him keep would cost him his life, I would have . . . I would have . . ." Matthias hung his head in shame, and Eliza's heart began to pound as she heard him sniffling and realized he was crying. She'd never seen him cry before. And why would she? They'd socialized a great deal, but never before had they shared such dramatic circumstances, and neither of them ever would have expected to. They'd hardly seen each other since Joshua's death. She'd seen some evidence of grief when he'd come with Simon to tell her that they'd identified Joshua's body and there was absolutely no doubt about his death. But it was Eliza who had fallen apart then, crying uncontrollably to the point of embarrassment. And Matthias had offered her comfort. Now his grief and sorrow were spilling out and Eliza felt helpless, not wanting to embarrass him. She wondered if his tears were more based in losing his brother to death, or the shame and regret he felt over his role in covering Joshua's misdeeds. Both, she suspected.

Eliza's gratitude to Simon was beyond words when he moved from one chair to another so that he was sitting directly beside Matthias and put a brotherly arm around his shoulders. "There, there, my friend," Simon murmured and offered Matthias a handkerchief, but the latter reached into his pocket and drew out his own, which he wiped across his face while he kept his head bowed.

Eliza exchanged a long, concerned glance with Mia before they both looked toward Simon. Eliza hoped the vicar might be able to silently communicate something to help them know how to best respond to Matthias's confessions and this unexpected expression of his sorrow. Simon offered a subtle nod, as if to say that they just needed to allow Matthias some time, and that Simon would manage the situation. Eliza had been grateful countless times that their dear friend was a vicar; he always seemed to know exactly what to say or do in difficult or awkward situations. Since Joshua's disappearance and the subsequent news of his death, Simon's skills of compassion and communication had been especially appreciated. But at this moment, Eliza concluded she'd never been more grateful for Simon's intervention and the special abilities of his character as well as his training. Eliza wanted desperately to also sit beside Matthias and throw her arms around him with some attempt at offering comfort. But she knew that doing so would hardly be considered appropriate, and even if she disregarded social convention given the extenuating circumstances, she felt certain that such a gesture at this moment would only make Matthias more embarrassed and uncomfortable.

Eliza put her trust in Simon to take the lead while she and Mia silently waited for Matthias to gather his composure. Once he had, he apologized profusely for getting so upset, but Simon offered a great deal of reassurance that it was only natural for him to be grieving over a great many things, and that he was among friends.

"I wonder how any of you can still consider yourselves my friends after everything I just told you," Matthias said.

"You've explained everything," Eliza said, "and it's evident that you have lost more than any of us due to Joshua's indiscretions. I would surely be a hypocrite not to forgive you, Matthias. I believed everything he ever told me without question. I look back now and realize how naive and foolish I was. I recall many little things that didn't ring true . . . things that made me uncomfortable, but . . . I ignored my instincts; I believed his lies."

"That does *not* make you a hypocrite, Eliza," Matthias insisted.

"I agree wholeheartedly," Simon added.

"Perhaps," Eliza said. "But certainly gullible, and certainly a fool."

"You wanted to think the best of him," Matthias said. "I see nothing wrong with that. You loved him."

"Yes, I did love him," Eliza admitted, looking down. "Although I can see now that love is never enough in and of itself. Love without trust . . . without integrity . . . without honesty . . . is doomed, is it not?"

"I thank God the marriage never took place," Mia stated.

"Oh, I feel the same!" Matthias said zealously, perhaps even with anger. "I knew that your money would become his." Again he looked directly at Eliza. "And I was so worried that his gambling would gobble up your fortune in no time. I don't know if you could ever believe me, but the morning of the wedding—after I'd not had a moment's sleep—I had decided to stop the ceremony. I had realized that when a man of God asks the friends and loved ones if there is any reason they know of why these people should not be wed, that I had to speak up or I would surely never find peace with God again. I could not have let him go through with it, Eliza, even though I knew he would have been furious with me . . . he likely would have disowned me. And you would have . . . well, I don't know how you would have responded, Eliza, but I suspect you wouldn't have believed me. At least not at first. I don't know how it would have come together, or rather . . . fallen apart. But I knew I couldn't allow the marriage to take place. I have never prayed so hard in my life as I did in seeking guidance to know how to publicly declare what I knew . . . and to make certain his debts didn't become *your* debts. But I never could have imagined such an outcome. I wonder sometimes if . . ." His voice quavered and faded.

Simon put a hand on his shoulder. "What is it, my good man?"

Matthias looked directly as Simon and asked, "Is it possible my prayers brought him to his death? His death prevented the marriage from happening. Could it be my fault that he—"

"Oh, my friend," Simon said with a compassion deeper than Eliza had ever heard him express, "Joshua's death was undeniably the result of his many bad choices. The timing was certainly a blessing in regard to sparing Eliza and Mia, but I don't believe for a moment that your sincere desire to prevent the marriage would result in any such thing. You must *not* think that way."

"No, you must not," Eliza added vehemently. "I'm glad to know you intended to prevent the marriage. I fear I might have been angry . . . might not have believed you. I didn't believe what you told me after the funeral."

"Which is understandable," Matthias said. "In fact, I wonder why you are all so readily believing everything I'm telling you now. Even as I hear the words come out of my mouth, they sound so . . . ludicrous. How can you possibly know that I'm not every bit as deceptive as my brother and that I'm simply telling you a version of the story that will keep myself in your good graces?"

"Your sincerity is evident," Eliza said, even while something deeply uncomfortable sparked inside of her, making her wonder if he *was* telling the truth. And she knew her sister so well that she could almost hear Mia thinking the same thing.

"Perhaps I'm a very good actor," Matthias said. "Perhaps such skill runs in the family."

Mia spoke up in a firm voice that betrayed the cynicism Eliza knew she had been trying very hard to subdue. "You sound as if you're trying to convince us that you're not being truthful."

"I swear to you that I'm telling the truth," Matthias insisted. "I simply wonder . . . how you can believe me when the truth includes an admission of how much I've deceived you in the past."

Silence followed his statement, as if everyone in the room had to measure and weigh it carefully, and Eliza sincerely didn't know what to say. She *did* believe he was telling the truth, but to try and convince him of that right now felt awkward and she couldn't find the correct words. Once again, Simon saved them all by saying, "It's been my experience that when trust is broken in a relationship, it simply takes time for it to mend. I'm of the opinion that the only way to learn to trust is to simply offer trust . . . but perhaps cautiously. People make mistakes; it is the nature of our humanity. If forgiveness and the rebuilding of trust were not possible, no relationship would ever last. I suggest that we let this conversation rest . . . that we all take some time to think about it . . . and that we go forward as friends and work on rebuilding our friendships on a new foundation, a foundation rooted in complete honesty and integrity and forgiveness."

"I think that sounds perfectly excellent," Eliza said and expected Mia to say something in agreement, but she remained silent, which was highly unusual. Eliza ignored her sister's lack of response and hoped she wouldn't regret it when she said directly to Matthias, "It's evident you are very much in need of friends. We would be terrible friends indeed if we turned our backs on you now . . . when your situation is so dire."

"I do not seek any pity," Matthias insisted, sounding mildly defensive. "My needs are being met and I will manage just fine."

"Will you, though?" Eliza asked. "It's ridiculous to think of the great abundance in our possession, and to know that you are living in such poverty because of Joshua's bad habits. We want to help you, Matthias."

"And I absolutely insist that I will not accept any such help," Matthias declared adamantly.

Again, Simon knew how to ask the right questions. "You said that your needs are being met and you're managing. Since we are all friends here, would you be willing to tell us more about what happened exactly with the financial situation? And how you *are* meeting your needs? There's no reason for you to be ashamed of the situation, not with us."

Matthias sighed loudly; it was evident he didn't want to talk about this at all, but he also looked resigned in a way that implied he had known when he'd come here this afternoon, he would need to share these details. He told them how multiple debtors had been making threats about collection for many weeks prior to Joshua's death; most of them had been legal creditors, and Matthias had been unaware of the less-than-legal means through which Joshua had borrowed money—which had been the precursor to his death. Following Joshua's death, all his creditors had *descended like vultures*—as Matthias described it—each wanting their fair share before the money was gone. Matthias had been working very hard to sell off every possible asset, every valuable possession, including the majority of his fine clothing and the home in which he'd grown up, in order to honorably pay off his brother's debts. He spoke of his new living quarters as if they were a blessing, and the job he'd found at a pub to be the same.

Eliza couldn't imagine what it must be like to have been raised a gentleman and then be reduced to such lowly labor in order to simply survive, but he'd already made it clear that he would not accept her help. Still, she ventured to ask, "What do you do exactly?"

"The most menial of chores," he said stoically, as if it took great strength to ward off any embarrassment. "I do whatever no one else wants to do, and I do it gratefully because I know work is not necessarily easy to come by for someone who has absolutely no skills whatsoever."

"I know this is a difficult conversation," Simon said, "but . . . may I ask if you were able to pay off all of Joshua's debts?"

Matthias hesitated and his face became rigid; Eliza knew he didn't want to answer. But he said firmly, "Almost. I am in agreement with two more creditors to make payments until the debt is free and clear, and yes, I have sufficient to meet my needs and make those payments. As I said, I am managing, although I thank you for your concern. I am very glad to know that I have friends who care . . . who would help me if I had need of help; nevertheless, I am fine. I find solace in knowing that my dishonesty never went beyond the necessary deception to cover up my brother's bad habits. I'd rather be poor and have integrity, than keep a single penny of what my brother owed to other people in the way of gambling debts. Perhaps my present situation helps me feel a little better in offering me the opportunity to pay some kind of penance for my part in all of this. And when the debts are relinquished, I will work on building a new life for myself. Right now, I can only take on one day at a time."

"Indeed," Simon said gently, "your grief over your brother's death—along with such a dramatic change in circumstances—must surely be overwhelming. You must promise us that if it becomes too much for you . . . that if you *do* need help . . . you will come to us, that you will be honest with us and allow us to help you."

"Yes!" Eliza declared almost ferociously. "You must promise!" The reality of his circumstances made her feel literally ill, especially when she considered the possibility that if it weren't for the miracle that had spared her from marrying Joshua, she and Mia could have ended up in a similar situation. But she couldn't think of that now beyond an acknowledgment of her gratitude that all of this had not turned out so much worse.

Again, Eliza could see that Matthias didn't want to respond. She could understand his pride over such an issue as providing for himself and honoring his brother's debts, but she believed he needed to understand that they could not stand by and know that he was going without the basic human necessities. She was about to attempt an explanation of her feelings when he said, "I promise." He let out a long sigh. "And now . . . I would like to take Simon's suggestion to heart and allow time for all of this to settle in. Might we simply enjoy each other's company and attempt some normalcy . . . just for one evening?"

"Excellent idea," Mia said in a way that was mildly forced, as if it were taking great effort for her to say the right thing, but she knew that she needed to behave appropriately despite the difficult circumstances. "And also owing to Simon's suggestion that we work on rebuilding our friendships on a new foundation, I believe that you should both come to tea or dinner—or both—as often as possible. When might we see you again?" she asked, looking directly at Matthias, since they both knew they would see Simon regularly.

"I'm afraid that Sundays are my only day off," Matthias said.

"Then we shall see you again next Sunday," Eliza stated rather than asked. "We shall make a habit of it."

"That sounds delightful," Matthias said. "Thank you. Seeing the three of you each Sunday will certainly help me get through my weeks . . . with something to look forward to."

"I'm glad of it," Eliza said, and they were able to shift the conversation into lighter topics, although it wasn't at all effortless and sometimes felt stifled. She knew it was good for all of them to at least attempt some normality, which would help them move beyond all that had happened and the dramatic changes in their lives; but at the same time there was no denying the grief they shared and its impact on everything else they shared.

Still, the remainder of Matthias's visit went well, and they had a rather enjoyable time. Mia even seemed to relax somewhat as the mood and conversation became more reminiscent of times gone by instead of focusing on matters of trust. When it was time for Matthias to leave, Eliza insisted that their carriage take him home since he'd reluctantly admitted that he'd walked from his flat earlier. She told him the carriage would come for him the following Sunday, since the distance between their homes was significant. Eliza could tell he felt mildly embarrassed over her offer, but he graciously accepted and kissed the ladies' hands as he thanked them for a lovely visit.

Simon stayed for a short while after Matthias left, and Eliza was glad for the way he frankly told her and Mia that he believed they were doing the right thing on behalf of Matthias, and they would not regret maintaining their friendship. Instinctively Eliza agreed, but she very much trusted Simon's judgment and discernment and she was glad for his added validation. Mia did not comment.

That night while Eliza was trying to fall asleep, she reviewed the most dramatic pieces of their conversation with Matthias, and more than once tears leaked from the corners of her eyes down into her hair while she stared into the darkness above her. She was deeply grateful for the way Matthias had been willing to candidly share what he knew, even though it had been difficult for him. And she was glad to know that despite the financial devastation Joshua had left in the wake of his death, Matthias was managing. She respected him for being willing to work to provide for himself and to follow through in paying off his brother's debts. But she hated to think of him living in such a way. If he had been born in different circumstances, being engaged in such lowly labor would have been an expected way of life. But to be catapulted out of a gentleman's life—not by his own choice—into the need to work surely had to be difficult for him. She wondered what exactly he'd meant when he'd said that he did the most menial chores, the things that no one else wanted to do. Because he never would have been taught any skills that would be useful toward employment, he apparently had no choice but to do work that required no skill.

Eliza's heart hurt for Matthias. As the hours ticked on and she found it impossible to sleep, she considered how she had always disliked him. It wasn't that she'd ever felt uncomfortable around him during the countless times they had shared meals and teas and attended the same social events. She'd simply viewed him according to everything Joshua had told her about him and had sized him up to be a cad and a scoundrel. But now she knew that Joshua was anything but the man she'd believed him to be, and it seemed that the same was true about Matthias. What surprised her most was how intense her desire was to be able to get to know him all over again, to give their friendship a fresh start with no judgment or bias based on anything she'd heard in the past. She was glad to know he'd be coming to spend time with them every Sunday and wished that the following Sunday didn't seem so far away. Without any warning, Eliza clearly recalled Matthias gazing at her as he'd shared his most vulnerable feelings, and her stomach responded with a giddy lurch at the same time that the beating of her heart quickened its pace.

"Good heavens!" Eliza murmured into the darkness, putting one hand over her heart and the other over the fluttering in her stomach, as if they had betrayed her and she might be attempting to scold them. But the sensations only heightened while the image of Matthias's anguish and regret and the way he'd gazed directly at her as he'd offered his most sincere apologies remained clear in her mind. Reminding herself that she was alone and no one could read her mind, Eliza finally allowed herself to admit that she felt attracted to Matthias. *Matthias!* Her fiancé's *brother!* Joshua's funeral had not been so very many days ago, and not many days before that Eliza had been prepared to marry him. And now she was feeling attracted to Joshua's brother? She felt like the worst kind of traitor! The very idea was so upsetting that she had to force her mind completely away from Matthias *and* Joshua. She mentally placed herself in the middle of a pleasant childhood memory, and in the midst of recalling her playtime in the garden with Mia, she finally drifted to sleep.

Eliza woke late but was glad that she'd been able to get the hours of sleep she needed. She knew from the clock as well as the angle of sunlight in her room that she'd missed breakfast, but she rang for Prudence, and a few minutes later she arrived with a tray of hot tea and warm scones, as if the teapot and a pan of scones had been kept on the stove just for her in anticipation of when she awoke.

"Thank you, Prudence," Eliza said as she tied a wrapper around her nightgown and moved toward the table where Prudence had set the tray.

Prudence curtsied slightly and said, "I'll return in a while to assist with your hair."

"Thank you," Eliza said again, wondering for the first time ever if she had taken those who worked in this house for granted, or if she'd ever been unkind to them. Sitting down to enjoy the warm scones which she slathered with the fresh butter and jam that had come with them, she was overcome once again with thoughts of Matthias. What was he doing now? How was he coping with his new way of life? He'd always had people waiting on him and helping with every little thing—just as she did. And now he was completely on his own. Her heart ached with sorrow and concern while at the same time quickening at the thought of him. But Eliza pushed away her traitorous thoughts and feelings, focusing instead on her gratitude for all that was good in her own life, and saying a silent prayer that all would be well with Matthias.

When Sunday came again, Eliza was glad to note that she was beginning to feel a little better every day as far as getting beyond Joshua's death and the shock of his betrayal. She and Mia had talked extensively about their feelings, and they both agreed that the information Matthias had given them had helped everything make more sense, which in turn made it easier to put the past behind them by fitting the pieces together more accurately. Although Eliza still sensed that Mia was finding it more difficult to truly trust Matthias, even if she didn't come right out and say it. Eliza wondered if she should urge Mia to talk about such feelings, but she felt that ultimately it was better to just give her sister time enough to see that Matthias was telling them the truth and that he could be trusted.

Eliza kept her more personal thoughts and feelings about Matthias to herself, certain they would pass and that it was nothing to be concerned about, and certainly nothing she wanted to admit aloud. Still, she couldn't help but anticipate seeing him and wondered if being in his presence would enhance or diminish the way she'd been feeling.

Eliza was pleasantly surprised to see Matthias at church, which made her realize that he'd not been there since Joshua's death. He greeted them kindly and asked if he might sit beside them. He and Joshua had been sitting with Eliza and Mia in church ever since Eliza and Joshua had begun courting. But so much had changed, and they all knew that people tended to create gossip out of the simplest and most benign situations. However, Eliza cared nothing about what others thought or said; she was only too glad to have Matthias join her and her sister. He had no family, and with his change of financial status—and the fact that he'd moved to another area of the city—he likely no longer had any friends beyond them and their mutual friend, the vicar.

Eliza enjoyed the service, and Simon gave an excellent sermon as always. But even as consumed as she was by the goings-on of the meeting, she was unduly distracted by the fact that Matthias was sitting next to her, and the effect that his nearness was having on her. More than once she had to stop herself from the impulse to reach for his hand the way she would have reached for Joshua's if he had been sitting next to her. But they had been betrothed! And not so long ago! Eliza could hardly believe this was happening, and she found only the tiniest degree of peace regarding such feelings when she considered how deeply Joshua had betrayed *her*. Had he not died when he had, she would have likely lost *everything* to his gambling habits, and he had been willing to enter into a marriage with her and not forewarn her of this possibility. She reminded herself that she was not a vindictive person, and whatever Joshua had or had not done did not excuse her own feelings or behavior. She felt more determined than ever to keep her feelings to herself, certain that with time they would dissipate. Still, she *did* enjoy sitting next to Matthias at church, just as she enjoyed having him join them for tea and dinner and much visiting in between. Sundays became a day she looked forward to on every other day of the week. It had always been her favorite day because she loved attending church, and she enjoyed the different mood in the house that existed on the Sabbath. And now with Matthias's regular visits—along with Simon joining them as he always had—Sundays became especially delightful.

After Matthias had come to visit a few times, it occurred to Eliza that he no longer smelled of cigar smoke—as he had for as long as she'd known him. When she commented on her observation, Matthias looked astonished and said,

"He told you that I smoked cigars? And that's why we both always reeked of the smell?"

Eliza and Mia both nodded, and Eliza could see the truth now, even before he said, "It was the other way around, Eliza; I hope you can believe me. I never smoked, and Joshua never smoked around you because you'd told him you detested the habit. So," Matthias blew out a long breath that seemed to be an attempt to let go of yet another layer of anger toward his deceased brother, "he told you that *I* was to blame."

"And we all believed him," Simon stated, rescuing Eliza from having to say it.

"Why wouldn't you?" Matthias asked. "It wasn't until his death that he gave any of you any reason to be suspicious of him." He let out a forced chuckle and added, "Well, I'm glad we have that cleared up." He then changed the subject immediately and they went on to have a pleasant evening, followed by many pleasant evenings each and every Sunday.

More than five months of Sundays carried them from summer, through autumn, and into the onset of winter. Eliza could feel her own grief and shock over Joshua's death easing peacefully and noticed the same with her sister and the two men who were such dear friends to them. The experience had been different for all of them due to their unique relationships with Joshua, but they had all grieved, and they were all slowly coming to terms with their loss.

Little by little Eliza saw Matthias becoming more like his old self. And Simon had been right about allowing time to help them rebuild trust in their relationships. As she got to know Matthias without the taint of Joshua distorting her view of him, Eliza found him to be nothing but a good man. Of course, she often reminded herself that she had no idea how he actually lived his life when he wasn't in their presence, but given that they were only friends, such things really didn't matter. She had come to know that he'd told them the truth about everything related to Joshua, and their friendship had become based in their common bond of having loved Joshua, lost Joshua, and perhaps most of all having been deeply betrayed by Joshua. As time passed, they were able to talk about these things with less drama and emotion, and the little group of friends were able to help each other immensely in healing and moving forward.

On a very cold and windy Sunday evening, after dinner was over and coffee was being served in the parlor, Eliza was surprised to hear Matthias say, "Eliza, I wonder if I could speak to you privately for a few minutes . . . and then we'll join the others."

Simon and Mia both looked a little surprised, but Simon motioned with his hand and said, "You know where to find us." He winked and added, "Although I would beg you not to leave the two of us alone for too long; Miss Mia would surely become terribly bored with only my company."

"On the contrary," Mia said. "I think we'll manage just fine."

Eliza nodded at her sister and attempted to keep her own surprise over Matthias's request from showing on her face. She smiled at him and led the way to the library, picking up a lamp from a table in the hall since she doubted that any of the servants would have anticipated that the library would be used this evening. Entering the room to find it dark and cold, her suspicions were confirmed, and she wished she had chosen to go to a different room.

"Oh, I don't think this is an optimal place to visit," she said to Matthias, determined to go back into the hall where there was at least a little warmth from the rooms where fires were burning and the doors had been left open.

"It's all right," he said, and she found herself standing face-to-face with him, holding the lamp in a hand that she realized was trembling. Looking up at him she had to acknowledge that her attraction for him had not diminished at all in the months since she'd first noticed it. She could only think that she felt a little less traitorous, given the time that had passed since Joshua's death. "What I have to say won't take long," he added, but then hesitated, and she realized he was nervous. She nodded in an effort to encourage him to continue. "I can't go another day without telling you what keeps going around and around in my head—let alone another week, which is when I will see you again." He drew in a deep breath and let it out slowly. "Eliza," he murmured with a slight quiver in his voice, "you have to know the truth. I feel like such a traitor, but . . . you have to know the truth."

Eliza gasped but found it impossible to speak, so she just waited for him to explain.

Chapter Six
TRUST AND TRUTH

WHILE ELIZA WAITED NERVOUSLY FOR Matthias to offer some further explanation—and his own nervousness seemed to be preventing him from doing so—she suddenly felt far too cold to remain in this room that had been closed off all day from any source of heat. Using the excuse of being cold as a valid reason to suspend the growing tension between them, Eliza said, "Forgive me, but it's far too cold in here. I . . ." She didn't finish as she turned and left the library, aware of him following her through the open door of a parlor where a fire was burning in the grate, even though the room was dark otherwise. Eliza knew this room was known for doing well at emitting heat into the hallway; therefore, a fire was almost always blazing here during cold days. Knowing from what little Matthias had said that this conversation could *not* be brief as he had implied, Eliza set down the lamp she was holding and sat in a chair near the fireplace, feeling a little unsteady as she tried to take in Matthias's confession that he felt like such a traitor . . . and that she needed to know the truth. What other horrible unknown factors to this situation were yet to be revealed? She didn't know if she could bear any more terrible news, especially when she was just starting to feel like they were really beginning to recover from Joshua's impact on their lives.

"Forgive me," she said as Matthias sat in the only other chair that was situated near the fire. "I should have come here to begin with; the library is far too cold." She took in a deep breath and tried to brace herself for the certain negative impact of Matthias's confession. "You told us all months ago that you'd confessed everything related to Joshua's death . . . and the situation . . . and now you're telling me there's more? Is that what you're saying, Matthias? And why the need to speak to me privately? I don't understand."

"I am prepared to explain, Eliza, even though it's difficult." She heard him sigh even though she was looking at the flames rather than at him, which felt easier. "What I'm trying to tell you now has nothing to do with Joshua's death. In fact, it has nothing to do with him at all, except for the fact that I felt as if I had betrayed him in the deepest way . . . long before he died . . . even long before the two of you became engaged to be married. It has nothing to do with money, or gambling, or the lies he manipulated me into telling on his behalf." Eliza felt rather than saw his eyes become more fixed on her, even though her own gaze remained on the fire. "It only had to do with you, Eliza. How could I have ever told my brother the depth of *my* betrayal against *him*? How could I have ever told him that I was completely . . . and irrevocably . . . in love with you?"

Eliza gasped as she heard a confession that was miles away from anything she might have expected to hear. She snapped her gaze toward Matthias, only to find him staring at her, his countenance vulnerable, his eyes filled with undeniable sincerity that couldn't disguise his obvious fear over how she might react. As their eyes met, Eliza's heart pounded so hard she feared he might hear it over the crackling of the flames. A storm of thoughts flooded her mind with such force that she felt certain it could take a thousand hours of deep introspection to come to terms with everything he'd just said and all of its deeper implications. Overriding all else was the incomprehensible reality that while she'd been fighting for months to suppress her growing attraction to Matthias, he'd been struggling much longer to contend with his feelings for *her*. And yet the only words she was able to articulate were, "And you thought this conversation wouldn't take long? Isn't that what you told me?"

"I . . . suppose I just hoped to be able to say what needed to be said and be done with it. I suppose I believed that . . . you needed to know how I feel . . . and you surely need time to . . . think about it and . . . well, the situation is complicated at the very least, and . . ."

"Well, *that* is certainly true!" she said, wishing it hadn't sounded so sharp. She looked back at the fire; feeling more heat from his gaze than from the flames, she feared she might melt if she looked at him too long. "And I certainly have a great deal to think about."

"Eliza," he said gently, tempting her to look at him again although she couldn't bring herself to do it, "forgive me."

"For what?" she asked, astonished, looking at him abruptly without even thinking about it.

"Perhaps it would have been better to keep my feelings to myself," he said. "If you don't feel the same, I completely understand, and the last thing I want is for this—or anything else—to taint the friendship we share. I consider it a miracle that our friendship has survived all that happened with Joshua, but now that he's gone . . . and some time has passed . . . I simply can't keep my feelings to myself any longer. I've grown so terribly weary of keeping secrets, and I don't want any secrets between us, Eliza, even if that means having you tell me that you could never love me. And if that's the case, then we never need to speak of this again. But I needed to say it. And now I have." He stood up. "Perhaps we should go back and—"

"Sit down," she said, and he did. Now that she'd had more than a moment to take in his confession, she wanted to take advantage of the opportunity of being alone with him to clarify at least a couple of points. "So . . . you're telling me that . . . even before Joshua and I became engaged . . . you . . . cared for me . . . romantically?"

"Yes," he said without the slightest hesitation.

"And you said nothing?" Eliza asked, wondering how different her life might have been if Matthias had come forward with such declarations a long time ago.

"Joshua repeatedly expressed to me the depth of his love for you," Matthias stated. "How could I tell my brother I was in love with the same woman? But more importantly, Eliza, I could so clearly see how very much you loved Joshua. I could only see the possibility that my admissions would create confusion and hard feelings. I didn't want to compromise my relationship with my brother— especially when it was already strained due to many disagreements between us. And I certainly didn't want to complicate *your* life and put you in a position where you felt like you had to choose between us. I don't believe anything would have changed, except that both of you would have always been uncomfortable around me, and therefore it would have damaged all the good things we shared."

Eliza dumbly attempted to take in everything he'd said until she realized that she couldn't; not here, not now, not like this. She erupted to her feet before she even realized she wanted to get out of the room as quickly as she could manage. "I . . . need time to think; I . . . I can't even . . ."

"Eliza," he said with compassion as he came and stood beside her, "I know this must seem . . . insane to you, and . . . I apologize for any difficulty my confessions might cause you. Of course you need time, and . . . if you decide this is best left . . . ignored . . ." He coughed on the word as if he couldn't bear the possibility but had known it needed to be said, ". . . then I will honor that.

If you prefer that we never speak of this again, so be it. I simply had to tell you how I feel . . . how I've always felt; I couldn't keep it hidden inside any longer. Enough said." He motioned toward the door. "Shall we return to visit with the others?"

"Yes," she said, grateful beyond words for his offer of an easy escape. She hurried toward the door and took up the lamp from where she'd set it. Returning to the parlor with Matthias close behind her, Eliza wanted to run—as if she could run away from all that he'd admitted to her. Or perhaps more accurately, she wanted to run from what this could mean in regard to *her* feelings for *him*—of which she felt certain he had no awareness whatsoever. Eliza also wanted to walk as slowly as possible if only to be alone with Matthias just a little longer. A part of her wanted to just stop walking and turn to face him and blurt out the truth of how thoroughly preoccupied she had been with thoughts of him for months now—long before any respectable woman grieving a fiancé should have been. She wanted to tell him how just thinking of him would cause her heart to quicken and her stomach to flutter, and that actually being in his presence only enhanced such reactions. But she just kept walking, determined to keep her feelings to herself—at least until she'd had a good long time to think about everything he'd just told her in light of all that had happened and all that she felt. She felt relatively certain that Matthias had to be unnerved by how openly he'd exposed his feelings, and she'd given him nothing in her response to help assuage any concerns he might have. Eliza felt bad about that, but not bad enough to be able to come up with any kind of appropriate response.

Eliza set the lamp down on a table in the hall and entered the parlor where Simon and Mia were both laughing. Whatever the reason, it must have been terribly funny because they were laughing very hard. Eliza and Matthias each sat down, and the others continued to laugh as if they were simply incapable of stopping.

"You must let us in on the joke," Matthias said nonchalantly, although Eliza was well aware of a vague and well-disguised tension in his eyes.

"It's a very long story," Simon said, wiping his eyes as he made an attempt to get his laughter under control, "and I doubt we could retell it well enough to do it justice."

"Although we could try," Mia said, also wiping her eyes, "but only if you share whatever secrets you've been discussing."

"Nothing important," Matthias said, much to Eliza's relief. The last thing she wanted was to draw attention to the enormity of what he'd told her. "I just needed to clarify something to Eliza—nothing for any of you to be concerned about." He swept his gaze over Eliza in a way that seemed to say that he especially didn't want *her* to be concerned about it, as if he would truly prefer that everything he'd said be forgotten. But she knew that would be impossible. She just didn't know what to do about it.

Eliza was relieved beyond measure when the men left for the evening, and she told her sister she wasn't feeling well and intended to go straight to bed.

"Do you need anything?" Mia asked with concern as they went together up the stairs.

"I'm certain a good night's sleep will put me right," Eliza insisted. "I'm just very tired."

"Very well," Mia said in a tone that implied she would have liked to argue with Eliza but knew it would accomplish nothing. "I'll check on you in the morning."

"No need for that," Eliza said. "Prudence takes very good care of me."

"She does," Mia said, "but I'm your sister, and I'll check on you in the morning. I won't disturb you if you're sleeping."

"I'll see you tomorrow, then," Eliza said and parted ways with her sister, desperately wanting to be alone in the privacy of her own rooms. It occurred to her that she felt extremely hesitant to share her feelings about Matthias with Mia due to the fact that she continued to sense a well-disguised but undeniable hesitancy on Mia's part to trust him, and Eliza didn't know how to talk to Mia about such a sensitive topic. Compounding this with the complication of romantic notions left Eliza all the more ambivalent about being completely truthful with her sister.

Prudence was waiting to help Eliza out of her dress, which buttoned down the back.

"Is everything all right, m'lady?" Prudence asked while she unfastened the necklace around Eliza's throat.

"I'm just very tired," Eliza said.

"I'll not disturb you in the morning until you ring, then," Prudence said.

"Thank you," Eliza replied and nothing more was said between them except for Prudence making certain Eliza had everything she needed to finish getting ready for bed.

Once Eliza had freshened up and gotten into her nightgown, she doused the lamps and crawled into her bed, and the moment her head hit the pillow she immediately found it difficult to breathe, and her heart began to pound painfully hard. Now that she was alone in the dark it was as if she were experiencing a delayed reaction to what Matthias had told her—the kind of reaction she never would have allowed herself to express in his presence. She gasped for breath with such vehemence that if anyone had been in the room they probably would have sent for a doctor.

"What's wrong with me?" she whispered between her heaving breaths. She wasn't concerned about her physical state, knowing well enough that her symptoms were a result of the emotional impact of Matthias's confession, combined with all its complications and implications—especially regarding her *own* feelings, about which he knew nothing.

Eliza worked hard at forcing herself to breathe evenly, but once that happened, she began to cry. She couldn't quite define exactly *why* she felt the need to shed tears, but they came out of her in torrents, not caring whether or not they were defined. Looking back to when she and Mia had first begun to socialize with Joshua and Matthias, she wondered how she might have felt if she had been able to look forward to *this* moment and foresee the complicated— even disastrous—web of confusion and chaos that had resulted. And now that it felt as if they were all finally beginning to heal from all that Joshua's life—and death—had done to their lives, Eliza was faced with an entirely different kind of complication.

Once Eliza's tears had settled into a contemplative silence, something joyful and giddy erupted inside of her as she recalled Matthias's confessions of love for her. Was it possible? Could it truly be possible? Had she been falling in love with a man who had been in love with her for years? She was a person who tended to believe in destiny above coincidence. Could this truly be some kind of destiny? How else could she explain two people coming to share the same feelings for each other? But then, she had loved Joshua—and he had loved her—and now she knew that marrying him would have only led to disaster. How could she possibly know—really know—that investing in these feelings she'd not yet admitted to for Matthias might not also lead her down some kind of disastrous path? She had come to absolutely believe he was telling them the truth about all that had happened, including his peripheral involvement. But here in her bedroom, surrounded by darkness and unable to sleep, she could see that believing in a person's integrity as an acquaintance or even as a friend was entirely different than doing so in light of admitting to any kind of romantic association. Romance and attraction *always* came with the assumption that the possibility of marriage would be taken into consideration.

And marriage meant legally turning over all her financial security—and that of her sister—to her husband. Mia would receive her inheritance at the time of her marriage, but if Eliza married before Mia, all their combined fortune would still belong to Eliza—or rather the man she married. After what had happened with Joshua, Eliza doubted she could even force herself to make such a decision. Therefore, even entertaining the idea that her feelings for Matthias—or his for her—could ever come to anything was simply not possible. He'd told her that it never needed to be spoken of again, and somewhere in the darkest part of the night, Eliza finally came to accept—after stewing and stewing over the matter— that it was all best let go of and forgotten. In light of every facet of the situation, there was simply no other feasible option. After what Joshua had done to her, Eliza just knew that she could never open her heart enough to trust *any* man enough to become his wife and potentially lose all that she had. Determined to put the matter away once and for all, Eliza was finally able to sleep.

Eliza awoke to find that she'd slept so late it was nearly time for lunch; therefore, attempting to have any kind of breakfast seemed pointless. She rang for Prudence who came to gather every piece of clothing Eliza needed while she freshened up. Prudence fastened the buttons down the back of Eliza's dress and quickly styled her hair so that she could be on time to meet her sister for lunch.

"Oh, there you are," Mia said with a smile when Eliza entered the room to see her sister just about to begin eating. "Did you sleep?"

"Eventually," Eliza said, taking a seat.

"And are you feeling better?" Mia asked.

"I think so," was all Eliza could say. She didn't want to admit that it had not been any kind of physical malady that had sent her to bed early, because she didn't want to talk about the dilemma taking place in her spirit. Despite having made a firm decision on the best way to handle the situation, Eliza couldn't deny some sadness over having to let go of the possibility of exploring these feelings she and Matthias had for each other. But she didn't want to admit *any* of it to her sister, so she hurried to spark a conversation about the novel she was reading, and the fact that they would be attending an opera the following evening with Simon and a few acquaintances who were also fellow churchgoers. The group would be gathering before the opera at the home of a Mr. and Mrs. Hull, who had arranged the tickets to the opera and were also hosting a dinner party preceding the performance. Eliza was looking forward to the event, and she generally liked all the people who would be involved, but she couldn't help wishing that Matthias would be joining them. She hated to think that instead of being able to attend operas and dinner parties—as he had once done frequently—he was employed at a pub doing the chores that no one else wanted to do.

Throughout the remainder of the week, Eliza did her best to go about her normal routine and not let on to how preoccupied she was with thoughts of Matthias. His confession had brought forward a myriad of strange thoughts as she found herself trying to review every scene of her relationship with Joshua and attempt to imagine how it might have been if she'd known that Matthias had been present more often than not, observing his brother's interaction with a woman he loved, knowing that Joshua was being less than honest. Matthias's dilemma—and the difficult feelings that had surely been continually present— left Eliza uneasy to the say the least. And as if that weren't bad enough, Eliza had her own feelings to contend with, while she wondered what to do about them when she truly believed that pursuing such feelings—or even acknowledging them—would only lead to disaster. Still, she couldn't deny how much she'd grown to care for Matthias. Her attraction to him often led to daydreaming that made her stomach flutter at the very thought of him. But beyond all that silliness, she truly cared about him and the terrible blow his life had been dealt due to his brother's appalling choices. Eliza became incapable of allowing very many minutes to pass without wondering how Matthias was doing, and in her mind she could clearly see that terrible place where he now lived, and she could only imagine the kind of conditions in which he was working six days a week. He'd purposely avoided sharing any details of the work he did, but Eliza had spent enough time in the kitchen of her own home to be able to imagine what the most menial tasks of working at a pub might entail. It wasn't right or fair, and she often felt angry with Joshua for all he'd done to mar her life—and especially for what he'd done to his brother. Eliza still had a plentiful and luxurious life with every possible comfort available to her continually. But Matthias had lost all of that and was merely trying to survive. She desperately wished that he would allow her to help him, and even took the opportunity on one of Simon's visits to ask if he knew of any way that she might do so anonymously.

"Forgive me, Eliza," Simon replied, looking back and forth between Eliza and Mia, who agreed over the matter of wanting to assist Matthias in any way they could, "but I've pondered the very same question a great deal myself. I'm certain I could glean information about exactly who his creditors are, and I could mediate on your behalf and help you pay off the debts anonymously, but—"

"Then, that's what we must do!" Eliza interrupted. "It's one thing for him to be forced into manual labor to provide for himself, but it's another thing entirely to be required to pay off his brother's debts in this way; he's already lost *everything* because of Joshua. Surely we can—"

"You must let me finish, Eliza," Simon said. "It can be done, but I strongly advise that you do *not* take action in this way." Eliza felt so confused and disappointed that she couldn't utter a syllable of protest—even as much as she wanted to—before Simon went on. "He's spoken with me privately, and of course I will maintain my integrity—both as his friend and as a vicar— in the feelings he shared with me. Simply allow me to say this: I do believe that a man—any man—who has a healthy sense of pride in wanting to be responsible regarding himself and his family, would likely be offended—perhaps even insulted—at the very idea of having *other* people step in to solve such problems. In such a case, I believe it's best to offer friendship and support and encouragement, but to remain uninvolved in a financial sense."

"But . . ." Eliza sputtered, then took a long moment to figure out what to say next; she only knew that everything inside of her wanted to protest. "As people who strive to be good Christians, we understand the value of giving aid to those who are struggling or suffering. What he's enduring is not through any fault of his own, but even if it were, he surely would deserve mercy and forgiveness from his friends. And . . ." Eliza searched for words to strengthen her case, "if Jesus taught us to assist those in need—such as the example given in the story of the Good Samaritan—are we not obligated to do so? If people in need are not willing to accept help, then how are those of us in a position to help meant to live these Christian edicts?"

"That is an excellent point, Eliza," Simon said to her with an amused smile, which she found annoying since the situation was anything but amusing. "And it is almost word-for-word of what I would . . ." She noted in his hesitation the need to not betray anything specific related to his private conversation with Matthias. ". . . What I would have said to someone in such a position, and yet neither you nor I have any control over how such an offer would be received." Simon sighed. "Perhaps with the passing of time he will be more open to the possibility of accepting assistance . . . or perhaps the debts will soon be paid off; I have no idea of their specific amount. But I do believe I've said more than I should; I trust that you ladies will keep my confidence. We must continue to offer Matthias our friendship, and to make certain that he feels safe enough with us to ask for help should the need arise. It's my opinion that if we are aggressive about offering help when it's not wanted, he's less likely to ask for it should the situation become more desperate."

"I'm sure you're right," Eliza said with a defeated sigh. "I don't like it at all, but I can't argue with your logic."

"Let's just be grateful," Mia interjected, "that we have an established routine of seeing Matthias every Sunday." Eliza studied her sister's countenance as she spoke and wondered if Mia's heart was softening toward Matthias—if she was learning to trust him more—or if she was simply striving to live by her strong Christian principles despite her personal doubts. "Having him here gives us the opportunity to not only see that he's fed well at least one day a week, but to be able to make sure he's all right. His life is difficult right now; of that we are certain. Although, there are still many people out there who have it far worse; we know that well enough. We've seen ample evidence of Matthias's gratitude that his situation is *not* worse. Perhaps we simply need to support him in such an attitude and allow him to make his way."

"I'm sure you're right," Eliza said, unable to argue with her sister's logic either, but deep inside—for reasons that Mia and Simon didn't know about— her heart ached so deeply for Matthias that sometimes she felt as if it would crack wide open.

That evening after Eliza was all ready for bed, she slid beneath the covers, turned up the lamp on the bedside table, and made herself comfortable leaning back on a pile of pillows stacked against the headboard, intending to read until she got sleepy. She didn't want to think about Matthias, or anything related to him; she only wanted to lose herself in the story she was reading and avoid thinking at all.

A knock at the door surprised her, since Prudence never came back to her room this late; but before she could call out, the door opened and Mia peered inside. "May I come in?" she asked.

"Of course," Eliza said and set her book aside as Mia entered the room and closed the door behind her. She was wearing a warm but elegant dressing gown over her nightgown, and she kicked the slippers off her stockinged feet before she sat on Eliza's bed, facing Eliza directly as she tucked her feet beneath her, which would help keep them warm. On such cold winter nights, the only way to be completely warm was to remain bundled up in warm clothing or blankets, or to remain very close to the fire.

"What is it?" Eliza asked her sister. "Is something wrong?"

"That's what *I* came to ask *you*," Mia said firmly. "Something has been wrong with you for days now, and I can't figure out what it is. I suspect it has to do with Matthias, given your obvious concern for him along with your desire to help him, but I think it's more than that—even if I can't imagine what. I keep thinking that you'll tell me; I'm your sister, and I thought you told me everything, but apparently not. You should know from a lifetime of experiences that I would never betray your secrets, but if you have a secret—and it's weighing on you—don't you think you should allow me to help you share that burden? If something is bothering you, dear sister, I do hope that you would trust me enough to tell me."

Eliza cleared her throat tensely and folded her arms tightly as if they might protect her from Mia's perception. Eliza had believed she'd been doing well at concealing her troubled thoughts and confused feelings, but obviously not well enough to fool her sister. But could she say it aloud? Could she tell Mia what Matthias had said to her? And perhaps what was even more difficult, could she admit to her own feelings for Matthias, especially when she wasn't entirely certain how Mia felt about Matthias after all that had happened? Still, she could see now that it wasn't realistic to be as close to Mia as she was and *not* have her sister figure out that something was amiss. And if the situation were reversed, Eliza would certainly want Mia to share her secrets *and* her burdens.

"It's not a matter of trust," Eliza began. "I trust you completely, of course. I simply . . . haven't wanted to talk about it; or perhaps . . . haven't wanted to admit it . . . or . . . well . . . sometimes it feels as if putting feelings into words makes them impossible to deny . . . as opposed to . . ."

"To what?" Mia guessed when Eliza hesitated too long. "Do you believe that allowing your feelings to spin around endlessly inside of you will help you make sense of them? Or make them go away? I thought we had an understanding to always talk about our feelings for the very purpose of helping each other make sense of them."

Eliza sighed, then gave her sister a wan smile. "You're right. I've just been so . . . overwhelmed . . . and certainly confused, and . . . perhaps I just didn't know where to begin. Forgive me. I was not intentionally shutting you out. I . . ."

"What?" Mia pressed when once again Eliza had difficulty finding the right words.

Eliza looked at her sister and stated something she had once taken for granted, but she could do so no longer. "I'm so grateful for the trust between us; so grateful we can tell each other the truth and never have to worry about . . ."

"About having to lie for each other in order to cover evil deeds," Mia said firmly as if she'd given that very idea the same kind of thought as Eliza. "And we never have to worry about one or the other of us ending up murdered and discarded in an alley because of such terrible misdeeds."

"Something like that," Eliza said softly. "I would hope that if I were doing something stupid, you would do everything in your power to stop me."

"And the other way around," Mia said vehemently; then her voice became sad. "Although, I suspect Matthias did everything in *his* power to try and stop Joshua from being such a fool. I'm certain he's only shared with us the tiniest portion of what actually took place between them. I must admit to many mixed feelings over the matter. At times I have trouble with wondering whether Matthias can be trusted, and I don't know if that's because of what Joshua did and said, or if Matthias's dishonesty in the matter might be more than he's admitted to." She sighed and Eliza was glad to at least hear her sister admit she was having the exact difficulty that Eliza had suspected. "Still," Mia went on, "I've been haunted by imagining a great many arguments between them . . . of Matthias begging him to be honest with you . . . and to stop taking such terrible risks with their financial security."

"I've imagined the same," Eliza admitted, "which makes my heart hurt all the more for Matthias being in the position he is now."

Mia looked down and cleared her throat as if she might be making certain nothing would hold back her voice as she prepared to say something difficult. She looked back up at Eliza and said, "If you and I are in agreement that we need to tell each other the truth about anything and everything, then I assume it's all right for me to tell you that you're either blind or a fool or both."

"I beg your pardon!" Eliza retorted, unable to keep from sounding defensive in response to such an accusation.

"Before you get all huffy," Mia went on, "please hear me out. Clearly we have no secrets from each other about anything that is untoward, but I do think there is something we should have talked about a very long time ago . . . and that's the obvious fact that Matthias is in love with you; he always has been, I think."

"What?" Eliza gasped.

"Oh, surely you know," Mia muttered with a smile that seemed to be trying to hide some measure of concern.

"I do *now*," Eliza said. "I mean . . . recently . . . but only because he told me and—"

"Matthias *told* you?" Mia gasped. "He admitted it . . . aloud?"

"He did," Eliza said, even more confused and overwhelmed with the realization that Mia had clearly observed things to which Eliza had been oblivious. "But . . . are you telling me that you knew?"

"For all of Matthias's efforts to manage his feelings appropriately . . . and to keep them concealed . . . I fear we just know him too well to not see past his façade. And of course, he never would have intruded upon the relationship his brother shared with you, but Joshua is gone now, and—"

"Wait, wait, wait," Eliza insisted. "What are you saying? And who is *we*?"

"Simon and I, of course," Mia said as if it were obvious. "We always agreed that Matthias would be a better match for you, but we also believed that it wasn't right or appropriate for us to intrude upon what you and Joshua shared."

Eliza suddenly felt angry without fully understanding why. She jumped out of bed as if some unseen force had pushed her, then she began to pace frantically, which was her typical reaction under stress. "Well, maybe you *should* have intruded! At the very least, perhaps someone—especially my own sister—should have shared such observations and allowed me to decide what was best. Clearly Joshua was *not* a good choice as a husband. Would you and Simon—and Matthias—have allowed me to leap headlong into a life of disaster and deceit?"

"Eliza, dearest," Mia said with concern as she too leapt from the bed and stood in front of Eliza to stop her pacing. Mia took hold of Eliza's shoulders and looked into her eyes. "For all that we knew Matthias had feelings for you, it was clearly Joshua whom you loved, and we had no desire to create any dilemma or unrest for you by complicating the situation. You can't judge our actions of the past on knowledge we have now that we didn't have then. If we'd known the truth about Joshua, of course we would have handled things differently. We may have had some suspicions, but we *didn't* know. Matthias knew, but he's already explained his position; he's humbly asked for our forgiveness and we have freely given it. All of that is in the past."

"Is it?" Eliza asked. "Is it truly in the past, Mia?" She took a deep breath and decided if they were sharing secrets, they should discuss what had been avoided for far too long. "You've been very kind to Matthias, and I believe you're trying to be appropriate, but . . . knowing you as well as I do . . . I sense that you don't trust him, and—"

"Simon has taught us that forgiveness does not necessarily equate with trust," Mia said with a defensive edge to her voice. "I have worked very hard to forgive Matthias, because he wronged us terribly. Even if his sins against us are not nearly so severe as Joshua's, he deceived us all the same. I do believe I've forgiven him, and I have compassion for what he's going through; nevertheless, it's true: I *don't* trust him, not entirely, at least. Although I'm willing to give myself time to keep working on that. I only ask that with whatever is happening you will be extremely careful and not entangle yourself into a situation that might only end up being much like the one from which you narrowly escaped."

Eliza felt hotly tempted to defend Matthias in every possible way, but she couldn't deny the validity of her sister's feelings, nor the caution she'd just offered. So Eliza just swallowed hard and nodded in agreement, but she didn't comment, not wanting her sister to know that she was suddenly fighting the threat of tears. She sat down on the edge of the bed and Mia sat beside her, saying gently, "But what is this about Matthias confessing his feelings? Did he actually say that he loves you?"

"He did," Eliza said, looking at her hands as she clasped and unclasped her fingers repeatedly. Taking a long moment to swallow the threat of tears and gain her composure, she finally added, "And what am I to do with such information?"

"I suppose that would depend on how you feel about *him*," Mia said, her tone betraying her hope that something magical and fairy-tale-like might evolve between her and Matthias, which seemed a direct contradiction to her caution about whether he could be trusted. Eliza believed Mia was just trying to be supportive, or perhaps she was as confused as Eliza over the matter.

"I believe it's far more complicated than that," Eliza said, still looking only at her hands. "After what happened with Joshua, I don't know if I could ever bring myself to commit my life to any man when marriage vows would automatically give my husband *everything* I have—legally and irrevocably."

"Are such laws not irrelevant when two people trust and love each other?" Mia asked, which seemed a logical observation, but her words only provoked Eliza's anger again.

"You're asking me such a question after you've just admitted that you don't know whether you can trust him?" Eliza wished she hadn't sounded so angry, but her emotions were running hot. "That would be the case if you *could* actually trust that a man was completely honest about every facet of his life. I believe I can trust Matthias, that he's a good man. But how can a woman ever be completely certain that a man is telling her the truth about everything? And if I can't be completely certain, I could *never* risk our financial security."

"Are you truly implying that Matthias is like his brother?" Mia asked, and Eliza wondered if that was how Mia felt but didn't want to admit to it;

therefore, it was easier to shift the question to Eliza's shoulders. "Do you really think he would deceive you like that? Deceive all of us?"

"How can I know for certain?" Eliza asked, finally looking at her sister.

Mia gazed into Eliza's eyes for a long moment as if she were searching for something; she then declared firmly, "You love him; you do. You love him and it frightens you because of what Joshua did."

Eliza felt suddenly cold and also wanted very much to put some distance between herself and her sister—or rather her sister's declaration that was far too accurate for Eliza's comfort. She climbed back into the bed and leaned against the headboard, pulling the covers up to her chin as if they might protect her from all that Mia had just said. Mia crawled across the bed and into the other side as if she too were cold. She lay on her side and leaned her head into her hand, gazing at Eliza in a way that implied she would do so until Eliza admitted to the truth.

Eliza sighed, then for more than a few minutes of grueling silence, she pondered all that had been said while Mia just waited, seeming confident that Eliza would eventually respond to her sister's speculations. Eliza finally sighed again and said, "I . . . cannot deny that . . . I feel something . . . for Matthias. I don't know if it's love, Mia; it's nothing like what I felt for Joshua. I thought I loved Joshua. I certainly wanted to be in his presence . . . I thought about him a great deal when we weren't together . . . and it just seemed right for us to marry, but . . . I feel things when I think of Matthias . . . or when I see him . . . that I've never felt before."

"Oh my!" Mia said with a little giggle as if she were willing to completely dismiss any concerns, at least for the moment.

"Now, don't do that!"

"Do what?" Mia asked, all innocence.

"Don't go making something out of this that may well be nothing at all! And it should go without saying that when I share something so personal with you, I'm trusting that you won't run to Simon and repeat what I've shared in confidence."

"Of course!" Mia sounded insulted that Eliza would even feel the need to mention such a thing. "I would never share anything personal with him or anyone else without your permission. You *can* trust me, Eliza, and that will never change."

"I know," Eliza said and reached for her sister's hand beneath the covers. "This is all just so . . . overwhelming . . . and confusing; those two words have kept recurring in my thoughts over and over—for months now."

"Months?" Mia echoed. "You've been feeling this way for months?"

"I confess that I have," Eliza said, "which initially made me feel guilty when Joshua had not been dead very long, but then . . . Joshua certainly did nothing to leave me with fond memories or any reason to remain devoted to him."

"That's certainly true!" Mia insisted, her anger toward Joshua evident in her tone. She let out a long, slow breath and added more gently, "And how long have you known how Matthias feels about you?"

"Only since Sunday," Eliza said.

"So, *that's* why he wanted to speak with you alone."

"Yes," Eliza admitted. "And he left not long after our conversation, so I've not spoken to him since. I don't know whether I should be dreading his visit on Sunday—or feel elated to see him; some of both perhaps."

"Does he know how *you* feel about *him*?" Mia asked.

"No," Eliza said as if that one word might express how deeply she never wanted him to know. "He told me he believed I should know how he felt about me, that he couldn't keep it a secret between us . . . but if I felt it was best ignored he would honor that; he made it clear he didn't want his confession to damage our friendship in any way. And I just . . . told him I needed time . . . and that was all really. I think I'm still in shock, because the very possibility of him feeling that way about me doesn't even seem real."

"Now that you've had some days to think about what he said, what do you think?"

"I think that it *is* best ignored," Eliza said firmly. "I think that it's best if I simply resign myself to a simpler life, and just—"

"Life as a spinster, you mean?" Mia asked, sounding angry as she sat up abruptly. "Are you truly telling me that you would spend your life alone because *one man* wronged you? Are you sincerely going to gauge the character of every man based on Joshua's deceit and lack of integrity?"

"How can I do anything else?" Eliza countered as if Mia's belief that she could feel any other way was nothing short of ludicrous. "You yourself just admitted you're not certain you trust Matthias. I never had any reason to doubt Joshua's sincerity, or his declarations of love for me. If I was foolish enough to have absolutely no clue about his true character, how can I trust myself to ever know if *any* man is being entirely honest with me?"

"Because you are wiser now . . . more discerning," Mia insisted. "You have learned a good deal from what Joshua did; we all have."

"And yet you began this conversation by telling me that I'm a blind fool," Eliza snapped.

"I was not referring to—"

"If I have been completely oblivious to the way Matthias feels about me for *years*, while you and Simon could clearly see the evidence, how does that help me believe that I am discerning enough to know whether a person can be trusted?"

"First of all," Mia said, "I think you need to start determining your ability to be wise and discerning from this point in your life going forward, rather than basing it on the mistakes of the past. I admit to having doubts, but I also believe that we are both capable of being able to discern the truth with time. And secondly, both Simon and I have learned a great deal through these experiences as well. We both love you, and we will both always be a part of your life. We should have shared with you the things we had observed instead of keeping them to ourselves. From now on, we *will* share our observations with you regarding the people with whom we interact, and that means you don't have to rely on your opinions alone. We can all do better, Eliza. But you absolutely must not resign yourself to some form of martyrdom regarding your future because of Joshua. You can't allow him to have that kind of say over your life. Even if he had lived and you had discovered his indiscretions, you would have ended the relationship, and I believe you would have had the strength to move on in a positive way and be happy. Surely with Joshua dead and gone and no longer around to complicate your life in any way, you can find a way to learn from the experience and create a good life for yourself."

Eliza thought about that for a minute or more before she said, "I *can* create a good life for myself. I just don't necessarily believe that means I will ever marry."

Mia let out a frustrated sigh and dropped her head onto the pillow as if Eliza's attitude had worn her out completely, draining her of all strength. While Eliza could understand her sister's frustration, she wondered if Mia could fully grasp how difficult it was for her to believe that she could ever fully trust *any* man after what Joshua had done. Her own mind told her it was completely illogical to judge others based on the bad behavior of one person, but her damaged heart told her something entirely different. And Mia's vacillating feelings over the matter only confused Eliza further.

Chapter Seven
THE ART OF CONVERSATION

ELIZA WAS GLAD THAT MIA didn't bring up the sensitive conversation they'd shared about Matthias, especially when she felt more determined than ever to remove any possibility of marriage from her future. And her determination was solid and firm until Sunday came and she saw Matthias at church. They had only a moment to exchange greetings before the service began, but that was all it took for Eliza to feel as if just being in the same vicinity as this man might make her melt into a puddle on the floor. There was nothing in his behavior or even his countenance that might betray the feelings he'd confessed to her, but now that Eliza knew the truth, she could see it in his eyes, which made her especially glad that they were able to sit down and face the front of the chapel so she didn't have to look at him at all. And she managed to carefully steer Mia to be seated between herself and Matthias; she didn't think she could bear to sit right next to him. The battle taking place between her heart and her head had taken her completely off guard; she didn't need any encouragement of her attraction to Matthias making matters worse. She intended to do exactly as he'd suggested: ignore what he'd told her, and her own feelings along with it. She simply hadn't anticipated that it would be so difficult. But she refused to allow her fanciful notions and irrational emotions to lure her into a situation that might very well compromise her security—and that of her sister. While Eliza hardly heard a word of the vicar's sermon and barely managed to sing the hymns, she reminded herself that she'd given Matthias no indication that she felt any attraction to him; therefore, she only needed to go forward maintaining that façade, and nothing at all would come of any of this. She would surely adjust to being able to spend time with him and not be so affected.

When the service ended, Eliza commanded her countenance to portray nothing but kind indifference as she smiled at Matthias and said, "I assume we will see you for tea as usual."

"As long as I'm still welcome, it would be my pleasure," he said, glancing back and forth between Eliza and Mia, and Eliza wondered if her sister noticed the mild trepidation in his eyes. Did he think that his confession would see him dismissed from their social gatherings? And did he wonder if Eliza had told Mia the truth? Or it was possible he had picked up on Mia's subtle lack of trust, even if she tended to vacillate back and forth on that matter.

Eliza hurried to try and put him at ease. "You are always welcome, Matthias."

"Your company is most pleasant," Mia added, sounding sincere.

"You are both as kind as ever," Matthias said before he was distracted by Simon wanting to speak with him.

Despite the countless Sundays Eliza had seen Simon wearing the robes of a vicar, it always felt a little strange in light of the time they spent together as friends when his clothes were more ordinary. If he was attending to any vicarage business during the week, he would wear the collar that represented his position, but he often dressed as normally as any other man. However, on Sundays it was impossible to ignore that he held an important and respected position. Eliza was glad to see the way that Simon interacted with Matthias in front of the other parishioners. His doing so was not at all unnatural given the friendship they'd shared for years, but Eliza still felt certain that Simon was making certain that people saw his acceptance of Matthias, given the likelihood that everyone surely knew by now that he had lost everything following his brother's scandalous death, and that he had also been reduced from the status of a gentleman to a menial laborer at a pub. There were people in this parish from every walk of life, and Simon did well at treating them all as equals. But Eliza believed he wanted to show by his example that Matthias's status as a human being and a member of the parish had not changed, even if his circumstances had.

Eliza felt a deep compassion for Matthias as she discreetly observed him talking to Simon, but she was also overcome with that increasingly familiar inner fluttering that often occurred when she saw Matthias. Even though Mia was engaged in speaking with an older couple about the birth of their newest grandchild, Eliza eased carefully through the people gathered in the chapel who were taking advantage of the opportunity to socialize after the service and made her way to the doors at the back. She went outside even though it was cold, but the chill in the air and the brightness of the sun in a brilliantly blue sky helped her push thoughts of Matthias away—along with the effect he had on her.

When a cold breeze made the chill in the air far too uncomfortable, Eliza walked to where their carriage was waiting and found Ferris and Clint both there. She knew they always attended the service as well, even though they maintained the expected, appropriate distance from their employers. And since they were accustomed to being on the outside of the carriage through their brief journey back and forth, they were more suitably dressed than Eliza or her sister to ward off the cold. They greeted Eliza kindly before Clint helped her step into the carriage where she was able to wait, protected from the increasingly strong wind. Mia arrived only a few minutes later and they were quickly on their way home.

"Are you all right?" Mia asked the moment she was seated across from Eliza.

Eliza sighed and debated for a moment whether she should be honest about her present distress, or just steer the conversation elsewhere. She decided on the former, certain it would take far too much effort to try and pretend with her sister; her efforts would be better served in putting up the proper front when Matthias was around.

"I suppose . . ." Eliza began, looking out the window, "being around Matthias is more difficult than I expected . . . now that I know how he feels about me."

"Then perhaps you should tell him the truth about how *you* feel, which would surely make it easier."

Eliza was astonished. "I cannot do that! I've already explained to you where I stand."

"Yes, you've certainly explained," Mia said with mild disgust. "But you can't truly believe that these feelings you have will just somehow dissolve simply because you want them to."

"With time, yes; I believe I will be able to see the situation more sensibly and not allow any silly notions to cloud my judgment. And *you*—having made it clear that you are not certain whether you can trust Matthias—have no right to be giving me advice over *my* decision regarding marriage."

Mia said nothing after that as if Eliza had made too strong a point to be protested, and they passed the remainder of the ride home in silence. They both went inside to freshen up before lunch, each going to their separate rooms without sharing any further conversation. Throughout the meal they both remained silent, which never happened unless they were unhappy with each other. Clearly

Mia's opinion regarding the way Eliza was handling this situation was stronger than Eliza had realized—although she wasn't certain if it was Mia's opinion that Eliza shouldn't give up on marriage, or if she didn't trust Matthias; or perhaps she was as confused as Eliza—but that didn't change the fact that Eliza absolutely knew she could never make a decision that could even remotely compromise their security.

After finishing their lunch, they each went back to their separate bedrooms, and Eliza attempted to take a nap. She dozed off and on while strange dreams that she couldn't remember when she awoke intruded upon her brief bouts of sleep; she only knew that she felt unsettled.

Eliza found herself dreading Matthias's arrival for tea and was glad when she was the last to arrive and found him already there and visiting with Mia and Simon. The men rose to greet her before they were all seated and resumed the conversation. It took Eliza only a few minutes to relax and mostly be able to forget about the matter pressing on her mind; and even though she couldn't completely forget, she was able to behave like her normal self, and she felt confident that no one would suspect that anything at all was any different than it had been before Matthias had come to her with his confession. More than once Eliza caught a glimpse of something in his eyes when he glanced at her, but she was quick to glance away and efficiently banish any related thoughts or feelings into the far recesses of her mind.

After tea, Simon instigated a rousing conversation about a principle from the Bible that he'd come across in his recent study. They all enjoyed Simon's enthusiasm over such things, and the insights he offered fascinated Eliza. By the time dinner was served, Eliza had noted that Matthias was not behaving any differently toward her than he ever had. He'd even stopped showing any indication in his eyes that he might be gauging her feelings—or perhaps more accurately her response to their last private conversation. It seemed that the matter had been settled, however silently, and they could go on as they always had. By the time Matthias and Simon had left for the evening, Eliza felt much more confident about going forward with her convictions. She told Mia so before they went to bed; Mia had nothing to say about the matter, but they talked about other things and it seemed that everything was back to normal between them as well—as long as they avoided any reference to Matthias's feelings for Eliza, and Eliza's determination to ignore them. And they entirely skirted around the fact that they both knew that Mia didn't really trust Matthias; it was as if she liked him but didn't trust him. Eliza could relate to that, especially when she thought of her relationship with Joshua.

The weeks of winter grew into months while they continued to see Matthias every Sunday, and Simon came to visit almost every day. Eliza was able to more easily distract herself from any thoughts of Matthias by focusing on the obvious growing attachment between Mia and Simon. There were many times when Eliza almost mentioned it to her sister, wanting to know exactly how Mia felt about the vicar, but a part of her wanted Mia to be the one to bring it up; she wanted to know that her sister trusted her enough to share such a personal matter.

When February was coming to a close and it had been nearly nine months since Joshua's death, Eliza finally sought out her sister just before bedtime, determined to know how Mia was feeling, even if that meant she had to instigate the conversation. She found Mia sitting in her bed with a book open on her lap. Eliza assumed she had been reading until she sat on the edge of Mia's bed and glanced at the book.

"How exactly do you manage to read when the book is upside down?" Eliza asked.

Mia looked down to see that Eliza was right before she slammed the book closed and set it beside her.

"Why did you feel the need to pretend you're reading just because I came to talk with you?" Eliza asked.

Mia sighed and folded her arms. "Because I didn't want you to know that I'm far too distracted to read, and I don't know what to do about it."

"And why wouldn't you want me to know?" Eliza asked.

"Truthfully?" Mia retorted.

"Of course!"

"Because I do not trust your judgment when it comes to matters of the heart; therefore, I'm not certain I want to share what's in my own heart." Eliza was astonished by what she'd just heard but couldn't think of a response before Mia went on. "When you are so determined to ignore what's in your own heart, how can I talk to you about what's in mine?"

"Oh, Mia," Eliza said with regret, reaching for her sister's hand and feeling relieved when she took it, "I never meant for my own difficulties to become *yours*. You must talk to me." She hesitated only a moment before venturing to just say, "It's Simon isn't it; you're in love with him." She made the statement confidently, based on months of observing the two of them together and the way they interacted.

Mia looked astonished, as if she were desperately searching for some way to insist that Eliza was wrong; then her expression melted into resignation and tears rose in her eyes. "Yes," Mia admitted with gentle sincerity, "I love him . . . and I do believe he loves me—although neither of us have said as much. But we always enjoy each other's company, and we have so very much in common; we share the same ideas and attitudes regarding almost everything, and when we *do* disagree, we do so respectfully. He reminds me very much of Father in the way he's always kind, and he holds a high regard toward women—which we know well enough is not always the case with men. I do believe I could make a good vicar's wife. I mean . . . well . . . I can't say it wouldn't be a challenge in some respects, and I know there is much that would be expected of me, but still . . . I believe with Simon at my side, knowing how supportive and kind he is, I could live that life and be happy."

"You've clearly given this a great deal of thought," Eliza said.

"I confess that I have." Mia sighed deeply, as if her breath were escorting her most personal feelings out into the open. "I think about him almost constantly, whether we are together or not. I *am* relatively certain he feels the same way about me, but I've wondered why he's said nothing. Does he only consider me a friend? Have I misinterpreted his acts of friendship as something more, simply because I want it that way? And what am I supposed to do about it? Surely, it's not appropriate for a woman to simply ask a man such questions. I certainly don't want to compromise our friendship by even hinting that I feel something more, and risk that he doesn't in truth share my affection."

"Then perhaps *I* should talk with him," Eliza suggested.

"What?" Mia asked, sounding horrified. "No, you mustn't say a—"

"Hear me out before you get all upset," Eliza said. "I too have been a friend to Simon for many years. Surely I'm capable of having a simple conversation with him in which I might be able to gauge his feelings on the matter. He can be very shy about personal matters, even though he exudes confidence in his role as a vicar. Perhaps he just needs some encouragement, or if it's true that he sees you only as a friend, I can ascertain that, and you will not have to keep wondering. I promise you that I can share such a conversation with him and not let on to anything you've shared with me about your own feelings."

Mia silently weighed what Eliza had said, staring at her sister as if she were carefully sizing up her ability to do what she had just proposed. "I want to believe you," Mia said, "but if we're being completely honest with each other—and we have sworn to be so—I can't deny some skepticism."

"Why?" Eliza asked, and as soon as the word left her mouth, she knew what Mia would say.

"If you are not able to honestly address your affection for Matthias—and his for you—then why should I believe that you have the ability to assist *me* in such matters?"

Eliza looked down, wishing the question hadn't pricked her so deeply. With the passing of time, she had truly believed her feelings would dissipate, but the opposite had happened—even if she didn't want to admit it, even to herself. However, she was willing to answer her sister honestly. "Because I am much more likely to see the situation between you and Simon with more clarity than I am able to see my own emotions—which quite honestly only confuse me."

"What is there to be confused about?" Mia asked. "Time has passed and it's evident you care for him very much."

"Is it?" Eliza asked, looking up again, fearful that she'd not concealed her feelings nearly as well as she had hoped.

"Oh, yes!" Mia said. "I can see it clearly. And it's equally evident that Matthias still cares for you."

Eliza sighed and looked down again. "That doesn't change the fact that—"

"There is no reason for you to repeat your ridiculous edict about the reasons you should never marry. It's more accurate to say that you are simply afraid of making such a commitment after all of Joshua's deceit. And that is certainly understandable, dear sister. But it is not a good reason for you to lock your heart away and spend the rest of your life alone. There are good men out there, and Matthias is one of them."

"Yes, he *is* a good man," Eliza stated, "and yet I believe that you are at least as confused as I am, if not more so. I don't believe for a moment that you completely trust Matthias, and yet you seem so determined for me to do so without question."

Mia looked immediately guilty; her contradictions had been pegged exactly and she knew it. "Perhaps . . . it's more the principle of the matter. I don't believe you should eliminate the possibility of marriage from your future. Whether or not Matthias can be trusted . . . and whether or not he is the right man for you is . . . well . . . perhaps still in a stage of experiment. I believe we should be . . . cautious, but . . . quite simply I can't bear the idea of your determination to never marry."

Eliza didn't like what she was hearing, mostly because she felt more and more convinced that Mia was more confused about Matthias than Eliza was. After Eliza remained silently thoughtful for a couple of minutes, Mia said, "I'll make a deal with you, Liza. I'll let you speak with Simon if you promise to at least let Matthias know how you feel about him." Eliza wanted to protest, but Mia kept talking. "There's no need for any kind of commitment in simply admitting to how you feel, but I believe you at least need to give yourself—and him—the opportunity to know whether marriage is possible, instead of simply deciding that it's not and locking your heart away without any explanation to him whatsoever. He did, after all, open his heart to *you*. It must have taken a great deal of courage to do so, especially when he knows better than almost anyone the full depth of what Joshua's indiscretions have done to your life. Surely you can exhibit the same kind of courage. And . . . perhaps you will only know whether he can be trusted if you start to have truly honest conversations."

Mia paused, allowing Eliza time to respond, but now she couldn't think of a single word to counter what her sister had just said. Still, she was surprised when Mia offered, "Or . . . I could speak to him. If you're going to speak with Simon, I could speak to Matthias."

"I'm capable of speaking to Matthias myself," Eliza insisted.

"Good, then do so," Mia said triumphantly. "And once I know you've shared a completely honest conversation with Matthias, you are more than welcome to talk to Simon about *me*—as long as you promise to tread carefully."

Eliza agreed to Mia's deal, but a few hours later, alone in her bed in the darkness and unable to sleep, she wondered what she had gotten herself into. She didn't feel at all nervous over the prospect of talking to Simon; he was probably one of the easiest men to talk to in all the world. And Eliza felt confident she could get him to discuss his feelings for Mia—whatever those feelings might entail—without any awkwardness at all. But the very idea of admitting to Matthias that she had grown to care for him—and to feel an enduring attraction toward him—felt tantamount to going to the gallows. She was able to sleep only when she reminded herself that she wouldn't even be seeing Matthias for days, and she had plenty of time to consider how to go about that conversation.

The following morning Mia wasn't feeling well and remained in bed. She had a stuffy nose and a slightly sore throat and felt tired, but since her symptoms were mild, they both agreed that she was not in need of a doctor and they hoped it would remain that way. Mia felt confident that if she got plenty of rest and indulged in the nasty herbal concoctions Mrs. Simpkin always offered in the face of any ailment, she would be up and about in no time.

Eliza spent most of the morning reading to her sister until Mia drifted off to sleep and Eliza left her in peace. After lunch, Eliza took a nap herself, feeling suddenly tired as a result of her inadequate sleep the night before. Following her nap and a quick freshening up, Eliza was about to go to Mia's room to join her for tea when a maid came to tell her that the vicar had just arrived. It wasn't at all uncommon for Simon to come by unexpectedly, and often at teatime or even for meals. Eliza and Mia had extended an open invitation to him years earlier, insisting that he was always welcome. As busy as he was kept caring for his parishioners, combined with the fact that he had no family, they were only too glad to provide meals for him and to enjoy his company whenever possible. True, he had a housekeeper at the vicarage who also provided simple meals for him when necessary, but she was the first to claim that her culinary skills were not the finest, and she was more capable in the areas of keeping the vicarage clean and orderly and managing the vicar's appointments for him. Therefore, she was as pleased as anyone when he was invited to share meals with his parishioners. And when Simon was not at the vicarage for meals, Peter usually was, so her efforts were always appreciated. And the Grenville sisters were blessed with Simon's company more often than anyone else, which was an amiable arrangement for all of them. Eliza knew now that his tendency to spend a great deal of time here was likely due to his affection for Mia, but at this point that was nothing but speculation—at least regarding Simon's motivation.

As Eliza went downstairs to share tea with the vicar, it occurred to her that this would be the perfect opportunity to speak with him about that very matter and not have the conversation feel maneuvered or contrived. She knew she had told Mia she would speak to Matthias first, but she doubted she would ever get a better opportunity than this to speak to Simon privately, and she would assure her sister that she would keep her promise to speak with Matthias about her own feelings—even if she presently dreaded doing so with all her soul and had no idea how she would go about it. But for now, she focused on speaking with Simon, and as always, simply enjoying his company.

Simon greeted Eliza amiably, as he always did, and expressed such sincere disappointment about Mia not joining them that Eliza's confidence was bolstered regarding her theory.

"Is she all right?" Simon asked with genuine concern as they were seated across from each other.

"She has a little cold," Eliza explained. "I don't think it's anything serious, but I promise to keep a close eye on her."

"Very good," Simon said with relief. "Please send word if she worsens at all, and of course I will be praying for her; I always do. And you of course; I pray for the both of you."

"That's very kind," Eliza said. "And you are always in our prayers, Simon. We know that your work is very important, and you are deeply committed to it. You surely deserve God's richest blessings for all the good that you do. But you are also such a very dear friend to both of us; I don't know what we would ever do without you."

"Oh, my dear Eliza," Simon said, "I can assure you that it's the other way around. You and your sister have always made me feel so welcome here. Your home has become somewhat of a refuge for me, I confess. Whenever the burdens of my work become too great, I feel as if I can always come here and find strength in your kindness and support, and gain some reprieve that helps me feel more capable of going back out there to continue doing the best I can to ease the suffering of others—although more often than not it feels as if it's never enough."

Eliza readily admitted, "I'm so glad that we've been able to help in such a way; I had no idea you felt such things. And I'm absolutely certain you do a great deal more that is good than you might believe. I've not only witnessed the good you do . . . and the way people are touched by your kindness . . . but I've experienced your support and compassion very personally."

"You're awfully kind," Simon said, showing a mild shyness over the compliment.

A maid came into the room to serve tea, creating a natural pause in the conversation. After the maid had left, Eliza and Simon chose dainty cakes and little sandwiches which they placed on small china plates in a matching pattern to the teapot and the cups and saucers they used to prepare their tea, each according to their own liking. Once they were settled again, Eliza felt compelled to just jump in and ask what might be considered a delicate question, but she and Simon knew each other well enough that she hoped he wouldn't find it offensive. Still, she would tread carefully, just as she'd promised her sister.

"Simon, may I ask you something . . . personal?"

"Of course," he said as if he weren't at all concerned.

"You don't have to answer if you don't want to, but . . . I've often wondered, and . . ."

"We're the best of friends, Eliza," he said. "You may ask whatever you like."

"Thank you," she replied. "I was just wondering if . . . well . . . surely you don't wish to remain a bachelor. I can't really imagine you without a wife and children; surely a vicar should have a family, and . . ." She paused to gauge his reaction thus far and he seemed as relaxed as ever. "Well . . . I'm just wondering if anyone in particular has caught your eye. You've never spoken with us about any romantic interests on your part, but . . . surely there must be a woman among your social circles you've felt drawn to; someone with the qualities you would consider suitable to be a good vicar's wife."

Simon looked at Eliza with a gaze of such severe inquisition that she began to feel as if he could see right through to her soul. She tried very hard to feign innocence as to the nature of her inquiries but had to look away when she felt certain he had discerned her motives. She was surprised to hear him chuckle, but not so terribly surprised to hear him say, "I know exactly what you're getting at Lady Eliza." She found it easier to look up at him again when he used her title with such affection; he knew she preferred that he simply call her by her given name when they were not in public; therefore, his speaking to her in such a way was never anything more than a form of endearment. "Should I be surprised that a woman as discerning as yourself has figured out the true nature of my feelings for your sister?"

Eliza admitted, "I couldn't be absolutely certain."

"Well," he drawled on the wave of a long sigh, "perhaps your bringing it up is an answer to my prayers, because I've been trying to gather the courage to ask your permission to officially court Miss Mia. In lieu of any male relative, it seems that speaking to you is the only proper course of action."

"That seems logical," Eliza said, "and of course you have not only my permission but my blessing. I completely respect Mia's judgment in this and will support her in any course she chooses for her life."

"Do you think she holds the kind of regard for me that would . . . well . . . do you believe she would agree to an arrangement of courting?" Simon's unusual expression of vulnerability in the question made it difficult for Eliza not to smile.

"Have the two of you never discussed your relationship in this way?" Eliza asked him.

"I'm afraid we haven't," he said a bit sheepishly.

"And yet . . . you must have some sense that she shares your feelings or you wouldn't venture toward courtship. I don't believe you would set your sights on a woman if you didn't have good reason to hope she shared your affection."

"I believe I have good reason to hope," Simon said, "although I'm not absolutely certain, and I . . . confess that the uncertainty is somewhat unnerving."

"Then as soon as Mia is feeling better, the two of you must have an open and honest conversation." Eliza *did* smile at Simon then. "How many times have you told me that proper communication in relationships is necessary? Do I detect some degree of hypocrisy in you, dear friend?"

Simon chuckled tensely. "Perhaps, but I hope to remedy that right away."

"And I will look forward to the outcome," Eliza said.

"Has she said anything to you?" Simon asked, clearly hoping she might say something to help ease his nerves.

"She has," Eliza said, "but I don't believe I'm at liberty to repeat her sentiments. She'll be feeling better soon enough, and the two of you can talk."

"Now that you and I have shared *this* conversation," Simon said, "waiting an hour to speak with her seems far too long."

"Patience," Eliza said with a teasing chuckle. "You're always preaching about that, as well."

"Go ahead, call me a hypocrite," he said, chuckling as well. "I can't deny it."

"I never would think of you as a hypocrite and you know it; however much I might tease you, I know what a good man you are. I also know that matters of the heart are much different than anything else we might confront in this life."

"I fear you have gained far too much wisdom in that regard," Simon said, his mood darkening.

"*Too much* wisdom?" Eliza countered. "How is it possible to gain too much wisdom?"

"Perhaps it is more accurate to say that your experience with Joshua exposed you far too much to the harshness and cruelty of the world. I don't want to see you become cynical because of it, or to lose faith in other people based on Joshua's bad behavior. I have seen a great deal of the terrible impact that bad choices can have on the lives of people and their loved ones. But I can also attest to the overall resiliency of humanity. Most people are good at heart, with nothing but the best of intentions. I hope you won't judge others according to the way Joshua deceived you."

Eliza hadn't expected—or wanted—their conversation to take such a turn, but a part of her was glad for the opportunity to speak to her friend—if not her vicar—privately about her feelings on the matter. "But I was such a fool, Simon. He was lying to me in one way or another every time I saw him; he was pretending to be a completely different person than he actually was. And I didn't see it; I didn't even suspect. How can I ever know whether I'm capable of accurately gauging the character of another person? I'm not talking about judging others; I know what the scriptures teach about that, and I know that only God knows the reasons why people do what they do. I've forgiven Joshua, and I've forgiven Matthias for the role he played in the situation. I know he was in an impossible position, and he's certainly paying a grievous penance for his brother's choices. I'm referring now to my own ability to be able to trust anyone ever again. I'm just not certain that I can."

"What are you saying, Eliza?" Simon asked, sounding surprised. "If you don't believe you can ever fully trust again, do you mean that you don't plan to marry? Because you certainly can't marry a man if you can't completely trust him."

Eliza shouldn't have been so amazed by his perception as he succinctly stated the premise of her attitude. "Yes, I suppose that's what I'm saying." She wanted to add that her sister's vacillating attitude about whether Matthias could be trusted wasn't helping matters any, but Eliza didn't want to speak ill of Mia.

"So . . . you would allow Joshua to rob you of any possible happiness in your future?" Simon asked, and Eliza gasped at the question and the way it pricked her heart. "After all the hurt he inflicted upon you in the past, would you really want to also give him your future?"

"I hadn't thought about it that way," Eliza admitted, then silently contemplated his questions for a minute or more before she looked directly into his kind, wise eyes and asked, "But how *can* I trust another man with my happiness? My security? All that I have? If I was so thoroughly fooled before, how can I know I'm not being fooled again?"

"You've learned a great deal, Eliza," Simon said with compassion. "Although, I think you need to perhaps alter the way you're viewing the situation. Before you can trust any man enough to give him all that you have—your heart and soul as well as your temporal belongings—you first have to trust yourself. In truth, I believe you've lost your ability to trust yourself to be able to discern the honesty—or lack thereof—in other people. You *are* wise and discerning, Eliza. Joshua worked very hard to fool you; he fooled all of us. Even Matthias was ignorant to the full depth of his problems and his level of deception. But I'm certain if you look back at your memories of him you would be able to recognize many signs that there were problems. You didn't pay attention to them because you had no reason to believe he wasn't being honest with you. Now you know that people can be deceptive; he robbed you of your innocence, but he also took away your naivete and your gullibility. You might consider that as some form of a gift, because you will never be naive or gullible again. I daresay you would be keenly aware of even the slightest hint that any man or woman might be lying to you about anything, large or small. You must learn to trust in yourself again,

Eliza. And you must also trust in God more fully. He has given you intelligence, wisdom, discernment, and He will guide you in using these things for your best good. He wants you to be happy; He wants you to remain protected from any kind of evil. Strive to put your trust more fully in Him, and He will surely guide you through your thoughts and feelings, and if you're asking for His help and paying attention, surely all will be well."

Eliza thought about that while Simon waited patiently for her to do so; he had a way of knowing when it was best to not speak at all. She finally said, "It's no wonder you make such a fine vicar. You have a way of saying just the right thing. You've given me a great deal to think about. Thank you."

"You know I'm always happy to help when I can," he said, "although I know that some challenges in life are just enormously difficult to overcome—and what you've been through is one of those things."

"And yet . . . as you said, I shouldn't allow Joshua to take away the happiness of my future."

"No, I don't believe you should," Simon said.

Their conversation lightened as they talked of trivial matters until he excused himself, explaining his commitment to be on time for an appointment with a woman in his parish who was in need of his support; he told Eliza nothing more about who it was or what the problem might be, and she always respected the way he was careful about keeping the confidences of those whom he served. He enjoyed talking about the typical news in people's lives that anyone would discuss freely, but when it came to personal problems and challenges, he likely wouldn't reveal a word on pain of death. And Eliza was glad to know that he would keep *her* challenges securely private, just as he did those of other people in his parish. He was a good man, and Eliza truly hoped that he and Mia would eventually marry; the idea of having him become a permanent part of their family was deeply comforting and perfectly comfortable.

Over the next few days, Eliza pondered deeply on the advice Simon had given her. She prayed a great deal about the matter, wanting to do as Simon had suggested and learn to trust more in God, and also to trust more in her own ability to be able to discern any kind of dishonesty in others. Slowly she began to feel this new perspective settle more comfortably into her mind *and* her spirit, and she felt lighter than she had since Joshua had failed to show up at the church for their wedding.

Mia felt much better after a couple of days' rest, and once she was up and about, Eliza wasn't surprised when Simon came to call and requested the opportunity to speak with Mia alone. The moment Simon left, Mia came to find Eliza in the library, almost literally beaming with happiness over the fact that Simon had asked for the privilege of officially courting her.

"He told me he'd asked you about it," Mia said, plopping down on the same sofa where Eliza was sitting. She absently reached for the hourglass and turned it over, smiling as she did so. "He said that in lieu of us having any male relatives, it was only proper that he consult my older sister, and that you gave us your blessing."

"And why wouldn't I?" Eliza said with a joyful laugh as she took her sister's hand. "He's a wonderful man, and the two of you are well matched."

"Oh, I agree!" Mia said.

"So, how do you feel about becoming a vicar's wife?" Eliza asked. "There are surely complications to such a life."

"I believe I can do it, even though some of it makes me nervous." Mia sighed. "But Simon is a patient man; I'm certain he will guide me well in helping me learn all that I will need to do to support him, and I will gladly support him in every possible way—because I know he would do the same for me."

"I'm certain you're right," Eliza said, then hugged her sister tightly.

Eliza had never seen her sister so happy—at least not since she had been a carefree child, prior to the deaths of their parents. She wore a perpetual smile, and her face very nearly glowed almost constantly. When Simon came to visit the following day, Eliza joined them for tea and then graciously went into the library across the hall, leaving the rooms to both doors open for the sake of propriety, but also allowing the sweethearts to talk privately. Mia had done the same for Eliza and Joshua a great many times. And there had been times when Matthias had played the role of chaperone when Eliza had spent time with Joshua at the home of him and his brother. While Eliza sat alone in the library, able to hear the distant voices of Mia and Simon but unable to discern what they were saying, her mind wandered back to the many months of her courtship with Joshua, and then the months of their engagement. She had felt every bit as happy then as Mia felt now—the difference was that they knew Simon was genuinely a good man and not putting on any false pretenses; the same could not be said for Joshua.

While Eliza allowed her memories to wander into painful places, she felt that instinctive temptation to lock away any desire for love and marriage in her future, but then she recalled all that Simon had told her recently about forgiveness and trust—and she knew that she not only needed to learn to trust herself and her own abilities, she needed to forgive herself. She'd not once willfully made any choice that required forgiveness, but since the truth had come out about the man she'd loved so dearly, she had been very hard on herself for being so gullible and naive. Eliza could now see that she needed to be more kind to herself regarding all that had happened. Joshua had set out to purposely deceive her, and he'd been very good at it. Now she just had to find a way to fully and completely let go of all the heartache Joshua had caused and try to find a good life for herself. She still wasn't convinced that marriage would be in her future, but she did find herself thinking about Matthias with an attitude that was more open to the possibility of at least acknowledging her attraction to him. She truly believed that she could trust him despite the mistakes he'd made in the past, but she had no intention of rushing into any kind of romantic notions, and surely it would take time to know if she could truly trust herself or anyone else. Her heart had been broken and it needed to heal. For now, she enjoyed hearing Simon and her sister laughing in the next room. If Mia could find such happiness in her life, Eliza felt nothing but thrilled, and for the moment she was content to focus on her sister's prospects of love and marriage, as opposed to worrying a bit about her own.

Chapter Eight
BARRIERS

On Sunday Eliza and Mia went to church as usual, although Eliza was keenly aware of how Mia couldn't suppress her ongoing glow of happiness. Without exchanging a word between them, Eliza highly suspected her sister was imagining how Sunday services might be when she became the vicar's wife and she would be engaged in greeting and visiting with parishioners as they came and went. Eliza was sincerely glad for her sister's happiness, but she was more preoccupied by the conspicuous absence of Matthias. She tried to be discreet in the way she occasionally glanced over her shoulder to see if he'd arrived, but the service began with no sign of him, and she had to force herself to stop looking toward the chapel doors when she knew that everyone seated behind her would be well aware of her every move. The further they got into the service, the more anxious Eliza felt regarding Matthias's absence. A part of her knew it was irrational to believe that his absence meant that anything untoward had happened, but given the fact that his brother had been murdered, Eliza simply couldn't help feeling some fear.

"Where do you suppose he is?" Mia whispered in Eliza's ear during one of the hymns.

"How would I know any more than you?" Eliza whispered in reply.

"Perhaps he's ill," Mia suggested. Eliza didn't like the idea of Matthias being ill and on his own, but it was a much better idea than thinking of him dead in an alley somewhere.

Eliza thought for a long moment about how to respond before she whispered, "If he doesn't come for tea as usual, we will have Simon go with us to make certain he's all right."

"Excellent plan," Mia said and the hymn ended, but tea felt like an eternity away for Eliza as she considered all the possibilities of why Matthias hadn't come to church; and of course her mind kept being drawn to the very worst scenarios.

After the service, it took them far longer than usual to get to the carriage because Simon urged Mia to remain by his side while he told a great many people that they were officially courting. While the happy couple received outpourings of congratulations and well-wishes, Eliza hovered discreetly nearby until her feet began to ache and she chose to wait in the carriage. When Mia finally stepped into the carriage with Clint's help, Eliza said to her sister, "If that's going to become a part of your regular Sunday duties, you're going to need very comfortable shoes."

"Amen to that," Mia said, removing her own shoes before she tucked her feet up on the seat beside her. But the smile on Mia's face made it clear she'd enjoyed herself very much, and the prospect of becoming Simon's wife—and all that would be expected of her—was nothing but pleasing.

All the way home Mia chattered about how kind and excited people were about the news of her courtship with the vicar, and how glad she was to know that their courting was mostly a formality; she felt completely confident that they *would* marry, and they simply needed to take the appropriate amount of time to do everything properly, which was especially important for a vicar. Eliza was glad for Mia's delight and the distraction it gave her from worrying about Matthias.

When they arrived home, Eliza hoped to be told that Matthias had sent a message to explain his absence, but he hadn't. She kept hoping a message would arrive, but they finished lunch and still had no idea why Matthias hadn't been at church. Eliza declared the need for a nap before tea, even though she doubted she could relax while she felt so worried. Curled up beneath the covers in her bed, it occurred to Eliza that the depth of her concern was a clear indication of how much she'd grown to care for Matthias. She knew Mia was concerned as well, but not nearly as much as Eliza. She didn't want to wait until tea to see whether he would show up. She wanted to go and find him right now. In fact, she was very tempted to just ask for the carriage to be harnessed and go by herself the moment it was ready. Ferris and Clint would be with her to make certain she was safe, and she could even take one of them with her into the building where Matthias lived while the other stayed with the carriage.

Eliza kept glancing at the clock and debating whether or not to take this action, vacillating between an intense worry over Matthias's well-being and scolding herself for getting so upset when his absence could very well have a plausible explanation. And having her carriage driver and footman go to so much trouble only to find out that Matthias was fine would be ridiculous if not embarrassing. Perhaps Matthias had simply worked very late the previous evening; he'd once said that Saturday nights were especially busy at the pub. If that were the case, then he could have simply been exhausted and overslept. Eliza settled on making herself believe that was the case, and he would surely come to tea as expected. She reminded herself that if he *didn't* arrive at the usual time, Mia had already agreed that they would have Simon go with them to check on Matthias. Eliza simply needed to summon some patience and try to relax. When napping became impossible due to her extreme restlessness, Eliza went to her sitting room and attempted to read, but she still kept glancing at the clock every few minutes, glad to note that it was now less than an hour until tea, which meant she would soon need to freshen up and make herself presentable for company.

Eliza entered the drawing room a short while before tea would be served, expecting to find Simon and Mia already there. Simon almost always arrived early in order to visit longer, and now that he and Mia were officially courting, Eliza knew he would take every possible opportunity to spend time with her. Eliza stopped abruptly the moment she entered the room. Simon and Mia were *not* there, but Matthias was pacing near the row of windows that looked out upon the street. Her heart quickened just to see him, and relief washed over her, finally knowing that he was all right.

"Hello," she said, drawing his attention to the fact that she'd just entered the open doorway.

Matthias stopped pacing and turned to look at her, provoking a pleasant quiver in her stomach and making her heart beat even faster. Impulsively she closed the door, wanting to speak with him privately.

"You're all right," she said, since her concern for him had been the most prominent thing on her mind for hours.

"Of course I'm all right," he replied. "Why would you think otherwise?"

"You weren't at church," she stated, and just hearing the words come out of her mouth made all her worrying seem ridiculous. "I'm sure there's a simple explanation, but . . . I admit I've been concerned."

"No need for that," he said, but he turned to look out the window and she sensed—however subtly—that his words weren't entirely true.

"Is something bothering you?" she asked. "Please . . . sit down."

Eliza was glad when he accepted her invitation and sat across from her so that she could see his face. He crossed his legs and asked, "Where are the others? Have they abandoned us?"

"I assume they've gone for a walk," Eliza said.

"But it's freezing outside," Matthias declared. "I'm very grateful on these winter days that you offer me the luxury of your carriage to transport me back and forth for our Sunday visits."

"We're glad to help," she said, then explained, "I suspect Simon and Mia are strolling through the halls of the house, likely wanting every possible minute alone in order to speak privately." Matthias lifted one eyebrow, accurately posing the obvious question, which Eliza answered. "They are officially courting."

"Oh my," Matthias said and chuckled lightly. "I can't say it's a surprise; I'm more likely to say that it's high time they made it official. I doubt it will be long before they announce their intentions to be married."

"I'm sure you're right," Eliza said and was surprised to realize Matthias was staring at her in a way he never would have if other people had been present. No words were needed for her to know that his feelings for her had not diminished since he'd first confessed them to her; if anything, she surmised from the intensity of his gaze that they had only continued to grow. The very idea enhanced the fluttering in her stomach, and she had to look away. A taut silence grew between them until Eliza feared she might embarrass herself by blurting out an admission of her own feelings. Instead she sought to ease her curiosity—especially since she'd allowed his absence to upset her so much. "May I ask why you weren't at church? You were very much missed."

"That's very kind of you," Matthias said, but there was a subtle edge to his voice. He sighed in a way that implied he meant to say something he'd rather not say. "I was there," he said, much to her surprise, "but I slipped in and out discreetly and remained at the rear of the chapel, rather than making a spectacle of myself by going all the way to the front of the chapel to sit with you and your sister."

Eliza thought about that a long moment, trying to understand, then realized that she didn't. "Is there a problem . . . with sitting on the same pew with me and Mia?" she asked. "You and Joshua have sat with us at church for a very long time and it was never a—"

"Now Joshua is gone," Matthias said, looking away abruptly, but Eliza saw the muscles in his cheek tighten. "And everything has changed. I think it's better . . . more appropriate . . . if I *don't* sit with you."

"Why?" Eliza asked, astonished.

Matthias looked directly at her with a combination of anger and shame showing in his eyes. Eliza hoped he was going to explain the reasons why he felt that way, because for the life of her she couldn't imagine what they might be.

"Because," he said, a distinct edge to his voice, "it's best that I sit at the back—with the servants and the poor; it's where I belong now."

"Matthias!" Eliza muttered his named breathlessly. "Surely you can't think that I or Mia—or even Simon—would ever hold to such an attitude!"

"No, I don't think that, Eliza," he said, "but I am *brutally* aware that many people in the congregation *do* hold to such attitudes. I've heard a great many whispers, and some comments have been made directly to my face." Eliza realized that these things must have been taking place without her knowledge, and something had likely happened recently to change his mind so drastically, but she didn't know how to ask such a delicate and awkward question, and was relieved when he continued to explain. "My station in life has changed dramatically, and it is not only inappropriate for me to publicly associate with you and your sister, it is a taint upon your reputations. I greatly appreciate your hospitality, and I do hope that our Sunday visits might continue because they are—quite honestly—the only thing in my life that gives me any joy whatsoever. However, I will mind my place in public, because I have already done far too much to bring scandal and difficulty into your life, and I will not create any further grief for you or for Mia."

"Well, I entirely disagree!" Eliza insisted, surprised by her own vehemence. "The very idea that the gossip and lack of kindness of other people would influence our choices in such a way is . . . *preposterous!*"

"It's *not* preposterous, Eliza," Matthias said firmly. "Mia is going to become the vicar's wife, and you need to maintain a proper reputation so that you will be able to find a suitable husband . . . someone you can trust; someone who will respect you and honor you the way you deserve to be honored—like a queen. I'm not so naive as to think that—"

Eliza didn't even think before she blurted, "How can I possibly care about such things when it's *you* that I love!"

Matthias became immediately as still as if a sudden, icy wind had frozen him right where he sat. His eyes were so wide that they had forced his brows into stiff arches that creased his forehead. Eliza felt tempted to look away, embarrassed by her outburst and certainly questioning whether she should have admitted to her feelings at all. But another part of her was glad to have it out in the open, glad that he knew how she felt. And if she looked away, she could miss whatever hint he might betray of his reaction to such a confession.

"No, Eliza! No!" he shouted softly and stood, moving abruptly toward one of the windows where he looked out toward the street, which left his back turned to her so she couldn't see his face at all.

Eliza quickly moved to stand at his side. Now that they had embarked upon this conversation, there was no turning back, and she needed to understand what he meant—and how he felt.

"What do you mean by that?" she asked, and he barely glanced toward her as if he wasn't happy to find her beside him. He continued looking out the window, but at least she could see his profile. "No? What do you mean by '*no*'?"

He answered more quickly—and more tersely—than she had expected. "When I told you how I feel about you . . . I hadn't thought the matter through enough to realize that the very idea is preposterous. Too much has changed, Eliza. I would never expect to share any kind of relationship with you. Under the circumstances, I don't believe we should even be seen in public together. I'm committed to being truthful with you, however . . ."

"And I'm committed to being truthful with *you*," she countered. "Would you have me hold such feelings inside? Keep them to myself?"

"I would have you give some serious thought to the present situation," he said, looking at her now, but his eyes were almost scolding. "We would be nothing but foolish to encourage any kind of . . . of . . . romantic notion . . . between us. I'm not the same man I used to be, and I can never go back to that life. We must—"

Matthias's tirade was halted when the door came open and Mia and Simon entered the room. In spite of Eliza attempting to appear nonchalant, Mia was clearly too perceptive to not pick up on the tension into which they'd just intruded. "Oh," Mia said lightly to Simon, "I think we just interrupted something. Perhaps we should come back when—"

"No need for that," Eliza said, taking hold of Matthias's arm whether he wanted her to or not. "We'll just go for a little walk and be back soon. Start tea without us; we won't be long."

"As you wish," Simon said, and Eliza rushed from the room, letting go of Matthias once she knew he was following her.

Eliza walked quickly to the library and closed the door before she stopped and turned to face Matthias. She wanted to be absolutely certain they wouldn't be overheard.

"I shouldn't have said anything," Matthias said before Eliza could even gather any words to continue their conversation. "I believed at the time it was important to be honest with you, but I can see now I wasn't seeing the situation realistically. I should have kept my feelings to myself."

"No!" Eliza said. "I'm *glad* you told me, because . . ." She looked down, attempting to find the right words and unable to do so while facing his intense gaze.

"Why?" he asked when she hesitated, but he still sounded angry.

"Because . . ." she went on, drawing the courage to look up at him, ". . . I was already falling in love with you . . . before you told me."

Matthias took an abrupt step backward as if he'd been physically struck.

"My feelings were already there before you admitted to yours," Eliza clarified. "I've struggled with many confusing emotions since Joshua died and his true character came to light. The passing of time has helped me put a great many things into perspective, and time has shown me that what I feel is not . . . just a passing fancy or . . . some kind of bizarre reaction to losing Joshua. I know my own heart, Matthias." She sighed and regathered her courage. "If you must know, I had decided very firmly that I would never marry . . . that after what had happened with Joshua, I could never trust *any* man enough to give away all that I have . . . and all that I am. But Simon has helped me understand that I need to learn to trust myself again . . . and I need to trust God to guide me in my life. I don't know where these feelings will take me . . . us . . . but I couldn't hide them from you any longer."

"I can't believe what I'm hearing, Eliza," Matthias said, no longer sounding angry but certainly not warm. "I absolutely disagree with your temporary decision to never marry; you *should* marry. You should marry a respectable gentleman who is deserving of all that you have to offer. But any fool can see I am *not* a worthy candidate."

Now Eliza felt angry. "Are you saying that your present situation—which was created by your brother, not by your own choices—is of more importance than the way we feel about each other?"

"I made my own poor choices, Eliza," he insisted. "I chose to not tell you or anyone else the truth about what was really going on in Joshua's life. And now I'm paying my dues. You are an innocent victim to Joshua's wiles; me, not so much. I am *not* deserving of you, Eliza. My present situation only makes the circumstances far worse when *everyone* knows that you are a woman with an enormous fortune, and I am destitute. Everyone would believe my only interest would be the abundant dowry that comes with marrying you."

"*I* don't believe that!"

"Well, maybe you should!" he snapped. "Because that was certainly my brother's preeminent interest in you."

Eliza gasped, then found it difficult to draw breath. "What are you saying?" she muttered, clearly seeing regret on Matthias's face. "I thought that . . ."

Matthias let out a harsh sigh and looked toward the ceiling, even though his eyes were closed. "Forgive me," he murmured and looked at her with sorrow overtaking his countenance. "Joshua *did* care for you, Eliza; he did! I have no doubt you were more important to him than any other woman he'd ever known, but . . . oh, Eliza. I've done my best to be honest with you since his death, although I cannot deny I have omitted certain truths with the hope of sparing your feelings. I regret letting that slip out. You didn't need to know."

"Know what?" Eliza snapped, suddenly light-headed. "That he loved my money more than he loved me?"

The very fact that Matthias was clearly taking time to measure his words carefully increased Eliza's light-headedness and she hurried to sit down on one of the sofas as close to the fire as she could get, fearing she might faint otherwise and only add more drama to a conversation that already had far more drama than she could manage. Completely preoccupied with the question she'd just asked Matthias—and her fear that it was true—she was barely aware of him sitting beside her until she felt him take her hand and she turned to look at him.

"He cared for you, Eliza; I know he did," Matthias said with compassion. "He often told me how much he loved you. It's . . . my own opinion that . . . he didn't really understand the meaning of real love . . . that he'd never truly felt the kind of love that would make a man want to be a better person. He clearly loved his gambling habit more than *anything* or *anyone* in his life; or perhaps it's more truthful to say that it had become such a powerful addiction that it overshadowed everything and everyone else. I believe he *intended* to be a good husband to you, but I *know* he wasn't capable of that, and I also know that it would have taken very little time for him to gamble away every bit of the dowry he would have acquired from you upon your marriage."

Eliza took all of that in while she managed to gain her equilibrium and breathe more evenly. She finally said, "I think I knew all of that. I didn't want to admit it; I wanted to believe he loved me, but . . ." she focused fully on Matthias, ". . . I look back and now think that I was terribly naive and immature, because . . . I'm not certain that I loved *him*, at least not the way a woman should love the man to whom she's willing to commit her entire life. I think I loved the way he always said just the right thing to make me feel adored and admired, but is that not just vanity? And now I know he was a very good actor, and I wonder if he only said what he knew any woman would want to hear. Did he manipulate me into falling in love with him? Did he just take advantage of my gullibility?"

"I don't know, Eliza; I honestly don't know." Matthias's voice deepened with compassion and she felt him squeeze her hand. "It's impossible to gauge how much of his feelings for you were sincere, and . . ."

"And how much he saw our marriage as a convenient means to gain access to a great fortune that would help feed his bad habits."

"Something like that," Matthias said, hanging his head. "I'm so sorry, Eliza."

Once again, she allowed herself to take all of this in, realizing even more that she'd instinctively believed this to be true ever since Joshua's true nature had come to light; she simply hadn't wanted to fully acknowledge it. Recalling where this conversation had begun, she looked up at Matthias and asked, "But what does that have to do with us, Matthias? You are not your brother, and you are not to be judged by his actions."

As Matthias erupted to his feet and began pacing, Eliza could see that her words had clearly upset him. "Oh, but I *am* judged by his actions," Matthias said with a barely concealed fury, "which is the very reason it's best for me to keep my distance from you in public, and—"

"And pretend that what you told me is no longer true?" she guessed as she hurried to stand and face him with all the indignation she was feeling, which forced him to stop pacing. She wanted to tell him how deeply she had struggled with her feelings for him, how much turmoil and pondering she had wrestled with. And now that she'd finally gathered the courage to open her heart to him, she could hardly believe what she was hearing. This was not at all how she'd expected this conversation to go.

Matthias stared at Eliza as if her words had cast a spell on him and he was incapable of moving or speaking. Determined to maintain her dignity—rather than groveling in any way—but equally determined to get to the truth, Eliza took a step toward Matthias and looked up into his astonished eyes. "If your feelings for me have changed since you last spoke them to me, then all you have to do is tell me; tell me you don't love me, and I'll never speak of this again. But don't you dare lie to me! Don't try to convince yourself—or me—that lying to me for the sake of maintaining some kind of ridiculous social expectation is for the best. What's best is for us to be honest with each other. We're both adults, and we've both been deeply wounded by the deceit of someone we held dear. Surely we are capable of determining the best course to take from here by being wise and forthright, instead of pretending we feel differently than we do, or ignoring the facts as they are. The situation Joshua left us in is far from ideal, and far from conventional. But I refuse to be governed by *his* bad choices any longer. There are some things that cannot be changed, as difficult as they may be. However, there are other things that I believe are simply a matter of our choosing how we manage the hand we have been dealt. And surely, we have the right to choose what we do with the way we feel, Matthias."

Matthias looked at the floor and put his hands on his hips. She heard him sigh at the same moment that she realized her heart was pounding as a result of her impassioned tirade. "Oh, how I wish it were that simple!" he said and looked up at her, his eyes sad. "After what you've been through, I don't think I could ever bring myself to complicate your life with the reality of my circumstances and the—"

"Just for a moment . . ." she interrupted, taking hold of his upper arms, which surprised him. She wondered if he would consider her doing so inappropriate, but then they had embraced many times as friends, and she felt the need to fully get his attention. "Just . . . for right now . . ." she went on, ". . . can we set aside the . . . *circumstances* . . . and simply talk about . . . how we *feel*? Please, Matthias. I only ask that you tell me the truth . . . and we will . . . properly discuss what to do about the circumstances . . . another time. If you—"

Eliza was entirely unprepared for the way he took hold of her upper arms, at the same time putting his face so close to hers that she could feel the movement of his breath on her skin, and see every detail of his deep-green eyes. Before she had even a moment to question his motives, he closed his eyes and pressed his lips tenderly to hers. The sensation was as exhilarating as it was matchless. Joshua had kissed her many times, but never had it made her feel like this. She was distracted with wondering why when he drew back just slightly and their eyes met. She could see him trying to measure her response, and she hoped that he could read in her eyes the profound relief and deep thrill overwhelming her. She assumed that he had read her response correctly when he kissed her again, this time letting go of her arms in order to wrap her in an embrace that somehow made the rest of the world—with all its hardships and limitations and challenges—fall completely away. Eliza felt perfectly safe and boundlessly filled with hope. To say that Joshua had never made her feel this way would be like comparing the flicker of a single candle to the power of the sun on the warmest of summer days. Their kiss seemed to go on and on, but then it ended, and Eliza realized it had actually been very brief. But much to her relief, Matthias didn't relinquish his embrace. Looking into her eyes he spoke in little more than a whisper, "I love you, Eliza. I do. I think I've loved you for as long as I've known you. But . . . that doesn't change the fact that there is far too much standing in the way of us ever being together."

"Surely those are just problems to be solved," Eliza replied softly. "If we choose to share our lives . . . I believe we can overcome anything."

Much to Eliza's disappointment, he let go of her and stepped back. "I admire your optimism; I do. But I'm not certain it's realistic. The situation I'm in is—"

"Let me help you, Matthias," she pleaded, not caring if she sounded desperate. "Joshua did this to *both* of us! We are in this *together*! Please, let me—"

"No!" he insisted. "Absolutely not! He's my brother, and I allowed this to happen. I have to take responsibility for—"

"What option did you have beyond allowing it to happen?" Eliza countered. "What would have happened to your relationship with your brother if you had not—"

"Would any alternative not be better than his death?" Matthias retorted, and Eliza saw something in his eyes she'd never seen before—torment.

"Surely you can't be blaming yourself for his death," Eliza insisted. "He chose to become involved with—"

"Yes, Eliza, he made some terrible choices," Matthias said. "But perhaps if I had stood up to him . . . perhaps if I had told the truth rather than lying to everyone we knew to help cover up his misdeeds . . . he would have been forced out of his bad habits a long time ago. Instead I did nothing but cover it all up, and now he's dead."

"He could be very intimidating," Eliza stated.

"And what does that make me?" he retorted angrily. "A coward?"

"That is not at *all* what I meant," Eliza said and closed the distance between them if only so she could look into his eyes and allow him to see the evidence of her sincerity. "You were in an impossible situation. You cannot blame yourself for his death . . . nor for the situation he left you in."

More gently he admitted, "A part of me knows that I did the best I could . . . that I could not have foreseen how bad it would get. Although, sometimes I have difficulty remembering just how intimidating he could be . . . especially when I miss him and realize he's gone. He was a scoundrel to be sure, but he's still my brother."

"Of course you miss him," Eliza said, taking both of his hands into hers. "Sometimes I miss him too . . . but not in the way I used to; not in the way I might have expected. There's nothing inside of me willing to pine away for a man who betrayed me so completely." Their eyes locked again, and she hoped that he knew her love for Joshua had been completely eclipsed by her growing love for Matthias. When he said nothing but continued to gaze at her, Eliza boldly acted on her impulse to lift her lips to his, longing to once again feel the magic that his kiss had ignited in her. She was soothed by the evidence of relief she sensed in him, and the fervor in his response when he let go of her hands in order to take hold of her face, as if he feared the possibility of losing her in that very moment if he didn't hold to her tightly. Eliza wanted to reassure him that she would always be there for him, that they could always be together, but she knew he wouldn't be convinced—at least not now, not under the present circumstances. She could only hope that with time his circumstances would change enough that he would be willing to share his life with her, despite all that had happened.

Matthias eased his lips from Eliza's with obvious reluctance before he murmured close to her face, "We should go back before they come looking for us."

"I suppose we should," Eliza said, but felt terrified to leave the room, fearful that despite his confessions—and their tender exchange of affection— he would hold fast to his determination that there were too many barriers standing between them. "But . . ." she hurried to say, tugging on his hand as he headed toward the door, "might we talk again . . . soon? I . . ." She stopped herself from saying that at the very least they could be friends, because she didn't want to set friendship as a limitation for their relationship.

Eliza was relieved to see him smile at her, even if there was still sadness in his eyes. "I'll be here every Sunday until you terminate the invitation."

Eliza was taken off guard by the image that popped into her mind of the two of them having grown old and gray while they shared nothing but decades of Sunday visits. She uttered a quick prayer in her heart that they would be able to share a much more fulfilling life than that before she hurried out of the room, knowing he would follow. She needed time to think before she said something she would regret. She already felt as if she'd exposed far too much of her heart to a man who had dramatically different views about how their present circumstances affected their relationship.

"Wait," he said, reaching for her arm to stop her. "Are you all right?"

"I don't know," she answered honestly. She considered the message he'd given her with his overt affection, and how he'd boldly contradicted that message with his declarations that too much had changed for them to ever be together. She concluded with a faltering voice, "This is all very . . . confusing." Suddenly wanting to get away from him before she started to cry, she hurriedly added, "I need . . . time." She wriggled her arm from his grasp and rushed out of the room, fighting for control over her emotions before she arrived in the parlor where she knew Simon and Mia would be having tea by now.

Eliza paused at the door of the parlor long enough to take a deep breath and force a smile onto her face. She heard no sign of Matthias behind her, and a quick glance over her shoulder showed that he wasn't there; perhaps he just needed a little longer to push away the dramatic results of their conversation—and affection—in the library. Thinking of the latter made her giddy and it took another long moment to push all that aside in order to be in the room with her sister and Simon without letting on to any hint of the turmoil taking place between herself and Matthias.

Eliza finally opened the door and stepped into the parlor, leaving it open, certain that Matthias would be arriving at any moment.

"There you are," Mia said, covering her mouth with her fingers since she'd just taken a bite of cake.

"We were about to send out a battalion to find the two of you," Simon added. He glanced past Eliza's shoulder. "Where is Matthias?"

"I'm not certain," she said quite honestly, which implied that perhaps they hadn't been together all this time. Perhaps that had been Matthias's intent in holding back.

Eliza sat down and poured herself a cup of tea, saying nonchalantly, "Now, tell me what you've been talking about in my absence."

"We've come up with the most wonderful idea!" Mia said with childlike excitement. "Simon was talking about what he considers the ongoing quandary—something he's certainly talked about often—of the inequality of people in the division of our social classes."

"It feels increasingly challenging," Simon said, "to stand before a congregation and give sermons that can offer equal meaning to those who are struggling under the weight of poverty, and those who are blessed with great abundance. Of course, the two of you have always been so generous in your donations to aiding the poor and—"

"I'd forgotten all about that," Eliza said and took a careful sip of her tea. "Our solicitor takes care of the details."

"I only wish that more people who are blessed with wealth would be willing to share those blessings with the poor," Simon said with a heavy sigh. "I will keep doing my best to encourage better attitudes about such things among my congregation, but no one can be forced to let go of their money if they choose to ignore the needs of others."

"How true," Mia said, overt admiration in her expression. She truly would make an excellent vicar's wife. "The thing is," Mia added, turning toward Eliza, "we thought it would be wonderful to host a fine dinner for all the people who work for us. Simon is confident there are people in our parish who would be happy to help us, especially if they can earn a little something for their efforts, which would allow us to help *those* people. We can honor the people who work so diligently for us with a fine meal, and with the help of some friends, we will take care of everything so they can relax and simply enjoy the event. What do you think?"

"I think it's a lovely idea!" Eliza said, glancing toward the door as she wondered where Matthias had gone. Turning back to the eager expressions of Mia and Simon, she added, "We know nothing about cooking, but if Simon can help us find people who do, I daresay we can do well enough at serving a meal and cleaning up afterward."

"That's exactly what we thought!" Mia declared with growing excitement.

"Don't give me the credit," Simon chuckled. "This is *your* idea, my dear. I'm only too pleased to assist in such an endeavor. Perhaps word of your generosity toward your staff will spread, and other wealthy households might be willing to host similar functions. I do believe that goodwill can certainly be contagious."

"Oh, what a lovely thought!" Mia said, once again admiring her sweetheart as they exchanged a long, loving gaze. Eliza longed to be able to do the same with Matthias in clear view of others, but the barriers between them felt so heavy and ominous that she wondered if they could ever be overcome. And his absence wasn't helping her feel any better. She wondered where he could be!

At that very moment Matthias entered the room with a smile on his face, as if nothing in the world was out of the ordinary. He offered no explanation for his delay before he sat down and asked, "What are we talking about? I didn't hear what Mia said last, but there was no missing her excitement. Do tell."

Mia repeated the entire idea in detail to Matthias. Eliza felt a little concerned about how he might respond to such a plan, given that he had lived his entire life among the privileged and wealthy, and now he'd descended into poverty. But he smiled and said, "I would love to help! However, I'm only available on Sundays, so . . . is it possible to . . ."

"I daresay," Simon said with conviction, "that we can comfortably follow the example of Jesus in this matter. He served others and performed miracles on the Sabbath; surely this is an appropriate activity for us to engage in on a Sunday."

"Oh, it will be such fun!" Mia said with enthusiasm.

Matthias chuckled comfortably. "You might not feel that way when you're washing every dish after serving a large meal to a great many people. I have some experience with that."

"Then I'm certain you'll be able to make certain I do it right," Mia said to Matthias.

"I'll do my best," Matthias said and glanced toward Eliza with barely concealed affection showing in his eyes. Eliza felt a quiver in her stomach and unwittingly put her hand over it, but a glance toward Mia and Simon showed that they were so enthralled with looking at each other that neither of them had noticed. Eliza smiled at Matthias and he returned it, giving her at least a measure of hope that perhaps with time they *could* get past the barriers that stood between them. Perhaps once he was able to pay off the remainder of Joshua's debts, and know that he had taken responsibility for what he believed was at least partly on his shoulders, he might be able to recall more clearly that they were far more alike than they were different. They'd grown up in the same social class, and they'd been friends for years. Surely his present circumstances were just a temporary setback. Eliza wanted very much to share her thoughts with him, hoping they might make a difference to his thinking, but that would have to wait. They'd already spent far too much time alone for one day and attempting to sneak away again to share private conversation would only arouse Simon and Mia's suspicion. But Matthias had told her he intended to keep taking advantage of her Sunday invitations, and now they had a wonderful project to plan and execute together. Eliza felt soothed by the prospect of being able to count on their Sunday visits, and to know that he would be involved in providing a feast for her staff. She felt calmer now about her feelings for him—and his for her— certain that time would prove they were meant to be together. He was a good and honest man; she knew it in her heart. Surely, with time, all would be well.

Chapter Nine

THE HOURGLASS

Eliza was surprised to realize how thoroughly she was *not* enjoying dinner with Simon, Matthias, and her sister. Now that Simon and Mia had officially begun courting, they no longer had to try and hide their feelings for each other, and their ongoing exchange of affectionate comments and glances began to be an irritant to Eliza, despite how happy she was for both of them. The very fact that she and Matthias had to hide their feelings for each other—and she wasn't certain they would *ever* come to light—started to make Eliza angry. She'd taken only two bites of her dessert before she stood from the table and said, "Forgive me. I'm not feeling well." Even though her discomfort was emotional rather than physical, she believed the statement to be truthful. "I'm going to have an early night and just go to bed."

Both men stood when she did. Simon looked concerned, but Matthias looked panicked and she wondered why.

"I do hope you get feeling better soon," Simon said with his typical compassion.

"Thank you," Eliza said.

Matthias muttered, "May I walk you to—"

"No, thank you," she said, offering him a forced smile. The last thing she needed right now was more time alone with Matthias to add to her confusion. "I'll be fine. Enjoy your evening, all of you. No need to worry about me. I just need some rest, I think." She hurried from the room before any more conversation could take place, and she didn't slow down until she was at the top of the stairs, knowing Matthias wouldn't have dared follow her into this part of the house. She then slowed her pace as she ambled toward her room, reviewing all that had been said between her and Matthias—and all that had happened. She felt deeply frustrated by the pride he clung to that prevented him from accepting her help in solving his financial problems. She sincerely believed that once he was free of his brother's debts and could go back to living in better circumstances, people would quickly forget all that had happened—although she didn't really care what people thought; she cared about her own happiness, and that of Matthias.

Prudence was waiting in Eliza's room to offer any help she needed. They exchanged the usual greetings before Prudence said, "You're here earlier than usual. Are you not feeling well?"

Eliza sat down at the dressing table where Prudence began to take the pins out of Eliza's hair. "I'm fine, thank you," Eliza said. "It was more that I didn't feel like socializing any longer this evening."

As Prudence efficiently continued to work, Eliza's thoughts regarding the strange division of social stations in their culture shifted to the relationship she shared with this devoted woman who was always on hand any time of the day or night, except for the rare days when she took some time off and another maid filled in for her.

Impulsively Eliza said, "Prudence, may I ask you something . . . personal?"

"Of course," Prudence said, and Eliza turned in her chair to look up at the maid, which forced her to stop working and left her looking a little alarmed.

"It's strange, don't you think?" Eliza asked. "The way that we live and interact with one another? I did nothing more or less than any other person that put me in the position of inheriting a generous fortune from my father, and you did nothing to warrant you being born into a life that requires you to work for your living."

"Yes, I suppose that's true," Prudence said.

"Do you . . . ever resent those differences between us?" Eliza asked. "Between our classes?"

"Oh, no, m'lady," she said vehemently and grabbed a chair, which she moved next to Eliza's so she could sit down to face her. "You are such a kind and fair employer. I feel very blessed to be able to work for someone like you. I know of many people who are not so fortunate in their employment."

"Our parents taught us to always be kind and respectful to *all* people," Eliza said, "and I hope that I've never inadvertently said or done anything that would make you feel unappreciated, because I *do* appreciate you, Prudence— and all that you do for me. But you see me in every mood I experience, however foul it might be."

"You've always been kind to me," Prudence said, then her brow furrowed, and her eyes filled with confusion. "I don't understand the problem, m'lady.

We are both well aware that we've been born into different stations in life, but it's never been something I've resented, and I don't believe anyone else who is employed here does either. It's just the way life is, is it not? I don't believe I've ever really thought about it much."

"You're a fine woman, Prudence," Eliza said, "and very good at your job. I'm very blessed to have you."

"That's very kind of you to say," Prudence said with a timid smile. "I feel the same about you."

"But . . ." Eliza's thoughts felt deep and difficult to express, but she still felt inclined to take advantage of the opportunity this conversation afforded to hopefully glean Prudence's perspective, "there are so many people in dire poverty . . . people suffering . . . who don't have fair employment. What of *those* people?"

"Oh, my," Prudence said as if just speaking of such people made her heart ache, "it is certainly a tragedy that some people come into this world in such circumstances, and then of course there are people who make bad choices that land them into terrible situations. But m'lady, you do so much to help such people. You are one of the few of your class to actually share your abundance with the poor."

"How did you know about that?" Eliza asked. "I thought it was kept secret."

Prudence laughed softly. "Oh, you mustn't be upset with such gossip in your household, m'lady. Those of us who work for you are very observant— some more than others." She tipped her head and smiled, as if she might be thinking fondly of people she worked with who were kind and good but not necessarily very bright. "But we don't talk idly of such things, and we don't speak of it to others outside of the household. Those who work for you have a great respect for you and your sister and the way you carry on the generous traditions established by your dear mother and father. We are proud of the way you quietly offer so much to the poorhouses and the orphanages in order to help make the circumstances there better."

"Again, you are very kind," Eliza said, "but I really do hope that such information *does* remain within our household."

"Oh, I can assure you that it does," Prudence said firmly.

"Going back to my original question," Eliza said. "Do you not feel any . . . strangeness about . . . the great differences between us?"

"Not at all!" Prudence said. "It's just the way life is, and I've been blessed with a very good life, thanks to you."

Prudence stood up and returned her attention to working on the tedious process of taking down Eliza's hair, which didn't take nearly as long as it took to put it up and style it perfectly in the mornings.

"You're very good at what you do," Eliza said, "and you always seem to predict exactly what I might need even before I think about it."

"That's my job," Prudence said with a smile. Then their eyes met in the reflection of the mirror and Eliza could see that the maid had picked up on the fact that Eliza was still in deep thought. "May I speak candidly?" Prudence asked.

"Of course," Eliza said eagerly, wanting more insight from this young woman. She wanted to understand why Matthias was so concerned about his change in social status and how it might affect her life, and perhaps Prudence might be able to help—even if Eliza had no intention of telling the maid her reasons for delving so deeply into this conversation.

"I don't envy you, m'lady, nor do many of my station; I know that some people who have to work for their living are envious of those who do not, but I for one—and I know I am not alone in this attitude—am glad to be able to work to provide for myself. I'm well aware that it's considered inappropriate and even looked down upon for someone of *your* station to work, and I think that would be a life empty of much satisfaction and fulfillment. I respect your position, but I do not wish to carry such burdens myself—of being responsible for a household, for so much money. I prefer to work; there's a certain pride in it that has meaning for me."

Eliza was quietly thoughtful for more than a few minutes, until Prudence said, "I hope I didn't speak out of line, or say anything offensive or—"

"Not at all," Eliza said. "You've just given me a great deal to think about."

Another few minutes passed in silence while Prudence brushed out Eliza's hair once it was free from all the pins, then she plaited it into a long braid that would prevent it from getting tangled while she slept. Once that was done, Eliza motioned toward the chair where Prudence had been sitting, and the maid sat down again. "There's something I want to tell you, and something I want to ask of you."

"Of course, anything," Prudence said as if she might launch herself between Eliza and any potential danger should it be required.

"I would simply like to ask that you remain observant of the attitudes and situations among the staff. If there is any problem whatsoever in the household that has escaped my attention, will you please tell me? If anyone who works for me needs assistance, I want to be able to help. If anything ever happens that adversely affects someone in the household I want to know so that measures can be taken to rectify any problems."

"It would be an honor to assist you in such a way," Prudence said with a warm smile. Eliza returned her smile and the maid added, "And what is it that you wanted to tell me?"

Eliza felt her own smile growing wider as she recalled what it was, and she impulsively took Prudence's hand. "I ask that you not share this with anyone else yet, because we want it to be a surprise, but . . . my sister and I were just speaking with our guests about this, and—"

"Oh, the vicar and Mr. Downing are such fine men!" Prudence declared with enthusiasm.

"Yes, they are," Eliza agreed, appreciating the maid's comment. It seemed that in Prudence's mind, Matthias's status had not diminished his character. She wished she could discuss that with Prudence but didn't feel it would be appropriate. "The thing is, we have decided to host a fine dinner for everyone who works here in the household, just a little something to express how much we appreciate all that everyone on the staff does for us."

"Oh, m'lady!" Prudence said, her mouth and her eyes widening into circles. "I've never heard of such a thing in all my life! How wonderful! But it would be such a great deal of work, and—"

"Don't you worry about that," Eliza said. "We'll take care of it; I just had the urge to tell you. And since we've hardly had a chance to put our plans into motion, we'll just keep it a secret for now."

"Of course," Prudence said. "I won't tell a soul, but . . . oh! Everyone will be so thrilled! We surely work in the finest household in London."

"I seriously doubt that," Eliza said, "although I *do* want those who work for me and my sister to know that we *do* see all people as equals and we always want to be fair."

"That is not a problem," Prudence said, "I can assure you."

"Thank you for talking with me," Eliza said and squeezed her maid's hand before she let go and stood, saying, "If you'll unbutton this dress for me, I can get myself ready for bed just fine and you can take the rest of the evening off."

"Very good," Prudence said, and a couple of minutes later she left the room after saying, "Sleep well, m'lady. I will see you in the morning. Ring if you need anything."

"Thank you," Eliza said and hurried to get ready for bed. She knew she couldn't sleep, but she crawled beneath the covers and allowed herself to simply relax and mentally review all that had happened today, and all that had been said, and how she felt about her conversations with both Prudence and Matthias, and especially the impact of Matthias's display of affection when they'd been alone in the library. Recalling his sweet embraces and tender kisses made her tingle and she wondered how she could ever live without having him at the center of her life.

When morning came, Eliza was awakened brutally when Mia burst into her room so upset that Eliza might have believed the house was on fire. Realizing she'd not been able to discern anything Mia had said since she'd been asleep only seconds ago, she attempted to sit up while she asked, "What did you say?"

"I said the hourglass is missing!" Mia blurted. "A maid went into the library this morning to do the usual tidying and saw that it was gone." Eliza looked at her, trying to take this in. "You know . . . the hourglass! The one that our father considered to be the most—"

"I know what you're talking about," Eliza said, propping pillows against the headboard so she could lean against them while she worked on becoming more fully awake. "But . . . how can it be missing? I was in the library yesterday afternoon and it was there."

"Yes, you were there with Matthias!" Mia said, her tone accusatory, and Eliza could now grasp her sister's implications. Mia's vacillating opinions on whether Matthias could be trusted had clearly just been given fuel to press her opinion boldly in the direction of considering him capable of theft. But Eliza knew better, and she would not allow her sister to think so poorly of the man she loved under any circumstances.

"You can't honestly believe that Matthias would have anything to do with this!" Eliza sat forward, now fully awake. "He is no thief!"

"Well, it's gone, and it's worth a fortune," Mia muttered hotly. "I daresay its monetary value would relieve Matthias of his debts, but he should know that to *us* it is priceless in its sentimental value."

"He *does* know that!" Eliza insisted, willing to defend Matthias at all costs. In her heart she just *knew* he wouldn't have lowered himself to stealing from her. "We've offered to help him, and for all his pride and determination to take responsibility for his own obligations, I'm certain he would ask for help before he would resort to such an act."

"I'm not so sure," Mia countered, her face growing red. "Perhaps his pride is more powerful than his integrity; perhaps he would steal before he would be willing to lower himself to asking for help."

Eliza couldn't deny that Matthias's pride over his financial situation was indeed extremely strong; it was the very reason he was so insistent that they could never share a relationship—or at least it was at the root of the problem. Still, there was one thing she knew for certain and she didn't hold back in saying it to her sister. "Matthias is thoroughly repulsed by all of Joshua's treachery and deceit. He would *never* do anything to put himself into that same category. I'm absolutely certain of it!"

"Then what?" Mia demanded, putting her hands on her hips, which might have looked intimidating if she weren't wearing an old dressing gown, with her hair gone wild from sleeping on it. "Are you saying that one of the servants took it? There's not a person working in this house who hasn't been with us for years. Do we trust any one of them less than we would trust Matthias, especially given the desperation of his present circumstances?"

"Of course I trust the servants," Eliza said, "and I trust Matthias, as well."

"Then how do you explain the fact that the hourglass is missing?"

"I can't, but—"

"Were you not with Matthias in the library yesterday?" Mia demanded as if Eliza were a criminal under interrogation.

"Yes," Eliza said, "and then we left the room together and joined you for tea."

"Except that he didn't arrive for several minutes after *you* arrived," Mia said, pointing a harsh finger toward Eliza, as if that fact alone would be enough to convict Matthias of theft.

"There could be all kinds of reasons for that," Eliza said, astonished. "He's been making himself at home here for years. He likely needed a few minutes to freshen up. He knows where to find a privy in this house when he needs one, and we've all excused ourselves at one time or another from social gatherings for that reason. You cannot possible equate his delay with guilt."

"Adding it up with every other factor," Mia said, "I think his guilt is obvious."

"I think you are jumping headlong into accusations without having even considered that there could be a great many explanations," Eliza said. "In truth, I'm finding it difficult to understand why you would believe this of Matthias; you have befriended him since Joshua's death. You've admitted that you have had difficulty knowing whether you can trust him, and yet you've encouraged me to pursue my affection for him. Your confusion is utterly confusing to *me*! How can you encourage me to pursue the possibility of marriage with him, and also believe him to be such a terrible person over one incident when we have absolutely no proof or information? Before you assume that you have everything all figured out, at the very least we need to speak with Matthias about it."

"Fine!" she said, her face still red with anger. "As soon as we've had breakfast we'll go and visit him. With any luck he will still have it in his possession, and we can get it back before he sells it to some ruthless vagabond and we'll never see it again."

"With any luck," Eliza echoed with sarcasm and was glad when her sister left the room. She hated hearing Mia defame Matthias in such a way. Eliza truly believed he would not have done any such thing. Even if he were to steal something from them in light of his present desperation, he knew the sentimental value of the hourglass and he surely wouldn't have taken *that*. Although she absolutely believed Matthias would not have resorted to stealing *at all*, and she couldn't understand why her sister was so thoroughly convinced that he would.

Eliza felt so infuriated that she slammed her fists into the bed. When Prudence came to help her get ready for the day, she might have wanted to engage in some pleasant conversation, especially after their very productive and enjoyable conversation the previous evening, but Eliza was far too distracted with Mia's accusations to feel like talking.

"Is everything all right, m'lady?" Prudence asked while she was styling Eliza's hair.

"My sister is upset about something," Eliza said. "It's not the first time we've disagreed; I'm certain we'll work it out, but . . . I confess it's put me in a rather foul mood."

"That is to be expected," Prudence said, then much to Eliza's surprise, she added, "I'm certain there's a perfectly logical explanation for the disappearance of the hourglass."

Eliza met the maid's eyes in the mirror for only a second while she accepted that of course the entire household would know about the problem, since it was one of the maids who had discovered that the very conspicuous ornament hadn't been where it had rested for a great many years.

"I do hope so," was all Eliza said, glad that Prudence finished her work without any further comment.

Eliza dreaded sharing breakfast with her sister when they were so angry with each other, but she resisted the urge to ask for her meal to be brought to her room, not wanting the household to think that this issue was keeping the two of them from being able to share a meal. Eliza wasn't surprised by the silence between them, but she still hated it. And the dread she'd felt about enduring this awkwardness with her sister was nothing compared to the dread consuming her over their intended visit to Matthias's flat, where they would . . . what? Confront him directly about stealing from them? The very idea made Eliza feel literally sick to her stomach and she found it difficult to eat much of her meal.

Before Mia could leave the table, Eliza said, "I think that perhaps we should discuss this with Simon before we accuse Matthias of—"

"We don't need Simon to help us solve this problem," Mia insisted, and Eliza resisted the urge to tell her sister that she likely didn't want the man she loved to see her so consumed by her anger. "We'll have Ferris and Clint to keep us safe. Now, let's go and get this over with. I've already asked for the carriage to be made ready."

"Wonderful," Eliza said with deep sarcasm, too softly for her sister to hear.

The carriage ride was even more disconcerting and awkward than breakfast had been. Eliza tried desperately to come up with words she could say to Matthias—or her sister—to help soften the situation, but she felt completely at a loss and terrified over what this might do to her relationship with Matthias. If they wrongly accused him of stealing from them, she doubted that he would ever come to their home again, and any possibility of a future between them would be gone for good.

Climbing the stairs to Matthias's flat, with Ferris right behind them, Eliza's heart was beating so hard she feared it might impede her ability to keep moving. When Mia pounded on Matthias's door, creating a sound that expressed all her fury, Eliza just wanted to melt away and disappear. She wished that she had declined coming with Mia so that her sister could be responsible for any accusations and she could have remained uninvolved. Then she could have had a reasonable conversation with Matthias at another time. But they were here, and she knew he would answer the door at any moment, and all her tender hopes for a future with him would crash down and shatter. But the door didn't open, and they couldn't hear a sound on the other side, even though there were many noises coming from elsewhere in the building.

"He's ignoring us!" Mia declared as if she knew that to be a fact. "He's hiding so we won't catch him at his thievery!" She pounded on the door again with her fist, and that angry redness returned to her face. "We know he doesn't work until later in the day," Mia said. "He has to be here."

"Do you not think it possible that he would go out for reasons other than work?" Eliza asked, trying to sound calmer than she felt. "To acquire food, for example?"

Mia glared at her, as if a reasonable explanation for Matthias's absence only made her more enraged, and Eliza wondered what else might be going on with her sister. She was behaving so irrationally—which was so unlike her— that Eliza realized now that perhaps this situation had triggered something else inside of Mia that was contributing to her anger.

Much to Eliza's dismay, Mia insisted on questioning other people in the building to try and find the whereabouts of Matthias and the priceless hourglass she was certain he'd stolen. Ferris assisted Mia in her quest to knock on other doors and ask questions, even though Eliza could tell he wasn't at all happy about being required to do as Mia had ordered.

After speaking to three people who were clearly irritated by the intrusion, they were given no information at all. It seemed that none of Matthias's neighbors knew him or took any notice of when he came and went. Then an ornery older woman said to Mia, "I doubt you'll find the door locked. He's gone."

"What do you mean *gone?*" Eliza countered.

"Gone," was all the woman said before she slammed her door.

Eliza followed Mia back to Matthias's flat where Mia tried the doorknob and it turned in her hand. She pushed the door open while Ferris remained close by her side, as if he would gladly ward off any potential danger that might be lurking inside the flat. When it became immediately evident that no one was in the small room, the three of them stepped inside to find the bed made up neatly, and everything perfectly tidy. But it was also completely devoid of any evidence of someone living here. There was not a piece of clothing, a comb, or any personal objects. *He was gone.*

"Oh, help," Eliza muttered under her breath only a moment before Mia declared what she considered the most obvious conclusion.

"You see!" she snapped at Eliza, as if Matthias's actions were all her fault. "He stole it and he's gone. He's probably already sold it and he's left the city and we'll never see him again."

"You're wrong!" Eliza insisted. "There has to be another explanation."

"Begging your pardon, ladies," Ferris said, gratefully interrupting the argument. "But I think it would be wise if we return home. 'Tis not wise to remain here, I think."

"Of course," Mia said and huffed out of the room and toward the stairs. Ferris offered Eliza a compassionate glance before he motioned for her to go ahead of him. He followed her and closed the door, a sound that made Eliza so sick at heart she wondered how she was managing to put one foot in front of the other. Joshua had deceived and betrayed her, and he was gone from her life forever. Had Matthias done the same? Had she been as foolish in her feelings for Matthias as she had been for Joshua? Had Matthias truly stolen the only object in her home that she considered priceless and irreplaceable? Would he really have done something like this to her after all his declarations of love for her? And what of all his confessions of regret, and his insistence that he was a man of integrity? Had it all been a lie? A part of Eliza just couldn't believe he hadn't been completely sincere with her. But she couldn't deny the tiny nagging voice in the back of her head that made her wonder if Mia's theories were correct and her anger justified.

The carriage ride back to their home was endured with a silence that was far more fraught with doubt and insinuations than those which Eliza had felt earlier from her sister. But the more Eliza thought about the situation, the more she instinctively believed there had to be a logical explanation—both for the disappearance of the hourglass, and Matthias's disappearance from his flat. Of course, anything she said to Mia would only sound like desperation, like a blind insistence on defending a man she'd fallen in love with. Eliza could say nothing without giving the impression that she was as blind to Matthias's behavior as she had been to Joshua's; and she could never adequately put into words that in her deepest self she absolutely knew the opposite to be true. Ironically, the bizarre combination of all that had happened—and all that had been said— since the previous morning when Matthias had not been at church, had only strengthened Eliza's belief that Matthias was indeed an honorable man and that she needed to trust him. Not only did she need to trust him, she needed to allow herself to believe that they *would* find a way to be together. She couldn't comprehend any other future for herself—or at the very least, any other future only looked bleak and sorely unfulfilled. The problem would be convincing her sister of that; the very idea of having to choose between Mia and the man she loved assaulted her with a hefty bout of nausea. She longed to speak with Simon; he adored Mia and could get through to her on any topic, and he was always motivated by a desire to do what was right and good. Eliza doubted that Simon would be impressed with Mia's vehement anger, although she knew he would be compassionate toward her—or anyone else—regarding anything they might feel. But perhaps Simon could find a way to understand why Mia was so upset, because Eliza felt only confused and incapable of even attempting to reason with her sister.

They arrived at the house to be informed that the vicar had come to call and was waiting in the drawing room. Eliza was so relieved she felt as if a great miracle had descended upon their household. They needed Simon's wisdom and compassion—as well as his perfect friendship—now more than they likely ever had. Eliza followed Mia to the drawing room while she murmured a quick, silent prayer that Simon would be able to help Mia calm down and convince her to be reasonable, and also that he could help them find out why Matthias had gone missing—again—and where they might find him. She also prayed that her instincts regarding Matthias were correct, and that he hadn't done as Mia believed—stolen the hourglass, sold it, and left the city for good. She was surprised to find that equivalent to her disappointment over the prospect that he would lower himself to such behavior, was her sorrow over the possibility of never seeing him again.

"Oh, Simon!" Mia said as he rose to greet them, and she slipped both of her hands into his. "I'm so glad you're here!" She said it as if he might save her from death itself. Eliza too was grateful to have Simon here, but her sister's drama felt annoying and again she wondered if there was more going on inside her than simply her belief that Matthias had stolen from them.

"I was surprised to find that the two of you had gone out so early," Simon said to Mia, then peered over her shoulder to address Eliza who was standing behind her. "Is something wrong?"

Mia sank into a nearby sofa as if she'd run the distance from Matthias's flat, and Simon sat beside her as soon as Eliza had sat down herself in a chair facing them. "What is it, dearest?" Simon asked, holding Mia's hand affectionately.

Mia launched into a detailed oration of all that had happened since she'd been informed early this morning that the hourglass was missing, including her beliefs regarding Matthias's guilt. She reported the fact that his flat had been abandoned, which made her feel all the more certain that he'd stolen the valuable piece and left town and they would never see him again. Eliza wanted to scream at her sister and insist that she calm down and consider other possibilities, but there was no opportunity whatsoever to interject even a word into Mia's tirade.

Eliza was grateful beyond words when Mia finished her story and Simon's immediate response was to ask her, "Why are you so upset, my dear? I understand that the idea of Matthias betraying you and your sister is upsetting, and the hourglass has great sentimental value, but . . . I also know that neither you nor your sister are the kind of people who set a great priority on material possessions. Dare I guess that in spite of the sentimental quality of the hourglass, you would gladly give it up in order to spare a friend from facing danger or destitution?"

Mia looked utterly dumbfounded, stunned, and unable to respond. Eliza knew that Mia deeply loved Simon and she also respected him more than any other person in the world. Simon had earned that respect from all who knew him by his continual ability to offer sound wisdom and keen insight into any difficult situation. His personality was perfect for his calling in life, and Mia knew it. But Eliza could see now that Mia's angry tirade had just been kindly contradicted by this man she loved and respected, and she had been shocked into silence, which gave Eliza the opportunity to say, "I'm not certain why Mia is so upset." Both Simon and Mia turned to look at her, but Eliza kept her gaze connected with Simon's, not wanting to face her sister's disdain over the fact that Eliza was about to offer a completely opposing opinion. "But I find it extremely difficult to believe that Matthias would do such a thing. I'm well aware that desperation can drive people to do things they might not normally do, but I *would* give him the hourglass if it meant sparing him from all that he's facing—which I suspect is far worse than he's let on to any of us. Of course it has sentimental value, but I believe our father—if he were here—would have gladly given it up to save a friend. In spite of all that, I just don't believe Matthias would have taken it. I know the only other possibility would be that one of the servants could have taken it, which hardly makes sense either, but . . ."

"Or," Simon suggested when she hesitated, "there is another completely logical explanation which simply has not yet come to light. I've learned that until people acquire all the pertinent information related to *any* matter, judgment simply cannot be made."

Eliza nodded and said, "I don't know why Matthias has disappeared, but I feel . . . very worried more than anything else, and—"

"That's because you're in love with him!" Mia interrupted, but her tone was accusing and angry and completely lacking in any warmth, taking Eliza freshly off guard. "He's blinded you with his sweet talk the same way his brother did, and—"

"What are you saying?" Simon asked Mia, looking back and forth between the two sisters.

When Mia remained smugly silent as if doing so would incriminate her sister, Eliza knew she needed to answer Simon's question, but she felt it was important to first remind her sister of a pertinent point. "Once again you are contradicting yourself. You encouraged me to pursue the possibility of a relationship with Matthias even while you frequently gave hints that you didn't trust him. Now it's come to this, and I'm having difficulty understanding why." Before Mia had a chance to counter such a comment, Eliza turned to look directly at Simon and said, "It's true. Matthias and I have grown to care for each other very much. He admitted to me that he's . . ." she hesitated, wondering how much to tell him, then reminded herself that he was completely trustworthy, and she had already told Mia everything—a decision she now regretted, never having predicted that her sister could take her personal confessions and use them against her this way. Even though Eliza suspected that Mia's reason for behaving this way was rooted in some kind of pain she wasn't admitting to, her betrayal of this confidence made Eliza feel all the more hurt and angry, one likely being a result of the other. Eliza took a deep breath and said to Simon, "He told me that he's loved me for a very long time but didn't feel that he could intrude upon the relationship I had with Joshua. And I confess that I have grown to love him, but he's been very firm on his belief that we cannot be together due to his change of social station. Considering all the personal conversations I have shared with him recently, I am all the more convinced he would never steal from us. I know he's a proud man, and asking for help is difficult for him, but it is for that very reason that I believe he would face his circumstances with integrity and dignity before he would take advantage of his friends."

"Well, I agree with you," Simon said.

"What?" Mia squeaked as if her beloved had just betrayed her.

Simon looked directly at Mia and said with compassion, "I can understand why you're upset, my dear, although I wonder why you are *so* upset. Perhaps there is more to this than you're willing to admit and we need to talk about it." Eliza felt another miracle settling over them as Simon picked up on the very same thoughts Eliza had regarding Mia's behavior. "But that is going to have to wait. I came this morning to inform you that Matthias has been arrested and—"

"For stealing?" Mia interrupted in a voice that expressed *no* compassion whatsoever while Eliza's heart began to pound with fear and her mouth went dry while her palms became moist with sweat.

Simon looked at Mia with mild astonishment but said calmly, "He's been taken to debtors' prison."

"Oh, no!" Eliza muttered and put a hand over her heart and another over her middle in an effort to quell a rise of nausea.

While looking back and forth between Mia and Eliza, Simon explained, "Apparently the debts Matthias inherited from his brother were far worse than he was willing to admit to us, or perhaps the amount of money he's been able to put toward payments to these creditors simply wasn't ample, or fast enough. His flat was vacated because he was given a very short notice to gather his belongings

before he was taken to the prison where he will remain until his debt is paid."
Simon let out a weighted sigh and Eliza saw caution in his eyes; she suspected
that he knew what he was about to say would not make Mia happy. "It's my
opinion that if he'd had anything of value in his possession that could have
paid off his debts, he would have been able to appease his creditors rather than
allowing himself to be arrested."

"But what other explanation could there be," Mia demanded, "for the
missing hourglass?"

Eliza felt so angry—that her sister would be so insensitive about Matthias's
situation—that it took great discipline not to shout at her. She was glad when
Simon spoke, which gave her a moment to take a deep breath and calm
herself.

"There could be a great many explanations," Simon said, "although I
believe we should be more concerned with the fact that our friend is in a
dire situation, and I came here this morning with the hope that the two of you
would accompany me to visit him, and perhaps we could take some kind
of offering from your kitchen; I know Mrs. Miles and Mrs. Simpkin are always
very generous when it comes to sharing the abundance of your household with
those in need."

"Are they not provided meals?" Eliza asked, wishing her voice hadn't
sounded as horrified as she felt.

Simon looked hesitant to answer the question, which implied that he
knew the situation of being in debtors' prison was not good. He answered the
question by saying, "People there rely very much on the generosity of others in
order to enjoy anything but the most meager sustenance."

Eliza was more careful now to not allow her voice to betray her terror on
Matthias's behalf as she asked, "And how long will he need to stay there? I assume
until the debt is paid?"

Simon sighed and switched the way his legs were crossed. "The terrible
irony of debtors' prison is that those imprisoned have no means of working
to pay off their debts. Those who have families reside there in dark, tiny
apartments *with* their families; family members are allowed to come and go,
but the prisoners never leave. They remain idle and without purpose while
they reside there, and they have no means of employment. Instead they rely
completely on the generosity of others to provide for them, and to pay off their
debts."

"But Matthias *has* no family!" Eliza declared as if they might not know. "He
only has *us!*"

"Which is exactly why I believed we should go and visit him," Simon said.

As Simon's explanation settled in more fully, Eliza asked, "How can they expect a person imprisoned for debt to ever make the situation right if they are not allowed to work? It's ludicrous!"

"Yes, it is," Simon said with a vehemence that implied this was not the first time he'd been close to someone in this situation. Eliza felt a fresh compassion for him and the fact that a vicar would continually be exposed to the difficulties faced by the people in his parish. Trying to help face such challenges surely couldn't be easy.

"We must go!" Eliza declared, erupting to her feet as if she suddenly couldn't get to Matthias fast enough. "Are you certain it's all right for us to visit?"

"Visitors are always welcome during daytime hours," Simon told her, rising to his feet as any gentleman would do when a lady was on her feet. "Although . . . I doubt Matthias will be happy to see us; or perhaps more accurately . . . he may be very happy to see his friends, but embarrassed by the situation, as he has been ever since Joshua left him in this position." Eliza nodded to indicate that she understood, but she was unable to express her gratitude to Simon, fearing that the sudden urge to cry would betray her.

"I think I'll stay here," Mia said, remaining seated and still looking angry.

"On the contrary," Simon said to her, "I think Matthias very much needs to see *you* as well. We've all been friends for a very long time; surely he should know that our friendship has not waned simply because his misfortune has deepened." He chuckled as if to purposely lighten the mood. "It's good practice for possibly becoming a vicar's wife, is it not? If you're going to marry me, I can assure you this will be far from the last time you'll be visiting such places by my side."

"Very well," Mia said more calmly; she obviously didn't want to see Matthias, still believing that he was a thief, but she would do anything to please Simon, which pleased Eliza deeply, knowing that Simon was the best of men and he would always treat Mia like a queen—even when she needed some gentle guidance regarding her own inappropriate attitudes. Eliza far preferred to have Simon help guide her, certain that Mia would be much less likely to express anger and defensiveness toward the man she loved than she would toward her sister.

Much to Mia's dismay and Eliza's relief, they were soon in the carriage and on their way to one of the debtors' prisons located within the city. Eliza felt nervous beyond comprehension about visiting such a place, and she was still horrified to think of Matthias being confined there. But her desire to see him—and to let him know that her feelings for him hadn't changed despite this terrible turn of events—surpassed all her fears and concerns. She was grateful beyond words for the knowledge Simon had of such things, and that his commitment to remaining abreast of the challenges in the lives of his parishioners had made it possible for Eliza to know where Matthias had gone; she wondered what kind of effort it might have taken to find him otherwise. Now, she just hoped that Matthias was not unhappy—or embarrassed—about their coming to see him. And she prayed silently that he might finally be willing to allow her to help him financially so that he could return to some semblance of a normal life, or at the very least, that he would allow her to help him eliminate whatever debt had landed him in prison. The thought of him being in such a place just felt too heavy to bear.

Chapter Ten
IMPRISONED

THE CARRIAGE HALTED IN FRONT of a grim building of gray stone with an iron door so heavy and imposing that it needed no words to proclaim that this was a place where many people entered only to never leave again. Before the carriage door was opened, Eliza admitted to Simon, "Oh, I'm terribly nervous. What if he *doesn't* want to see me? This must be so very difficult for him, and I don't want to make it more so by—"

"Eliza, my dear," Simon said in his vicar-like way, "I personally believe that coming here and letting him know you still support him and care for him far outweighs the risk that he might be unhappy about your visit. It's my opinion that even if he is initially unhappy about it, in the end he will be glad that his friends came to see him."

Eliza nodded and took hold of the hamper beside her on the seat. Mrs. Miles had prepared it for Matthias, and she knew it was filled with a variety of baked goods, a bottle of preserves, and some apples and carrots from the cellar. Ferris opened the carriage door and held out a hand to help Eliza step down. While she stood looking up at the formidable structure they were about to enter, she heard Mia say from inside the carriage, "I prefer to just wait here, thank you very much."

"I know that you prefer it," Simon said to her, "and I know that you're upset, dearest. However, I don't believe we have all the information necessary to know what has really taken place. Matthias deserves our compassion, don't you think?" Eliza thought how clever he was to have worded the last as a question, which would appeal to Mia's natural sense of humanity; Eliza knew that Mia was a good person with a good heart, but for some reason this situation had made her more upset than Eliza had likely ever seen. And Simon knew her well enough to be able to see the same evidence.

"Oh, very well," Mia said, and Simon stepped out of the carriage before he turned to take Mia's hand and help her down.

Simon stepped to the door of the prison with the ladies behind him and used a large knocker as if he'd had considerable previous experience. The duties of a vicar living in such a city as this were taking on a much deeper meaning for Eliza. The sound of the knocker reverberated ominously through the heavy door, as if their arrival were being announced to the entire building, enormous as it was.

Eliza was startled when a small rectangular space in the door opened abruptly and scowling eyes peered at them. "Who's there and what's yer business?" a husky voice growled.

Simon calmly stated their names and that they had come to see Matthias Downing.

"He the new one?" the gatekeeper questioned, sounding a little less fierce now that he had been properly informed of their purpose. "Just come this very morning?"

"Yes," Simon stated.

The man behind the door moved his eyes back and forth a few times, as if to thoroughly survey the visitors so he could assess whether they were worthy to enter. He remarked coolly, "Not often such fine ladies come t' *this* place." Then much to Eliza's surprise, he added with kindness in his voice, "But not t' worry; tis perfectly safe, and I'll see t' that, mind ye."

"Thank you," Eliza said. The man nodded and slammed shut the tiny door through which he'd been peering. They heard the opening of two different locks, then the huge, heavy door swung inward on squeaking hinges. The man they'd been speaking to didn't look nearly as intimidating as he'd seemed when only his eyes had been visible. He was dressed in ordinary clothing rather than any kind of uniform, and he held a large ring that held a great many keys. He actually smiled as he motioned with his arm for them to enter.

The man closed the door and locked it noisily behind them before he said, "I'll take ye t' the courtyard since the weather is fair; it's a good place for the occupants t' get some fresh air."

Eliza didn't comment as she followed this man and Simon—with her sister beside her, still exuding her irritation over this whole affair. It occurred to Eliza that the sky was clear today, but it was cold outside. And she also wondered if this courtyard was the only place where the occupants had any access to open air; the thought of being imprisoned here for an indefinite period of time and having very little opportunity to even see the sky left her far more chilled than the outside air warranted as they stepped into the courtyard, the floor of which was constructed of the same stone as the four walls that banked it on each side. The walls rose up four stories, with windows that were apparently the quarters for the occupants; she supposed that was a better word than referring to them as prisoners. Surrounding the edges of the courtyard were a few roughly hewn benches and a few tables with chairs surrounding them. Seated around one of the tables was a group of men too engaged in a game of cards to barely notice the visitors, which suited Eliza just fine. There was a woman sitting on a bench knitting, and she barely glanced up as they passed by to be seated at one of the tables according to the jailor's suggestion.

The jailor glanced at the basket Eliza was holding and said with a crooked smile, "Ye ain't got no contraband in there, does ye?"

Eliza felt a little alarmed by the implication and feared that he might insist on searching the contents of the basket that were beneath the cloth tucked over the food.

"No," Eliza said timidly.

"That's all fine and well, then," the man said, apparently taking Eliza at her word. She wondered then if people actually smuggled weapons or other forbidden items into this place, hidden inside innocent-looking baskets and hampers.

After he left them there to go and get Matthias, Mia whispered just loudly enough to be heard by Eliza and Simon, "I hate this!"

"It's a terrible place," Simon stated, even though Eliza knew that wasn't what Mia had meant, but she suspected Simon knew that as well. "Of course, it's not nearly as bad as the prisons where criminals are kept—dreadful places!" He actually shuddered, and Eliza wondered how often he had visited people in such dreadful places. "I do believe having to live in a place such as this would make more sense if there was some way the occupants could work off their debt, as opposed to being so idle, which I believe contributes to a sense of hopelessness— even despair. The system is completely ridiculous, in my opinion. But I'm only a lowly vicar and have no control over such things. I can only do my best to offer hope and compassion where it's needed."

"And you're very good at it," Eliza said, wishing her sister could pull her thoughts away from her own anger enough to see the growing evidence of Simon's fine character. But Eliza forced her own thoughts away from her sister's bad attitude to wondering how Matthias was doing, and her anxiety over seeing him suddenly blossomed as she realized he could appear at any moment, and he was more likely than not to be displeased to see her here.

Eliza had barely entertained the thought when she saw Simon stand. Eliza glanced over her shoulder to see Matthias entering the courtyard with the jailor who motioned toward Matthias's visitors with his hand before he walked back, presumably to keep watch over the door.

Matthias stopped walking when he saw them, but Simon walked confidently toward Matthias, who gave Simon a wan smile before he looked past Simon to see Eliza standing there, and Mia, who had remained sitting. He looked more embarrassed than upset, but Eliza was mostly preoccupied with how glad she was to see him, to know that in spite of his landing in this horrible place, he was all right—relatively speaking, at least.

Eliza was grateful for the way that Simon immediately grasped Matthias into a brotherly embrace, expressing perfect acceptance without saying a word. He then took hold of Matthias's shoulders and said, "We were terribly upset to hear you'd been brought here, and we felt the need to make certain you're all right. How *are* you, my good man?" Eliza felt near tears just to hear Simon call him a *good man*; Matthias *was* a good man, and Eliza knew it. She only wished her sister would be able to look past Matthias's circumstances and see his heart.

"As well as could be expected," Matthias said to Simon, then he looked again at the ladies. "I suppose you all deserve an explanation." He motioned to the table where Mia was still sitting. The rest of them seated themselves, huddling into their coats in an attempt to ward off the chill in the air.

Matthias leaned his elbows on the table, clasped his hands, and hung his head, as if he couldn't bear to look at them while he spoke. "I sincerely believed the payments I was making to my creditors were sufficient, and—"

"You mean *Joshua's* creditors," Eliza corrected, which warranted a quick glance from Matthias, but he didn't comment before he looked down again and went on.

"But apparently one of them decided my payments were not large enough or coming to him quickly enough, and he changed his mind about the agreement we had made, and since that agreement was not in writing, he was legally within his rights to declare me indigent, and . . ."

"What is . . . indigent?" Mia asked in a tone that implied she wanted to understand the word so she might be able to use it against him.

"Impoverished," Matthias said with a glance toward Mia that showed courage in his eyes, as if he sensed her attitude toward him and he was willing to face it with integrity. "Unable to meet my financial obligations." He sighed deeply. "Therefore . . . I was given only a few minutes to gather my belongings, which was plenty of time since I have little more than a few changes of clothing." He pressed gloved hands down the front of his coat. "Thankfully I was allowed to keep sufficient clothing to remain warm."

"Thankfully," Eliza said with compassion, overcome once again with that sick feeling in the pit of her stomach.

"Before I say anything else," Matthias said, looking directly at Eliza, his tone imperative, "I need to tell you . . . before anyone notices and thinks the worst . . . that I moved the hourglass last night." Eliza noted from the corner of her eye how Mia sat up straighter and her eyes widened. Simon showed the barest hint of a smile. Eliza maintained her mutual gaze with Matthias and waited for him to go on. "I assume it's all right to speak candidly in front of Mia and Simon about . . . us."

"Yes," Eliza said, unable to even recall in that moment exactly how much either of them might know, but she wanted them to know everything. She didn't want any more secrets in her life, at all.

"It's just that . . . we've had many confusing conversations, and . . . I know the situation is impossibly difficult, but . . . when we were in the library, I noticed the hourglass, and I recalled how much it meant to you, and I thought of how we have both mentioned the need for time . . . to come to terms with all that's happened; time to consider our feelings . . . and our circumstances, and . . . well . . ." He chuckled uncomfortably. "I suppose it sounds rather silly now, but last night it all made sense in my mind, and . . . I moved it to a corner in the hall—hidden behind that enormous vase of silk flowers—just outside the parlor where we always have coffee after dinner, and I was going to speak with you privately for just a moment—or so I'd hoped before you left so abruptly—to tell you that I just needed some time . . . to get my life in order, and . . . I thought using a tangible object, especially one of such great value to you . . . might help make my point, and that you could look at it every day and it might remind you . . . and give you some hope that we might be able to eventually—with time—put all of this behind us, but . . ." He hung his head again and a cloud of shame seemed to descend over him. "All of that is irrelevant now. Being in here . . ." he glanced around himself quickly, "is . . . well . . . now I cannot even work to pay off my debts, and . . . this changes everything."

"It changes *nothing*," Eliza insisted, prompting Matthias to look up again. "This is just another terrible consequence of Joshua's unconscionable behavior, and you are a victim more than anyone else. You *cannot* blame yourself for this! And you need to lower your pride enough to allow others to help you! Without the help of your friends, you will never get out of here!"

"If you mean allowing *you* to help me," Matthias said with just the tiniest edge of defensiveness, "I simply cannot accept such help. You were dealt a terrible blow from my brother; he used you in the worst way, and I can only thank God that he never had access to the dowry that would have come to him had you married. I will *not* take money from you, Eliza. Never!"

Eliza felt so frustrated that she had to stand up and move some distance away, but she felt alarmed when Matthias followed her rather than remaining at the table where she had hoped that Simon might help explain to him that he was allowing his pride to potentially ruin the remainder of his life. She was even more alarmed when he took hold of her arm and guided her into a stone corridor, one of three that branched off of the courtyard. She noted that he took her far enough that the light from the courtyard would not reach them so they likely couldn't be seen by Simon and Mia. He took hold of her shoulders and gently pressed her back to the wall so that she couldn't move and couldn't leave.

"Listen to me," he murmured in an imperative whisper, "I love you too much to allow you to taint your good money by rescuing me this way."

"And I love *you* too much to allow you to waste away in here when the amount of money it would take to set you free is something I would not even miss. I wish you *had* stolen the hourglass, if it would have given you enough to free you from debt so that we could get on with our lives—together."

He looked stunned and she wondered why until he said, "So you *did* notice it was missing. And you thought I had stolen it?"

"No!" Eliza insisted. "I knew that you would do no such thing!"

"And Mia?"

Eliza chose her words carefully. "Mia . . . wondered. She doesn't know you the way I do. But she will in time; there's that word *time* again. Simon never doubted you; we knew there was a logical explanation for its absence, and so there is." She took a deep breath and pleaded, "Let me help you get out of here, Matthias. I can't bear to think of you in here; I need you in my life and—"

Matthias put his fingers over her lips to stop her. "Might we not talk about money right now?" He sighed. "I'm so glad that you came. I hate having you see me in such a place, but now that you're here . . ." He kissed her rather than finishing his sentence and Eliza took hold of his arms only a moment before he wrapped her in an embrace so warm that the coldness of the corridor became nonexistent.

"I love you, Matthias," she murmured close to his lips.

"I love you, Eliza," he replied in a whisper and kissed her again.

"Then let me help you," she whispered.

"No," he muttered and kissed her still again before he stepped back, took her hand, and led her back to the courtyard where Simon and Mia were still sitting in the same place, but they were clearly not sharing any conversation. Simon appeared to be lost in thought, most likely because Mia had retreated into silence, which was evidenced by a deep scowl on her face. Eliza wondered if she felt embarrassed over her bold accusations about Matthias being a thief now that they knew the truth, or angry that she had no practical evidence to hold against Matthias's character. Eliza knew she needed to have a direct and serious conversation with her sister, but she dreaded it. She would prefer that Simon talk to her first, but they obviously weren't talking now.

Simon and Mia both looked up as Matthias and Eliza approached the table, then their eyes went to the way that Matthias and Eliza's hands were clasped.

"Thank you for coming," Matthias said with glances that included all of them. "I truly appreciate your visit. However, it's cold out here and . . . well, thank you."

Eliza felt a little panicked at the prospect of leaving him here, wondering how long this would go on, how often it might be appropriate for her to visit, and most of all infuriated with him for not being willing to accept her help. In order to avoid getting upset, she focused on the obvious and took hold of the basket she'd left on the table, handing it to Matthias. "Just a little offering from our household. We hope you enjoy it; we know how you love Mrs. Miles's baking."

"Oh, I do!" Matthias said, showing a smile. "This is very thoughtful. I will enjoy it very much. Pass my gratitude on to Mrs. Miles; and I suspect Mrs. Simpkin was involved."

"Yes, you're correct," Eliza said. "I'll tell them."

"Take care of yourself, good man," Simon said, having now come to his feet to place a hand on Matthias's shoulder. "I will check on you as often as time permits, but do not hesitate to send word if you need anything—anything at all. As your vicar *and* your friend, I can't tolerate having you go without the necessities."

"Thank you," Matthias said. "I will."

Matthias kissed Eliza's hand and nodded toward Simon and Mia before he walked hastily away, as if he didn't want to drag out their farewells any longer. Eliza hated the image that came to her mind of Matthias alone in some cold, tiny room, perhaps even crying over the terrible situation he was in. Oh, how she wished he would allow her to help him!

In the carriage on the way home, the three occupants remained unnaturally silent until Mia cleared her throat especially loudly and stated, "It would seem I was wrong." She cleared her throat again and seemed to have trouble forcing herself to look at Eliza. "I apologize for my assumptions against Matthias."

"Apology accepted," Eliza said, then resisted the urge to say anything else. She still suspected that her sister's overly dramatic response was rooted in something deeper, but now did not feel like the appropriate time to address such a matter. She was only glad to know that the hourglass was safe, that Matthias had not let her down in regard to his integrity, and that Mia had been humble enough to apologize. If only Eliza could feel even the slightest degree of peace regarding Matthias's situation. To think of him in debtors' prison—with no hope of ever getting out if he wasn't willing to accept help—made her want to just curl up in bed and cry like a baby.

By the time they arrived home, her emotions were even closer to the surface and she told the others she needed to be alone.

"That's fine," Mia said, leading Eliza and Simon down a long hall that led off of the main foyer, "but not until we . . ." She went straight to the silk floral arrangement Matthias had referred to, almost as if she wouldn't be completely convinced of his honesty until she saw the proof. But the hourglass was there, just as he'd said it was.

"Well, that's settled," Simon declared with a little laugh. "Funny how a little communication can solve a big problem."

"Yes, that *is* funny, isn't it," Eliza stated and left to go up to her room, hearing Simon say as she departed that he would only be able to visit with Mia a few more minutes before he needed to leave to keep an appointment with another parishioner.

As usual, Eliza found Prudence waiting for her to make certain she had what she needed. Perhaps it was the comfortable conversation they'd shared that made Prudence feel safe in asking, "Is Mr. Downing all right?"

"As well as could be expected," Eliza said to her as she turned her coat, gloves, and hat over to the maid. "Thank you for asking." She then took advantage of the opportunity to have Prudence let everyone else in the household know that the mystery of the missing hourglass had been solved. She quickly gave Prudence an explanation for Matthias having moved it that referred only to his need for time in order to solve the problems left to him by his brother. Prudence was pleased to hear that the hourglass had been found, and Eliza felt certain that before lunch the entire staff would know the story. She wondered if any of them would suspect there was a budding romance between Eliza and Matthias, but she honestly didn't care. Given how her heart had changed, she wanted everyone to know.

"I do feel rather drained of strength," Eliza added. "I believe I'll rest for a while before lunch."

"An excellent idea," Prudence said kindly while Eliza sat down to remove her shoes. "I'm certain the day's events have been very difficult."

"Yes," Eliza admitted and felt the temptation to cry coming closer to the surface. "Thank you, Prudence. You're very kind, as always."

"Is there anything else I can get for you now?" Prudence asked.

"No, thank you," Eliza said, and Prudence left the room.

Eliza crawled into her bed, even though that meant messing it up when it had recently been neatly made. The moment her head sank into the pillow tears began to flow. Scattered memories of her encounters with Matthias dashed back and forth in her mind—going all the way back to when she'd first become acquainted with him and his brother. But she had been drawn to Joshua's charm and charisma while Matthias had remained in the background of her awareness, quieter and less flamboyant than his older brother. And now she could look back and see that Matthias had been less pretentious and arrogant than Joshua. Eliza had just been too blinded by her attraction to Joshua to be able to objectively assess the dramatic differences between the two brothers, and to face the fact that she had attached herself to the wrong one. She could easily feel guilty over the depth of her relief that she'd been spared marriage to Joshua, especially when her escape had come due to his inauspicious death. Now that Eliza had come this far and learned so much regarding her poor choices concerning Joshua, she could see that Matthias had always held himself to a higher standard of behavior and ethics. He'd done nothing to deserve his present circumstances, and she felt brutally angry toward Joshua for doing this to his brother. After many tears and a great deal of contemplation, Eliza determined—not for the first time—that being angry with a dead man would serve no positive purpose; she needed to forgive Joshua and simply focus all her attention toward solving the problems of the present. She'd worked hard on her forgiveness, knowing it was the right thing to do, and also knowing that she would feel more at peace once she was able to fully let go of the horrible impact that Joshua's criminal behavior had had on his loved ones—most especially Matthias.

As it was nearing time for lunch, Eliza hadn't slept a wink, but she *had* gained fresh determination to find a way to help Matthias. She just had to! She loved him and needed him in her life. She didn't care what people might think of him or her decision to associate with a man who had been subjected to a dramatic lowering of his social station. She understood why Matthias would hold to a desire to provide for himself and relinquish the debts that had fallen into his lap, but she could also see that he'd been put into an impossible situation and he simply could not solve the matter on his own. She wasn't exactly certain how to go about helping him, but she knew that she had to find a way. She intended to make it her highest priority and to speak with Simon about it the next time he came to visit, which she knew wouldn't be too long. Surely a vicar would have some ideas and perspective on how to appropriately offer assistance to those in need. However, Eliza knew that her first priority was to talk with her sister; hopefully they could put to rest the tension that had been between them earlier. She hated not having things right between herself and Mia; they were irrevocably connected, and they needed each other, and Eliza was determined to do everything in her power to preserve the closeness they shared.

After Prudence helped repair Eliza's hair from the time it had spent wrestling with her pillow, Eliza freshened up and went downstairs to find Mia already seated at the table where they always shared lunch, although no food had been served yet and she was just staring toward the window, looking sad.

"Hello, sister," Eliza said as she entered, and Mia looked toward her.

"Hello," Mia said and appeared to be searching for the right words, but Eliza wanted to speak first.

"Allow me to say," Eliza sat across the corner of the table from Mia and looked directly at her, "that we don't always have to agree on everything in order to maintain all that we share as sisters. If you disapprove of the way I feel about Matthias, and my determination to help him, I completely understand. I only hope that you can still find it in your heart to support me in my decisions, even if you don't agree, and—"

"Wait," Mia interrupted and put her hand over Eliza's where it rested on the table. "I was wrong; that's obvious now. I'm so terribly sorry. And I feel like a fool for making such a fuss. You and Simon were both right about acquiring more information before making such assumptions. I'm grateful for your patience with me . . . and Simon's as well; I will tell him when I see him. I can see now that I was . . . well . . . I think that perhaps . . ." Her voice cracked with emotion and Eliza tightened her fingers around her sister's. "I suppose I hadn't dealt with my anger toward Joshua—and what he did to you—nearly as much as I'd believed. And when I had what I thought was evidence that Matthias was taking advantage of you . . . of your feelings for him . . . I became unreasonably angry. I can see now that I must be very careful not to allow my emotions over one matter to distort my perspective over other matters that are entirely unrelated. I can see now that I've been . . . confused at the very least, and likely very confusing in the things I've said that have been full of contradictions."

"I appreciate your perspective . . . and your apology . . . more than I can say." Eliza's words urged a wan smile onto Mia's face. "Although, I understand; I do. The matters are not entirely unrelated. It's been difficult for me to learn to trust again after all that Joshua did, but Simon helped me. And I've come to know in my heart that Matthias is a good man."

"I do believe he is," Mia said as if she weren't entirely certain but was willing to trust Eliza's judgment. "Which means we need to find a way to help him. We must talk to Simon; he'll know what to do."

"I had exactly the same thought," Eliza said, and they paused their conversation when a maid and a footman brought lunch into the room and set it out for Mia and Eliza. Once the sisters were alone again, Eliza added, "He's very wise and quite accustomed to aiding those in need; surely he will have some ideas of how we might help Matthias without wounding his pride."

"Simon *is* a good man," Mia said, her eyes growing distant. "I think of how I behaved this morning—and the way I was feeling—and I truly question my ability to be the wife of such a man."

"Not at all!" Eliza insisted. "We are all human and we all learn from each experience we encounter—or at least we can learn if we choose to do so. You are a wonderful woman, Mia, with a good and loving heart. You have so much to offer! You will make an excellent vicar's wife!"

Mia sighed and picked up her fork. "I do hope so." She sighed again. "I hope Simon feels the same way after this morning's events; he can't have been very impressed by my childishness."

"He's not only wise," Eliza said, "he's very forgiving. Everything will be fine; I'm certain of it."

Mia nodded and once again smiled weakly before they focused on their meal. Eliza felt relieved beyond words to have finally put this issue with her sister to rest, and she prayed that they would be able to work together to help Matthias.

Eliza wasn't at all surprised when Simon returned nearly an hour before they normally had tea. He asked to speak privately with Mia, and Eliza made herself comfortable in the library, certain they were sharing a valuable conversation filled with apology and forgiveness and wise advice.

When it was time for tea, Eliza joined them in the parlor, and by the smiles on both their faces she knew all was well between them. While Mia was pouring out the tea, she declared with enthusiasm, "We must find a way to help Matthias. His pride is understandable; nevertheless, we cannot allow our friend to languish in that place when we have the resources to help him."

"My thoughts have been much the same," Simon said, "although I believe we must tread carefully, and if you will permit me, I would like to point out some thoughts on the matter that might be helpful in knowing the best way to treat the matter, delicate as it is."

"Of course," Eliza said. "We always trust your insights, Simon; there's no need to ask for permission to speak your mind—not with us."

"Thank you," he said. "I *do* know that; perhaps it's the . . . sensitivity of the situation . . . and the fact that Matthias has been a friend to all of us for quite some time that makes this problem more . . . challenging than many I have faced in my line of work."

"What do you mean exactly?" Eliza asked.

"Most people who land in debtors' prison are only too eager to accept merciful donations that will allow them to leave that dreadful place. Donations from the outside are the only way to ever be free, which I consider a ridiculous irony." Simon sighed and sipped his tea. "I believe that Matthias is so deeply troubled by his brother's behavior—and what he sees as his own contribution to the problem by simply remaining quiet about what he knew—that he feels the need to personally atone for the problem."

"Even if it means languishing away there for the rest of his life?" Eliza asked, unable to hold back the tint of anger in her voice. "If that's the only solution dictated by his pride, then I heartily disagree."

"Pride is an interesting word," Simon said, "which has different meanings in our language, and I for one have wished that it could be clarified more accurately. For instance, we use the word love in many contexts. There are a great many different kinds of love, and yet we only have that one word; therefore, we have to clarify it into categories such as romantic love, or brotherly love, or maternal love."

"Oh, I see," Mia said, so fixated on Simon she almost appeared to be in a trance.

"And so it is with pride," Simon went on. "I believe there is a very healthy kind of pride, such as the pride we feel when our loved ones achieve success or accomplishments. There is the pride we might feel in having done something good ourselves. Taking pride in one's work, one's charity toward others, and so on, is a good thing, as long as it is coupled with humility. However, there are also other types of pride that can be damaging to one's spirit, and I'm afraid our society encourages these kinds of pride. Focusing on the problem at hand, I believe Matthias was raised to believe that he should not take charity of any kind, and that he would feel like less of a man if he were to do so. I believe that for him, remaining imprisoned is preferable over feeling the need to be rescued by the charity of others—especially you." He pointed at Eliza. "He knows that Joshua was very interested in marrying you because of your great wealth; the dowry that would have come with your marriage was highly valuable to Joshua. For Matthias to even consider being a beneficiary of your wealth is likely the worst thing he can imagine, *because* he loves you."

Eliza didn't realize tears had spilled down her face until she felt Mia's hand in hers, and heard her say, "What is it, dearest?"

Eliza hurried to wipe a hand over her cheeks. "Then what can I do, Simon? It's only money. It means nothing in light of the love people feel for each other—*any* type of love."

"I agree completely," Simon said kindly, "and if you must know, I intend to go and speak to Matthias about the different kinds of pride, and hopefully help him see and understand that it truly is all right to accept assistance from others. The thing is . . . the Bible teaches us to give and to serve those in need, and as I see it, if no one was ever in need, those who have abundance would never have the opportunity to give. Being on the receiving end of charity can be very difficult for some people, but more than once I have seen that when people realize they are the means for others to have the opportunity to be blessed by giving, they are more willing to accept help."

"Oh, that's brilliant!" Mia declared. "You are surely the cleverest vicar in all of England!"

Simon chuckled with mild embarrassment. "I'm certain that's not true," he said humbly, "but I do try to be inspired on behalf of those who need my help." He looked directly at Eliza. "It may take some time, and I would advise you to be patient, but I sincerely believe that we will find a way to help him, and all will be well."

"Thank you, Simon," Eliza said, feeling much better. She hated the thought of Matthias being in that prison for even a day, but she knew the situation could be far worse, and Simon was right: she needed to be patient and trust that everything would work out.

With the passing of days, Eliza had to admit—at least to herself—that patience was not one of her better character traits. She thought of Matthias locked away in debtors' prison almost every waking moment, and even her dreams were riddled with vague uneasy images and discomforting feelings about his situation. Whereas Sundays had been her favorite day—made more so by Matthias's visits—she now came to dread Sundays; it was always nice to attend church and she enjoyed Simon's sermons, but the absence of Matthias later in the day always left her lonely and sad. She went with Simon and Mia to visit him again, taking another offering from the kitchen that Simon was certain he would greatly appreciate; at least they could do *that* to help him. But their actual visit was extremely brief since the weather was laden with a frightfully cold wind and the courtyard was the only place where the prison's occupants could visit with guests. Eliza believed that Matthias appeared to be fine physically, but he couldn't hide the growing despair in his countenance. Despite his despair, he made Eliza promise that she would not spend any of her money to help him, and without hardly realizing what had happened, she realized she'd inadvertently made that promise; and once she had, Matthias wouldn't let her back down on her word. She wanted to sneak into the corridor again and have him kiss her as he'd done on her previous visit, but no such thing occurred, and she felt especially disheartened as they left the prison and returned home.

Conversing with Simon only left her more discouraged when he told Eliza and Mia that he had some ideas of how he might prompt his parishioners to help Matthias in an appropriate way, but given his knowledge of their attitudes and circumstances, he wasn't necessarily hopeful that it would solve the problem. On the following Sunday he gave a sermon on Jesus's teachings to help care for the poor, and he did it beautifully—as was his gifted ability. Eliza suspected that if Matthias had been present, he would have needed to be more careful and discreet in order to avoid having Matthias feel like the sermon was being presented on his behalf. But since Matthias was painfully absent, Simon came right out and said that there were members of their parish who were in dire need, and that donations would be appreciated in order to offer them assistance. Eliza imagined the collection box filling up with an ample amount of money to free Matthias from prison, but two weeks later Simon reported that with all donations accounted for thus far, there was enough to pay off one of Matthias's two debts—albeit the smaller one—and not nearly enough to begin to pay off the largest of the two, which was the very debt that had landed him in prison.

Simon reported with sorrow more than disdain his frustration that members of the parish who had the most to give either gave nothing or very little, holding to the attitude that those who struggled with poverty—for whatever reason—had surely brought it upon themselves and were not deserving of their assistance. Their lofty attitudes went so far as to believe that those born into poverty had somehow actually done something to deserve being born that way, as if a newborn baby might have some power over the circumstances into which they had landed. Simon reported that in contrast, many parishioners had given with a glad heart all they could possibly spare. There were people with very little extra, and yet they had given that extra on behalf of those in need, not having any idea who they might be assisting or why; it was clear that such information didn't matter. And there were people who lived in the category of those who were barely getting by, or who needed help themselves and therefore had nothing to give. But Simon reported with an emotional cracking of his voice how touching it was to hear such people express their keen desire to help and their wish that they could. He declared that such people would be greatly blessed for simply *wanting* to help, as opposed to those who had great abundance and held tightly to it with their judgmental opinions on those they considered unworthy of any assistance.

Eliza felt both deeply touched and frustrated, just as Simon did. She made the decision, with Mia's blessing, that even though they couldn't help Matthias—because of the ridiculous promise she'd made—she could help others in need. With her solicitor's assistance, she put a large amount of money into Simon's hands for his careful distribution among the parishioners who were in need. She'd never considered before that her regular donations to assist with some particular orphanages and workhouses had overlooked the needs of those with whom she attended church every Sunday. Since people knew that the vicar was collecting funds to help those in need, the families who received assistance would all be given aid to ease their want, and both Eliza and Mia felt good about that, but it still didn't solve the problem of Matthias's debt. They all went to visit him every few days, taking a basket of food, which Matthias always appreciated, but their visits were brief and filled with tension and Eliza desperately longed to just be able to share lengthy conversations with him in a warm, comfortable room. She never could have imagined that such a simple pleasure would have been snatched away from them so cruelly.

Simon reported that he had spoken to Matthias privately more than once about the issue of his pride preventing him from accepting the sincere offerings of people who wanted to help. He was grateful for the donations from the parish that had helped pay off some of his debt, but he still insisted that he would not accept any help from Eliza or her sister. Eliza felt increasingly frustrated and sometimes angry over this—especially as weeks passed and she continued to only be able to see Matthias every few days, and all she could give him was a hamper of food from their kitchen. He expressed great appreciation for such offerings but continued to refuse any other assistance. It became somewhat of a habit for the two of them to sneak away into a dark corridor for a few minutes where he would kiss her and express his ongoing love for her. Eliza was grateful for such moments, even though they only added to her frustration over having him stuck in this place when it would be so easy for her to provide what would set him free. But she'd promised she wouldn't use her money to help him, and he often reminded her of this—an issue they had to avoid discussing because it only made them argue.

Simon kept reminding Eliza to be patient and allow God to work His hand in the matter, and that surely her prayers would be answered and a miracle would unfold. "Sometimes," Simon said on a rainy afternoon over tea, "if we step in too quickly to help, we deny God the opportunity to provide a miracle."

"I never thought of it that way," Eliza said, and Simon's theory remained prominent in her thoughts over the following weeks as she continued to visit Matthias and take him food, loving the precious moments they were able to spend alone when it became increasingly evident that their love for each other was only growing deeper. But as spring warmed into summer, she found her patience wearing very thin, and she wondered how long it might take for her prayers to be answered. She longed to have Matthias free so that they could pursue a life together. But given the enormity of the situation, and Matthias's ongoing stubbornness, she knew that it would truly take nothing short of a miracle to fix this problem.

As summer settled over London, Mia reminded Eliza that they had not yet followed through on their plan to provide a fine dinner for the household staff. Eliza had not been unaware of her procrastination in making the event happen; in fact, it nagged at her incessantly. But she admitted to Mia that she couldn't imagine carrying out the occasion without having Matthias involved, and it had been her hope that a miracle would see him set free so that he could be involved in the planning and execution of the event, just as they had discussed when it had first come up and he had been visiting every Sunday.

"I understand why you would want him to be involved," Mia said with obvious compassion, "and I know this situation is likely almost as difficult for you as it is for him—given the way you've grown to love him. Nevertheless, we have no idea how long this will go on, and I believe we need to go ahead with our plans. Simon has already spoken with people in the parish who have the skills to help us and they are more than willing to do so. All we need to do is set a date and make more specific arrangements. I believe it would be a good distraction for all of us—but especially for you. Perhaps if you put your attention toward giving to others as opposed to wallowing in your own sadness, your spirits might be lifted."

"I have not been wallowing!" Eliza insisted, disarmed by the defensiveness in her own voice. She sighed and added more softly, "Very well, I admit that I've been trying very hard not to wallow, but I'm not likely succeeding nearly as much as I'd like to think." She sighed again. "I'm certain you're right. Let's talk to Simon and get our plans underway. If nothing else, it would be nice to not have to feel guilty for having put it off for so long."

"Excellent," Mia said with enthusiasm, and the next time Simon came to visit they set a date for their special dinner and discussed specific plans. Eliza and Mia would talk to the cook and the housekeeper to make certain the staff was properly informed of the event so they could look forward to having some hours free from having to work, and to enjoy a fine meal together. And Simon would share details they had decided upon with those who were willing to help. Beyond that, the three of them mostly just had to be present for the event and help in any way they were needed; they planned on assisting with serving the meal because they wanted the opportunity to interact with the recipients of their offering, and afterward they would assist in cleaning up, even if it took them half the night to wash all the dishes—given their combined lack of experience in such things. Eliza chose not to think of how Matthias had lightly spoken of the experience he had gained working at a pub and how willing he'd been to help with this project.

On their next visit to see Matthias, Simon initiated telling him about their plans. Eliza had been reluctant to do so, knowing that Matthias would have preferred to be there to help, but Simon told her and Mia later that it would be unkind not to inform Matthias of what was going on in their lives, even if it brought him some sorrow. Eliza couldn't dispute Simon's reasoning, but she felt far too much sorrow of her own. Still, Mia had been right about the positive effect of focusing on something besides her concern for Matthias, and she began to feel excited about hosting this grand dinner, especially as the coming together of their plans became more evident.

Less than a week before the scheduled event, Eliza awoke while it was still dark and recalled that Matthias had been in her dreams. She began to cry as his absence in her life completely consumed her. She felt angry and frustrated and deeply sorrowful all at once. The passing of time had solidified her absolute knowledge that he was a good man, and that her love for him—and his for her— had the potential to offer a good life together. But as long as Matthias stubbornly refused to allow her to help him be free of his debts, this separation could go on indefinitely, and the best years of their lives could simply waste away.

Trying to be more positive—and considering all that Simon had said about miracles—Eliza turned her mind toward an effort to prayerfully consider any possible way of helping Matthias that she might not have considered. Even while she was telling herself that if there was anything she could possibly do she would have thought of it by now, an idea appeared in her mind seemingly out of nowhere and she gasped aloud before she allowed it to settle in more fully. By the time she was out of bed and ready for the day, she was so excited about her idea she could hardly sit still. She told Mia about it over breakfast, and was thrilled when her sister shared her enthusiasm—although they both agreed that they needed Simon's help, and Mia sent a message for him, asking that he come to visit at his earliest convenience.

Simon arrived less than an hour after the message had been sent. Eliza was grateful beyond words that he'd not been busy elsewhere, since she wanted so desperately to get Matthias out of prison—and her new idea was threatening to make her go mad if she couldn't see it put into action right away.

After telling Simon about her ongoing hopes and prayers for a miracle—and her state of mind very early that morning—she hurried to explain her conclusion. "It occurred to me," she said, the excitement in her own voice making her all the more excited, "that you had said there are a great many people in debtors' prison simply because of difficult circumstances over which they had no control. Of course, there are those who have purposely engaged in deceit and taking advantage of others—people like Joshua. But what of the people who are stuck there through no fault of their own? I'm assuming that in contrast to the vast fortune left to Mia and myself that their debts are likely insignificant. I daresay we could pay off the debts of a great many people and our bank balance would hardly notice."

"I daresay you could," Simon said, his eyes wide with pleasant surprise and his countenance beaming, as if the very idea of being able to do so much good thrilled him beyond words. "But how would this help Matthias if—"

"Allow me to clarify," Eliza said, "that this idea certainly came out of my desire to help Matthias, but now that it's come to me, I sincerely want to help those who are in genuine need of assistance, and I know that you—as a vicar, and with the help of our solicitor—would be able to determine who those people are and make certain the funds are distributed wisely and discreetly, and that our donations can remain anonymous. And it's something I want to continue doing as part of our father's desire for us to use our abundance for good."

"Yes, I can do that!" Simon said with enthusiasm.

"And if an anonymous donor is providing the means for *many* people to be relieved of their debts, and Matthias just happens to be one of those recipients, then . . . he won't feel singled out, and—"

"It's a lovely idea, Eliza," Simon said, "and I want to get started on it right away. But . . . I must say that, would this still not be breaking your promise to him that you wouldn't help him financially?"

Eliza sighed. "I have considered that," she said. "I can only say that I believe Matthias needs help even if he isn't willing to accept it, and since no one but the three of us and my solicitor—a man we trust completely—will know about this endeavor, I can sincerely say that my conscience is comfortable with taking this step. I won't lie to Matthias, and if he asks about my possible involvement, I'm willing to let him be upset with me for a time—but at least he can be free while he's upset with me, and if he loves me as much as he claims, he will forgive me and we can move forward with our lives."

Within just a few days Simon reported that with the help of Eliza's solicitor great strides had been taken already to help free some families who were living in the prison because of debt. Simon had made the decision to enlist the aid of another local vicar—a man he knew well and trusted completely—in order to visit with some of the occupants in the prison and assess their circumstances and needs. With Simon allowing his colleague to make the majority of these prison visits while Simon assisted him in ways that would help lighten his load, Matthias wouldn't see Simon wandering around the prison, and Simon could honestly say that he was not entirely responsible for this project of seeing people set free from their debts and being allowed back outside the prison walls. Peter, Simon's assistant, had been put to work helping these people find gainful employment and places to live, and the generosity of Eliza and Mia's anonymous donations was assisting these people not only with eliminating their debts but with helping them get by until they could reestablish themselves financially. Simon and the other vicar also had the idea that they would meet regularly with these people so as to help guide them in making changes in their lives so they didn't accrue more debt and end up back in the same situation.

Eliza was thrilled with Simon's report, but had to ask, "And what of Matthias?"

Simon sighed and looked hesitant to answer the question. He finally said, "Despite all our efforts to remain discreet, he is a sharp man and has figured out the most likely source of so many people being freed of their debts. He *is* upset with you, Eliza, and he's made me promise not to tell you anything more."

Eliza wasn't surprised, but she was still extremely frustrated. "Is he out of prison?" She felt the need to ask in order to be absolutely clear on that point. "Were his debts taken care of along with those of the others we helped?"

"Yes, and yes," Simon said, "and that's all I can say."

"You can't tell me where he is . . . or how he's doing?" Eliza asked, her frustration growing.

"Forgive me, Eliza, but he made me promise not to tell you anything. I'm certain he just needs some . . . time." Eliza thought of the hourglass, and tears stung her eyes. *Time.* So much time had passed, and yet barriers still stood between them and the love they shared. "I truly believe he will come to terms with all of this, and he will let go of his wounded pride. But this has all been terribly difficult for him . . . in ways I don't think any of us can fully understand. Please be patient with him, Eliza. You know he's a good man; he just needs . . . time."

Time, Eliza thought again and forced back her tears, not wanting to cry in front of Simon. But now that Matthias wasn't in prison, and he didn't want her to know his whereabouts, she couldn't even go and visit him. She missed him so much that she felt physical pain, and the very idea that he was unhappy with her added to that pain. She reminded herself that she had expected he might be upset, and she truly believed with time he would forgive her. But she was weary of trying to be patient and wondered how long it might be before she saw her precious Matthias again, and she could only hope and pray that he *would* forgive her—with time.

Sunday arrived and the grand dinner party for the staff came together beautifully. Eliza couldn't keep herself from missing Matthias and wishing he was there as they had originally planned, but she genuinely enjoyed serving a fine dinner to those who had worked so hard to care for her, her sister, and her home. When she announced that it would become an annual tradition, everyone applauded. She loved hearing their conversation and laughter as they enjoyed the exquisite meal, with no rush to finish in a hurry but rather an encouragement to savor their time over the meal and to enjoy each other's company in a setting that had nothing to do with work.

Eliza was surprised to have Simon pause in his filling water glasses to speak in his sermon tone, asking that everyone give him their attention. He then motioned Mia to stand beside him before he announced that Mia had agreed to marry him, and they were officially engaged. Everyone cheered and applauded, and some people stood to offer their congratulations to the vicar with hand-shakes. Mia remained by Simon's side for a few minutes, then hurried to where Eliza was standing to embrace her tightly.

"I apologize for not telling you," Mia said, "but he only asked me a little while ago and he wanted it to be a surprise."

"I'm so happy for you!" Eliza said and hugged her sister again. "And it's not at all a surprise to me."

They both laughed and hugged one more time before they got back to work so the meal could be served before any of the food had a chance to get cold.

The honored guests remained at the tables enjoying coffee and tea long after they had finished their dessert and the dishes had been cleared away. Eliza and Mia turned their attention to cleaning the dishes and began giggling for no good reason as they washed and rinsed plates and goblets and utensils.

"It's good to see you happy," Matthias said, and Eliza gasped as she turned to find him standing nearby; she'd not even noticed him entering the kitchen.

"What are you doing here?" she demanded, her heart pounding and her insides all aflutter from just the sight of him.

"Do you want me to leave?" he asked, lifting one eyebrow while his visage expressed that he was sincerely worried she might ask him to go.

"No! No!" she insisted and impulsively threw her arms around his neck, not caring who might see them, and not caring that her hands were wet. Her relief deepened when she felt his arms tighten around her. "I'm happier to see you than I can say," she said softly near his ear. Just feeling him in her arms, knowing he was free from that dreadful prison, and that he had come to her home—participating in this wonderful project no less—made her happier than she believed she had ever been.

"I can say the same," he said, easing back to look into her eyes. "We have so much to talk about, but . . . for now . . . I just want to help. Let's get these dishes cleaned, and then . . . perhaps we could go for a walk. Even though it will be late, it's rather pleasant outside."

"That sounds divine," Eliza said, praying that whatever he had to say wouldn't diminish the joy she was feeling to have him back. She only wanted to share her life with him and hoped with all the hope within her capability that they could come to an agreement that would make them both happy.

"Good," he said, his smile deepening her hope; she doubted he would look so happy if he intended to tell her—as he'd done in the past—that they simply couldn't be together.

Matthias quickly made himself busy at the sink, washing dishes with an efficiency that evidenced his recent experience with this kind of work—and which demonstrated in contrast Eliza and Mia's limited experience with such things. But Eliza sidled up beside him to assist and sincerely wanted to gain more experience; it occurred to her that perhaps they needed to host such events for the household staff more frequently than once a year. It was something she would have to discuss with her sister. She'd nearly forgotten Mia was standing on the other side of her still rinsing freshly washed plates. Then their eyes met, and Mia gave her a gratified smile as she glanced past Eliza to where Matthias was washing dishes. Mia winked as if to imply that she was witnessing a happily-ever-after in the making. Eliza couldn't deny that she hoped and prayed such was the case, and she could barely endure every forthcoming minute between now and having everything in order so that she and Matthias could talk.

It seemed forever before everyone attending the party finally dispersed for the night so that the final cleaning up could be done. Eliza would consider it disrespectful to these people if extra cleaning was left for them the following morning due to a party that had been held in their honor. She wanted everything to be left in perfect order. Thankfully, all the people who had been enlisted to help were efficient and ambitious, and everything was soon put right. Once all had been declared in order, Clint and Ferris left to safely deliver home those who had worked so hard to assist them. Eliza thanked everyone and watched the carriage roll away before she turned to find Matthias standing beside her, holding up a shawl that she'd been wishing she'd brought outside with her. It was indeed a pleasant evening, but still slightly chilly.

"Where did you get that?" she asked as he placed it around her shoulders and she drew it tightly around herself.

"Prudence is very helpful," he said with a smile, then motioned toward the gardens not far from the drive where they stood, which led from the carriage house to the street. "Shall we?" He then offered his arm and she set her hand over it, loving the opportunity to share such simple contact with him—away from that dreadful prison, which was the only place she had seen him for months now prior to this evening.

"I'm certain you have a great many questions for me," he said, beginning to stroll and she matched his slow pace, "so I will do my best to explain what's happened since I saw you last, and then you can ask me about anything I might have missed."

"I would like that very much," Eliza said, wanting no secrets between them—and certainly no difficult feelings.

"I have been staying with Simon," he said. "I asked him not to tell you anything, and I know he respected my request; I also know you weren't happy about that."

"On that last count, I would like to be able to say that Simon is a gossip—except that he is anything but." There was a hint of laughter in Eliza's voice.

"So true," Matthias said, glancing up at the waxing moon which lit their way rather well.

"I needed some time to adjust, I suppose. I think I'd made up my mind that I would spend the rest of my life in prison, and freedom took me off guard.

I also confess to indulging in some anger over my wounded pride, because I knew you were behind the scheme of having myself—among many others—set free. Many conversations with Simon helped me understand all the reasons that a person should never resent the well-intended assistance of others when in trouble. He taught me that life is full of people being on both sides of that situation—of being able to offer help and needing help. He brought up the point that even very wealthy people can have health problems, or deal with traumatic experiences, and money cannot solve those issues—but they are still in need of assistance." He sighed loudly, and Eliza recognized his courage in sharing these deep confessions. "I can see now, Eliza, that while it's important for any person to take responsibility for their actions, and to face with dignity the consequences of their choices, a person also needs to have humility in these things." He sighed again and let out a small, mirthless laugh. "I suppose what I'm trying to say is that . . . humility is an element I have been missing completely. I certainly felt humbled by all that happened—or perhaps humiliated is more accurate. And yet when it came to addressing the problems left to me by Joshua, I have been greatly lacking in humility. Simon also taught me a great deal about mercy, and the importance of having mercy toward others, but also toward ourselves. I confess this principle has helped me a great deal in being able to forgive Joshua— and also forgive myself, which has subsequently helped ease my guilt over my mistakes, and to understand more fully where I've come to and why." He drew in a deep breath and let it out slowly. "I am attempting to formally apologize for that, and also to thank you for your generosity in assisting me so that I can start my life over with some dignity." He paused and Eliza searched for the right thing to say, but before she could form any words he added, "Before you speak, please allow me to finish. I've been trying very hard to think of how to express all that needs to be said, and I hope you'll let me do so before I lose my momentum."

"Of course," she said and just listened as they ambled deeper into the gardens.

"I continually find you more and more remarkable, Eliza," he said, and the comment took her completely off guard.

"Whatever can you mean?" she asked. "I am merely an ordinary woman who—"

"Not ordinary, by any means," he declared vehemently. "Now that I have been on the other side of this strange social spectrum of our society, I can tell you that seeing your efforts to help those in need—which is something you've been doing for years—has taken on an entirely different perspective. Added to that, the event you hosted this evening was quite amazing."

"It was just a simple dinner and—"

"I don't believe that anyone who was the beneficiary of your kindness this evening considered it simple," he said with a firm glance in her direction. "I doubt any other grand household in this city has ever done such a thing. I'm trying to tell you that I admire your efforts. Don't be so prideful about it." He said the last with another small laugh, but this time his humor was genuine, and she could only smile. She'd scolded him for his pride; she would be a hypocrite to not graciously accept what he was saying now. "And most importantly," he went on, "the fact that you gave financial freedom and a new start to more than a dozen families is something that. . ." His voice cracked, and it took him a long moment to continue, but Eliza allowed him the time to compose himself. "The hopelessness in that place, Eliza, the inability for a man to provide for his family or work off his debts is just . . . ludicrous! Now that I have felt that, and seen it firsthand, knowing what you did for all those people is just . . . well . . . I admire you for such acts more than I can say. And that brings me to the point that I have gotten past my foolish anger and pride and I want to . . . need to . . . humbly express my gratitude to you for setting me free. I could never repay you for what you've done for me—not just in a monetary sense, but for all that you've taught me about truly living a Christian life and giving of your resources to do so much good. I am grateful to be among the beneficiaries of your benevolence, and I am even more grateful to know you personally. So . . . thank you, Eliza."

He seemed finished and Eliza felt it would be best not to make any fuss over all he'd just said. Instead she just held his words close to her heart, treasuring his changed attitude, and simply said, "You are most welcome, Matthias. It gives me much joy to know you have a chance to start over. You're a good man and you deserve that chance."

"You're very kind, as always," Matthias said, then he asked as if they'd been discussing the change of season, "And how have you and your sister been doing?"

"All is well," she said. "Better now that you're back." He smiled in her direction, then looked straight ahead as they continued to walk. "Simon and Mia are officially engaged," she told him, surprised that she had to search for words to fill the silence.

"High time," Matthias said with a laugh. "I confess that Simon told me of his intention to make it official this evening. I'm glad to know that he did. Not that anyone would have been worried about the possibility of Mia refusing his proposal."

"No," Eliza said, "I do believe she's the happiest woman in the world." Eliza longed to be as happy as her sister, to have a proposal of marriage from this man she'd grown to love so deeply, but it seemed that Matthias had said everything he'd felt the need to say.

They ambled mostly in silence back toward the door of the house where he turned to face her. "It's late and you must be exhausted. I am currently without employment; therefore, I'm not restricted to visiting only on Sundays. Would it be all right if I call on you tomorrow?"

"Oh, of course!" Eliza said. "You should know that you are always welcome." Realizing she wanted her invitation to sound more personal, she added, "I always enjoy your company, Matthias. You never need an invitation."

"Thank you," he said.

"Still . . . might I invite you to come for lunch? And stay for tea . . . and dinner if you like. I've missed having you in my home more than I can say."

His smile gave her hope that his efforts to start a new life included a more viable relationship with her, but she surely needed to once again exercise patience and allow him to heal from all he'd suffered.

"And I have missed being here . . . most especially being with you." His words heightened Eliza's hope. But he added, "However, there's something I need to take care of in the morning and I'm not certain I'll be finished by lunch. I will come as soon as my business is seen to, and I will absolutely be here for tea . . . and I would love to stay for dinner—just like our many Sundays shared in the past."

"Except it will be Monday, which could be a delightful change of pace."

"Indeed," Matthias said, and much to her relief, he kissed her. "It's so good to be back," he said and kissed her again, leaving Eliza with an abundance of hope before he bade her good night and left her with the promise of seeing her the following afternoon. Before Eliza made it into the house and up the stairs to her room, she was already counting the hours.

Eliza slept better than she had since Matthias had gone to debtors' prison. Now he was free and the things he'd said before he'd kissed her good night had given her great hope that they might yet share a future; she simply refused to think about the possibility of their relationship not working out.

She awoke to find fog pressing against the windows, which made the room feel chillier than it had the previous day when the sun had been shining.

But Prudence quickly appeared, as if she had some kind of supernatural ability to sense when Eliza was awake. The maid lit the fire and assisted Eliza in preparing for the day, while she talked more to Eliza than she likely ever had about how lovely the previous evening had been, and how much the entire staff had enjoyed the event. She also declared how pleased everyone was with the announcement of Mia's engagement to the vicar, and how it was a unanimous opinion that they were very well matched and would be extremely happy together. Eliza was pleased to hear all that Prudence was saying, while she secretly hoped and prayed that she too might eventually have the same kind of support and enthusiasm from her household staff regarding her own engagement. Eliza reminded herself to be patient; Matthias had come a long way, but that didn't mean he would be proposing marriage anytime soon. They'd never even officially courted; that would be a grand step in the right direction, and she couldn't help hoping that he might soon make this request so they could go forward without having to be secretive about it.

In spite of what Matthias had said about needing to take care of some business, Eliza still hoped he would get done early and be there for lunch, but he wasn't. Simon was also absent for lunch, which gave Eliza and Mia the opportunity to talk about the success of the previous evening's event, the pleasant surprise of Matthias's appearance, and the exciting announcement of Mia's betrothal to Simon. There was so much to talk about that their conversation went on long after lunch was over and they moved into the library where they sat on one of the sofas near the hourglass, facing a blazing fire that waged war with the dark, damp fog pressed tightly against the windows. They speculated over their mutual hope that with time Matthias would come to see that he and Eliza should spend their lives together, and they began to discuss wedding plans for Mia and Simon, which made Mia so giddy she could hardly talk for giggling, which in turn made Eliza giggle. All in all, they both felt indescribably happy and abundantly hopeful for a bright future.

In spite of very much enjoying her conversation with Mia, Eliza couldn't keep herself from glancing frequently at the clock, wondering when Matthias would come. He had promised to be here for tea, but that felt so far away, and she hoped he would arrive before then so they might have some time to talk privately. If they even had a few moments alone, he might very well kiss her, which made her tingle at the very thought. Fearing Mia would notice how distracted she was and comment on it, Eliza forced herself to focus her full attention on her sister, trying not to think about Matthias at all—which wasn't easy. She was surprised when only a minute later a maid came to tell them that Mr. Matthias Downing had arrived and he wished to speak with Lady Eliza privately.

"Oh, my," Mia said with a wink as they both stood. "I suppose I shall see the two of you at tea. And Simon has promised to be here as well."

"How delightful," Eliza said, feeling terribly envious of Mia's betrothed state. And again, she reminded herself to be patient, and to be grateful for the progress that had occurred between herself and Matthias. They had made remarkable progress, and she truly *was* grateful!

"I'll go and make myself busy until he arrives," Mia said and winked at Eliza. "I trust the two of you don't need a chaperone."

"I can assure you we do not," Eliza said, tingling at the thought of Matthias kissing her, and certain she would not want her sister or anyone else observing such a thing. But she was equally certain that Matthias was a gentleman and nothing untoward would ever happen between them, chaperoned or not.

Mia glided out of the room as if she were floating on her own happiness. She went one direction and Eliza the other in order to go to the drawing room where Matthias would be waiting. Her heart quickened at the thought of just seeing him, and a violent fluttering erupted inside her when she entered the room and he stood, wearing a smile that made it clear he was equally glad to see her. But Eliza was taken aback to realize he was not alone. Another gentleman stood as well, and Eliza immediately recognized him as Mr. Bigsby, her solicitor.

"Mr. Downing," Eliza said, greeting Matthias properly in light of their not being alone or among close friends.

"Lady Eliza," Matthias said, nodding.

"Mr. Bigsby," Eliza said to the solicitor and sat down, after which the men took their seats again. "What brings you here?"

"I invited him," Matthias said, increasing Eliza's surprise *and* her curiosity. "I've known for many years that he is your solicitor and that you trust him completely. The solicitor whom Joshua used for business is a man I would *never* trust; therefore, I made an appointment with Mr. Bigsby to assist me with a matter of business we would like to discuss with you."

"Very well," Eliza said, unable to even begin to imagine what this could be about. But she gave the men her full attention, hoping they would explain quickly before her curiosity jumped out of her in some kind of embarrassing exclamation.

"I've explained our situation to Mr. Bigsby," Matthias said with some caution. "*All* of our situation."

"Oh," Eliza said, realizing he meant that Mr. Bigsby had been made aware of the romantic relationship between Matthias and Eliza. A quick glance at the solicitor revealed a cheery smile on his face, as if this fact gave him nothing but pleasure.

"Since everything related to money has been a sensitive issue between us," Matthias said, "Simon suggested that perhaps it would be wise to enlist the aid of an unbiased third party who has the skills and knowledge to guide and advise people on such matters, and that perhaps doing so might help remove this issue from our relationship."

"I see," Eliza said. "Simon is a wise man, as always."

"Indeed he is," Matthias said. "I explained the situation to Mr. Bigsby, and also my feelings on the matter. I found his insights very enlightening and helpful; therefore, I would like him to explain his ideas to you directly."

"Of course," Eliza said, her heart quickening as she began to realize Matthias would not have taken such measures if he were not serious about pursuing marriage. She fought to keep her expression steady as she turned her attention to the solicitor, anxious to hear what he had to say, and silently praying that his ideas would indeed put all issues regarding money completely to rest between her and Matthias so that they could share a future together.

"First of all," Mr. Bigsby explained, "I have assured Mr. Downing that his present financial situation is not of his own making, but rather the poor choices of his brother, and he should not blame himself for the difficulties he's endured."

"And did he believe you?" Eliza asked while she tossed Matthias a somewhat mischievous smile, "because I've been trying to convince him of that for months."

"Perhaps it was all your convincing that helped me believe Mr. Bigsby," Matthias admitted humbly, then motioned with his hand for the solicitor to go on.

"I also explained to Mr. Downing that I have been aware of many marriages among those of your social class where a woman's significant dowry has saved the groom from financial devastation of one form or another; unfortunately such marriages are often based on the benefits of the financial arrangement rather than love. But it's not uncommon at all and is not necessarily looked down upon—although I know both of you well enough to know that the opinion of others is not of any concern."

"Indeed," Eliza said while her mind was stuck back on the moment Mr. Bigsby had referred to *marriages*. Was that the purpose of this strange meeting?

Oh! If she thought about it too hard, she might not be able to breathe! She forced her attention to remain on the solicitor, fearing if she looked at Matthias too long, she might indeed start gasping for breath.

"Given these facts, I assured Mr. Downing that he shouldn't be concerned about marrying a woman who is known for having inherited a great fortune—especially if love is at the core of the situation, which I have been assured is the case."

Eliza *did* steal a glance at Matthias and found him smiling, which made her heart pound. She forced herself to look away, truly fearing she might make a fool of herself in front of her solicitor.

"Still," Mr. Bigsby went on, "Mr. Downing made a very unique request of me when we met a few days ago. I have now designed a document that has met with Mr. Downing's approval, and he has asked me to explain it to you so that you understand exactly what it entails, and then I believe he's hoping you will add your signature to the agreement beside his own, and I will sign it as a witness."

Eliza felt her eyes go wide, unable to imagine what this *document* could possibly be. She couldn't speak due to the tight knot gathering in her throat, but she nodded toward Mr. Bigsby and he opened the leather case he'd brought with him to pull out a piece of parchment, which he set on the low table in front of him, although he didn't even glance at it as he explained what it entailed.

Motioning toward the page filled with rows of neat penmanship, Mr. Bigsby said, "Mr. Downing wanted a legal and binding document that states clearly that he has no access to your fortune beyond an appropriate monthly allowance that would enable him to see to certain needs of a gentleman without having to defer to his wife; the most important reason for this—upon my advice— is to allow him to interact normally among society without drawing any attention from others regarding this unique financial arrangement, since that is a private matter. Of course, when Miss Mia marries, she will receive her portion of the inheritance your father intended for her, and I know from having recently spoken with her that she intends to use that money to do some repairs and expansions on the vicarage, and to aid their cause in assisting those in the parish who are in need. I'm certain your parents would be pleased with her use of all that's being left to her. As for *your* fortune, m'lady, I will continue to oversee your various distributions to aid the poor. That is not what *this*," he again motioned toward the document on the table, "is about. Mr. Downing also wanted it stipulated in writing that if you agree to the marriage and this financial arrangement as it's written here, that in the event you pass away before your husband, all of your money will be distributed equally among your potential children. In the event that there are no children, it would all go to your sister with the exception of an allowance that is sufficient for your husband to live on until the time of his death." Mr. Bigsby sighed, exchanged a glance and a nod with Matthias, then looked at Eliza and said, "I believe that explains everything. You may of course read it before you sign—if you choose to sign."

Eliza's heart was pounding so hard she feared the others would hear it as Mr. Bigsby looked at Matthias with a humorous smirk and said, "I believe the rest is up to you, Mr. Downing."

Matthias looked directly at Eliza. Their eyes connected and locked. He smiled, and his eyes sparkled as if flames had actually been ignited in them. "I know this is far from how it's done conventionally, Eliza, but I hope you will understand why I needed to do it this way. I confess that something occurred to me recently, which helped me come to this arrangement. I know that you and I share the belief that all people are equal in the sight of God, no matter their social station, and if such is the case, money surely has nothing to do with human relationships, which is why I felt strongly about legally removing any financial issues from *our* relationship. It also occurred to me that—in light of the same belief—men and women are surely equal in the sight of God, which means that it doesn't matter if the financial needs of a family are provided by a man or a woman, and I should not be so prideful about such a thing." He drew in another long breath. "If you need more time, I understand but . . . I still have to ask . . ." He took in a deep breath and the sparkle in his eyes was enhanced by the glimmer of moisture gathering there. "Will you marry me?"

Eliza gasped, then had trouble catching her breath. Her hand went to her heart as if that might help her breathe. She finally managed to speak, although her words came out as a breathless whisper. "There was no need for all of this, Matthias." She motioned toward the document on the table. "The answer is yes; of course, yes; under any circumstances, yes. I want nothing more than to share my life with you. All that I have is yours!"

Matthias laughed with perfect delight and discreetly wiped away a tear that had slid down his cheek. "All I really need is your heart, Eliza. Nothing else matters."

Eliza was barely aware of Mr. Bigsby standing as he said, "I think I'll leave the two of you alone for a few minutes. I'll be in the foyer when you're ready to sign."

The solicitor slipped out of the room. Matthias and Eliza both stood at the same moment and each took a few steps before their arms wrapped around each other and their lips met, as if some invisible magnetic force brought them together perfectly. Eliza felt tears rise into her eyes and slip down her face while she soaked in the bliss of Matthias's embrace and the splendor of his kiss, made all the better by knowing that they would always be together.

Epilogue

MIA AND SIMON WERE MARRIED on a warm summer day. The vicar from a neighboring parish—the same one who had assisted Simon with charitable projects in the past—performed the ceremony, and there was much celebrating afterward with the entire parish gathered together. The vicar and his new bride then departed for a honeymoon while Simon's friend and assistant Peter helped keep everything at the vicarage under control, and the neighboring vicar was on hand to help where needed.

Less than a week after Simon and Mia returned from their honeymoon, Matthias and Eliza were married, with Simon performing the ceremony and the entire parish in attendance, including everyone who lived and worked in Eliza's household. The celebration at the house had been arranged so that everything had been prepared ahead of time and no member of the staff would have to do more than minimal work. Eliza wanted them to be a part of her wedding celebration, and it all came together beautifully. She was barely aware of anything going on around her, since she could hardly take her eyes off Matthias. She felt like the luckiest, happiest, most blessed woman in the world to have won the heart of such a good man, and to know that he loved her with his whole soul. Nothing was more important to Matthias than Eliza's security and happiness.

Eliza hardly thought about Joshua at all anymore; her experiences with him were a piece of her life story from which she'd learned a great deal and was now able to put it away. When she *did* think of Matthias's brother, she only felt gratitude that God had spared her from being bound to such a man, and that she had instead been blessed with the miracle of being able to share her life with Matthias, a man whose integrity was as strong and pure as his love for Eliza; she could see it in his eyes and feel it every time he spoke.

The wedding celebrations were concluded with tea being served at the usual time. Only minutes after Eliza and Matthias had finished enjoying the afternoon ritual, they were together in the carriage, en route to a destination a few hours away where they would spend their wedding night at a fine inn and then set out the following day in a hired coach to enjoy a lengthy honeymoon before they returned home to officially begin their life together. Eliza sat as close to her new husband as she possibly could and he put his arm around her, easing her closer still as she settled her head onto his shoulder. She'd never felt so safe, so secure, so happy.

"I've waited a long time to become Mrs. Downing," she said with a small laugh, "although I'm *extremely* relieved to have acquired the name by ending up with *you*!"

"I can sincerely say that I doubt your relief is any stronger than mine," he said with a chuckle and pressed a kiss into her hair. "Your last wedding day was not nearly as idyllic as this one."

"No, it certainly wasn't," she said with the tiniest hint of sadness. "But that's all behind us now, and we are going to be deliriously happy."

"Indeed we will," he said, chuckling more deeply. "Shall we have four children, or five? Six, perhaps?"

Eliza laughed with him. "I daresay we should have them one at a time and focus on more important matters of the moment."

"Like what?" he asked.

Eliza looked up at him. "Far too many minutes have passed since you kissed me," she said, and he smiled.

"As you wish, m'lady," he said and pressed his lips to hers, wrapping her tightly in his arms with an embrace that reminded Eliza they were now husband and wife. Oh, how delighted she was to finally be Mrs. Downing!

About the Author

ANITA STANSFIELD HAS MORE THAN seventy published books and is the recipient of many awards, including two Lifetime Achievement Awards. Her books go far beyond being enjoyable, memorable stories. Anita resonates particularly well with a broad range of devoted readers because of her sensitive and insightful examination of contemporary issues that are faced by many of those readers, even when her venue is a historical romance. Readers come away from her compelling stories equipped with new ideas about how to enrich their own lives, regardless of their circumstances.

Anita was born and raised in Provo, Utah. She is the mother of five and has a growing number of grandchildren. She also writes for the general trade market under the name Elizabeth D. Michaels.

For more information and a complete list of her publications, go to anitastansfield.blogspot.com or anitastansfield.com, where you can sign up to receive email updates. You can also follow her on Facebook and Twitter.